Theodore S. (Theodore Strong) Van Dyke

The Rifle, Rod, and Gun in California

A Sporting Romance

Theodore S. (Theodore Strong) Van Dyke

The Rifle, Rod, and Gun in California
A Sporting Romance

ISBN/EAN: 9783744652506

Printed in Europe, USA, Canada, Australia, Japan

Cover: Foto ©Andreas Hilbeck / pixelio.de

More available books at **www.hansebooks.com**

TO

Those Kindred Spirits

TO WHOM THE COUNT OF GAME AND THE

SIZZLE OF THE FRYING-PAN

ARE

THE LAST AND LOWEST

OF THE

PLEASURES OF FIELD AND STREAM,

This Book

IS RESPECTFULLY DEDICATED.

CONTENTS.

RIFLE, ROD AND GUN

IN

CALIFORNIA.

CHAPTER I.

BLACK BRANT AND CURLEW.

WHAT lake is this that so peacefully sleeps in its green girdle of hills on this February morning, sweet and fair as the brightest day of June? Over its glassy face rolls bright and sparkling the beaded water from the dripping oar, as our boat glides along. Around us, the merganser and the loon rise and disappear, and far away, water-fowl, white and black, loom up in the mirage. On the slope of land behind us lie some indications of what is to become a city, and beyond, the country rolls backward and upward into a table-land. As we recede farther and farther form the shore, white mountain-tops appear in the distance; then we see the dark blue below the snow-line; then behind, to right and to left, lower peaks of blue and gray rise in sight.

It is a wild and tumbling sea of land; "a lanp where it seems always afternoon;" a land far beyond the orbit of the tramp, the chromo man and the insurance agent; where the spinster is not a burden and the voice of the lightning-rod man is not heard ; where the beggar can afford to ride, and to breakfast at ten ; a land where one is forgotten by some of his old friends, and by others remembered the more kindly ; where nothing is certain but death, and even that is a remote contingency ; a land yet inviolate by Limburger, the Bologna, or any other flavor of European civilization ; a land of bees, birds, and rabbit-fed bachelors.

This fair sheet of shining green water, so deep, so long, so safely locked against all storms, is the harbor of San Diego ; and the town that lies on yonder slope is "the future seat of empire of this vast western——" half of San Diego County anyhow.

And who are these two young gentlemen in the boat now gliding over the bay : the one bright and blooming of countenance, with dark hair and soft black mustache, with a smile rippling around the corners of a well-cut mouth, and a twinkle of good-humor in his bright black eyes ; the other of more sober and intellectual face, once decidedly handsome, but now sunken and sallow ? The first is Dr. Belville, a young physician from San Francisco, who has come down to enjoy a few weeks of the winter shooting of Southern California. The other is Charles Norton, a young Bostonian, who has come to California to cure his consumption, which, has not yet advanced so far as to preclude good hopes of recovery. Norton and Belville met on the steamer from San Francisco, and having arrived and got settled, Belville is now taking his new acquaintance across the bay of San Diego, to

show him some of the coast shooting of this part of
the State. Belville has been from boyhood an ardent
sportsman, has made several hunting tours in Southern
California, and is familiar with its best game and fish
preserves. Norton, in his school-days, when he used
to spend part of his vacations at his uncle's farm, had
a decided weakness for distressing gray squirrels with
the flavor of cheap powder from the ancestral single-
barreled shot-gun, nearly as ancient and long as the
old clock on the landing in the stairway. But during
many years of business life, he had not even touched
a gun, and had everything to learn that a sportsman
should know.

On the steamer Belville had given Norton what so
few, even of old and experienced physicians, seem able
to give—good advice about amusing himself out of
doors. "The worst of all enemies," he said, "with
which an invalid has to contend at a sanatarium, or
resort for the effect of climate, is *ennui.* Wherever
you may go, whether to San Diego, Colorado, Florida,
Mentone, Egypt, or Algiers, this fiend will follow you.
It is the same everywhere : a few days' sight-seeing,
a few days' riding about, and then the everlasting sit,
sit, sit, mope, mope, mope, relieved only by finding
fault with the climate for not producing an immediate
cure, and by almost hourly comparison of symptoms
and feelings with every other invalid you happen to
meet. Meanwhile, the face grows daily longer, the
ribs thinner, and the cough deeper. The "sights" lose
all their interest ; the scenery is a bore ; you lose your
appetite ; and hypochondria fastens itself upon you,

and hastens your down-hill speed. Such is the fate of many whom mistaken kindness sends away from the comforts of home and friends, only to die among strangers in a far-off land. Of course, many come too late to be helped by anything ; but a large number also die through sheer ignorance of how to improve climatic advantages."

"I have little doubt you are correct, though I had not thought of it before," was Norton's reply. "But what amusements are there in this fag-end of creation ?"

"The very best of all for an invalid—light and easy hunting, with plenty of game. The game is indeed inferior to that of the East. No royal grouse with hoarse resounding wing goes booming like a shaft of darkness through the tangled brake. No long-billed beauty goes upward through the sapling grove with the whistling pinion, swift, twisting flight, and aristocratic colors that used to make me think that the preacher of old when he said, 'Vanity of vanities, all is vanity,' had never inspected an autumn woodcock over the rib of a good hammerless breech-loader loaded with Dittmar powder. And dear little Bob White!—excuse me, I can't go on. It is saddening to think of the difference."

"Then there can't be much pleasure."

"Oh, yes. Though inferior, it is game nevertheless. And, moreover, what the sport lacks in the nobility of the game is more than made up by the great ease with which it may be followed. To be able to travel in almost any direction with

a buggy or with the aid of a saddle-horse—
an article very cheap here—to stroll beneath soft,
clear skies, over green sod and flowery hillsides,
with no mud to flounder through, no briers or saw-
grass, with no chilled fingers, wet feet, or mosquito-
riddled face, and in two or three hours have all the
shooting that a man should desire, and that without
going quarter of a mile from your buggy or horse,
for one who has recovered from the foolish youthful
pride in being 'tough,' 'a tireless tramper,' and so
on, is hunting *par excellence*. And such is winter hunting here."

"I once liked hunting, but never was anything of
a shot. And I have not tried it for years," said
Norton.

"Once in the field, I will warrant you a quick return of the old love, and in flood-tide too. There is,
probably no part of the Union where a tyro can meet
with such speedy success as here. When we get to
San Diego, I will take you across the bay and introduce
you to some of the feathered gentry. One glimpse of
black brant will wake you from your long sleep like
an electric shock."

Belville then took Norton to his state-room and
showed him his new hammerless, self-cocking breech-
loader with all its shining accoutrements, fancy coat,
etc., and as Norton gazed upon them and heard their
owner explain their various excellences, and wax elo-
quent over the virtues of Dittmar powder, choke-bores,
and chilled shot, he began to feel strange emotions
springing up from some hitherto unknown corner of

his soul.   And when Belville took him to where his dog, Prince, a sleek pointer of liver color and white, was chained on the lower deck, and saw the dog lick his chops, lash his tail, and stretch his claws on the floor; and heard him, with sparkling eyes fixed on his master, whine and yelp with joyful recollections as Belville told how the veteran had pointed woodcock in New Jersey swamps, sniffed the fragrance of the ruffed grouse in Pennsylvania, skimmed the frosty stubbles in Maryland; how many pinnated grouse had fallen before him in Minnesota, and how many ducks he had retrieved in an evening from the dense tules of the Sacramento, Norton's faint emotions broke into a decided tumult.

"I'll have to try some of that sport right away," said he. "I'm sorry now I didn't bring a gun with me."

"You can get pretty well fitted out in San Diego," said Belville. "They have gun-stores, and indeed all kinds of stores, far better than you would suppose. And you can soon get from San Francisco anything they cannot furnish you at San Diego."

It required but a short time, after Norton got well rested at San Diego, to equip him with a fair breech-loader and plenty of cartridges, a coat and hat of the color of sea-weed, and a pair of rubber boots. From one of the many hospitable and accommodating sportsmen there Belville soon borrowed a boat, twenty-five or thirty black-brant decoys, and a light box, low and broad, and of sea-weed or mud color, to be used as a blind. This was not a regular sink-box, or floating battery, but a movable blind, light and dry, easily shifted from place to place along the wet and muddy shores.

With this outfit, our friends were now crossing the bay, the box containing the decoys being towed behind the boat. Under the vigorous strokes of Belville, who was used to rowing, they soon crossed the bay, and turned into Spanish Bight just as the tide began to ebb. A few moments more brought them to a narrow place near the upper end of the Bight, half a mile or so from where the surf was booming against the sand spit that formed the end of the Bight. There they anchored the box at the outer edge of the grass and sea-weed that fringed the shore, and placed the decoys in the water some thirty yards farther out. Collecting more sea-weed, they made the fringe complete, so as to hide the box, and Norton took his seat in it, while Belville took the boat away several hundred yards along the shore. Then returning, he ordered Prince to lie down in some weeds on shore, and the well-trained dog obeyed. Then Belville got into the box, and he and Norton laid themselves in it lengthwise and opposite to each other, the bottom of the box resting on the mud.

After they were thus disposed, some ten minutes passed away with no signs of game. Life enough there was, but not of the kind they wanted. Around them, the gull winged his unwearied flight; little fish-hawks of almost pure white shot from on high into the water ; divers, shags, and fish-ducks of various kinds dove, swam, or "skittered" along in front ; the gray pelican with his long lancet out-stretched, poised in his dignified flight, dropped with a heavy *chug* into the water, and coming up again bolted with true American expedition the breakfast he had caught; while bunches of small snipe went hissing by with rapid wing. But they had not waited long, when Belville suddenly said :

"Down close now ! Here comes a flock of curlew. The tide is now low enough for the birds to fly."

Swiftly up the Bight came a flock of birds about the size of small teal, and winding around the turns in the shore, in a moment were almost over the blind. With breasts of light buff, wings nearly the same color underneath, and long bills outstretched, the birds looked like gigantic woodcock whose bills had been warped into crescents by the dryness of the climate. Their clear "*teet-a-leet, teet-a-leet*" went ringing across the Bight, as Belville raised his gun, upon which they pitched and wheeled in all directions. But one descended with a splash at the crack of the first barrel of the gun, and as it struck the water the second barrel rang out, and another bird came whirling down with his wings broken and sprawling.

Prince still lay in the grass, head up, awaiting his master's order to fetch the birds. At the word he bounded into the water and started first for the wounded bird which he brought to the edge of the box, his eye sparkling with satisfaction, and delivered to his master without a feather ruffled. He then brought in the other, shook the water from his dripping coat, and went back to lie down at the command.

After they had waited a few minutes more, another clear, penetrating "*teet-a-leet, teet-a-leet*" came ringing from the distance, and a larger flock than before came rapidly following the sound of the cry, now massing like an armed host, now scattering like leaves before the wind, then closing up again in solid column. As they flew low, and close to the box, Belville whispered to Norton to take the first shot.. As Norton raised himself a little to shoot, the penetrating cry of the flock, still repeated, so startled him that he missed the upward-darting and swerving birds, first with one barrel and then with the other. But as they hurried off in alarm, Belville pacified one with his first barrel, and materially enhanced the speed of the rest with the other.

Another flock came winding up the line of the shore, just as Prince was bringing in Belville's prey; and seeing the dog, the birds swung out some fifty yards from the box. Norton fired again, and from the rear of the flock a bird settled with a cerebro-spinal incongruity into the water.

"A good long shot, that!" exclaimed Belville. "If you had held at the front line of the flock, you would have got more, perhaps. However, one is good enough. But here comes another bunch. With this ebbing tide they are flying fast now."

Low along the water, and not twenty yards from the box, this flock drifted by, their long, curved bills, dark eyes, and brown backs shining in the sun, thirty or forty of them, all advancing in even and swift array. Norton felt a strange sensation as along the smooth, trim barrels of his gun he saw the sickle-bill and brown wings of the foremost bird ; and his heart beat hard as he pulled the trigger, and saw through the smoke the fast-sailer lower its jib, reef in its sails, and anchor in the shallow water.

"Isn't this splendid !" he said, as he took down his gun.

"I think them pretty good game, though they are little hunted here," said Belville.

"Do they fly like this every day ?"

"At ebb tide they do. At low tide they are busy feeding on the flats, and at high tide they are on land, or up the inlets waiting for the ebb. There are thousands of birds on this bay, and in the tide-waters of California generally ; but they are hard to get at except in this way. There is another kind larger than these, but so much slower and tamer, that there is really little fun in shooting them. | At least, all I have seen were so. They are of a dark cinnamon color, with dark bronze wings, glossy as those of a wild turkey. I think it is too early for them yet, as I never have seen them much before April. I have seen them in May at San Luis Rey, tame enough to shoot with a pistol—provided one was a good shot, of course."

And what is this dim line of dark bodies fast looming over yonder sand spit to seaward, and which our friends are too busy talking to see? The line, rapidly rising in the western blue now changes into two long converging strings, and the V-shaped train bears swiftly down. It is not strange that you cannot name them ; for rare is the man who has ever seen one east of the Pacific coast. They are too small for geese; their stroke of wing is too fast, and they cleave the air too swiftly. Nor are they ordinary brant : their stroke of wing is still too fast. Nor are they mallards ; for they are much too large, are nearly black in color, and grow blacker yet and more shiny as they approach.

Now they sweep by about one hundred yards out, and change color fast. A white collar appears around the glossy black neck, and the dark breast shades swiftly into white. Like a procession of sable gentlemen in black broadcloth, white neckties, and long white aprons pinned around behind, they glide past with a "*wah-oouk, wah-oouk*" that arouses Belville from his carelessness, and he leaves to Norton's imagination the conclusion of a joke he has been inflicting on him.

"So much for not watching! We must be careful now, for when these chaps once start they come fast. Keep close down, and don't move your gun or head until they are near enough, and then be quick," said Belville.

"Those were brant, I suppose," said Norton.

"Yes, the black brant, the finest of American waterfowl. They are never found inland, and will not cross even a point of land if they can fly around it. It is said that this bay and False Bay, four miles above, are the only places in California where they are found. But it is a California weakness to like a monoply of anything good, so it is permissible to doubt this statement. But it is certainly a rare bird anywhere but here and the bays of Lower California.   They are coming in now from the sea as the tide goes down."

Another dark line was fast rising above the high sand-bank that shut out the grumbling breakers toward the west, and both men dropped low and were silent. On came the birds, widening out their line and growing darker and larger every second as they plied their swift black wings.   In a slow but even curve they swept in toward the decoys, and the soft hiss of their stiffened sailing wings was becoming audible, when Norton, getting anxious, turned his head a little to get a better look before rising to shoot. In a twinkling, there came from a dozen of the advance-guard the warning "*wah-oouk! wah-oouk!*" and instead of the black broadcloth vests and swallow-tailed coats, the expectant hunters saw only the snowy fluttering of the white skirts of fifty nether garments fast sheering away from them across the Bight.

"You see they are gamey enough," said Belville, laughing. "You must be careful not to move until ready to shoot."

"Are they very hard to shoot?"

"Not hard to *hit*, if they once get close enough ; for although quicker far than any other kind of goose, they are still slower than a duck. But they shed shot as subscribers do editorial appeals to pay up, and even when they get a good charge, often bear up under it as patiently and bravely as a school-boy under his headache when school is out.

"Down low now !" he added quickly, as another line of black dots appeared in the west. "We'll let these light, so as to give you .a good shot. Don't move till you hear them settle in the water."

· Swiftly the dark ranks advanced down the Bight, nearly a hundred strong. In two long, diverging lines, with a heavy bunch at the apex, they glided past, low down along the water and just out of shot, winnowing the still warm air with the rapid but gentle stroke of their glossy wings, their black necks, breasts, and white underwear pictured in the glassy surface below.

"Don't move an inch!" whispered Belville. "They will come back."

For two or three hundred yards they sped straight on, then curling upward and sideways, they turned with long and graceful sweep, and with stiffened wings came sliding swiftly down the air, straight toward the decoys. But just as they were curving their wings to settle, and the air began to hiss with their swiftness, one among them cried "*wah-oouk!*" and in an instant the air throbbed again with the heavy beat of strong pinions, and in a confused huddle of black and white they dashed outward toward the sky.

Bang! went two barrels almost at once, and the aspirations of one ambitious colored gentleman culminated and declined. Bang! bang! went two more shots, and another concluded to join the minority. The majority wheeled off down the Bight, and soon looked like an away-going flight of revolving arrows feathered with white and black.

There was not long to wait for the next shot, for when these birds fly at all they generally fly thick and fast as the shades of night in this southern land, and another flock soon loomed up in the west.

"Now possess thy soul in patience, until you hear them light," cautioned Belville.

Both crouched low in the box, and in a few seconds a silken rush was heard, then the hiss of wings, and finally a long *swish*, as they settled into the water. Dull as a home without a baby must be the soul of him who could be cool and collected on the first day of his introduction to such noble birds as these; and Norton was a gentleman of refined sensibilities. His hands trembled as he raised his head and gun over the edge of the box; his pulse bounded, and a strange joy thrilled him like an electric shock, as he planted a full charge of shot fair into the thickest part of the flock——of decoys !

Like a flash the air above the decoys was filled with a wild medley of flapping wings and cries of "*wah-oouk.*" Two black-and-white bustling bodies dropped into the water with a splash at the crack of Belville's gun, while Norton's second barrel roared vainly at the rest as they dashed away, until, from far across San Diego's bay, the flutter of their white raiment faded into the distant glimmer of the water.

"I was a little too greedy," said Norton regretfully. "I'll look sharper next time."

Large flocks of curlew still winged by, with their ringing note ; bunches of snipe whisked over the box almost within arm's reach ; sandpipers, willet, shore-plover, and waders of various kinds scudded past; but all these looked contemptible now, and were allowed to pass on unhailed.

"Here come some more," said Norton's friend and guide. "Don't move until I do. They're coming straight for us."

There were fifteen or twenty in the flock, moving in a crescent-shaped bunch. When they were almost over the box, Belville suddenly rose, and at the crack of his gun a ghostly display of linen in *dishabille* instantly took the place of the trim, sable robes in which the visitors arrived, and two heavy birds came whirling down into the mud, one to each barrel. Norton raised his gun and saw a white-and-black climbing body in line with it ; he pulled the trigger; a distinct *chiff !* was heard, and a few snowy feathers parted from their owner, which twisted, wiggled, lowered, swung off to the right, lowered again, then finally rose and flew off to join his companions.

"It took him some time to make up his mind," said Belville. "He was pretty hard hit, but they are tough."

Soon half a dozen lines and bunches rose in the horizon, and widening out and then closing up, stringing out and then bunching again, they came in a long procession down the Bight, all black as they approached, white and black as they passed just out of shot, and nearly white as they faded in the sheen of the distant water. Then came a single brant, fast fanning the air with a lonely "*wah-oouk*," and bobbing his black head and neck about, looking for company. At last, seeing .the decoys, he swept around in a graceful curve, set his wings, and rode down an invisible incline, as swiftly and softly as a falling star.

Bang ! went one barrel of Belville's gun, the shot skittering over the water beneath the bird. The brant swiftly picked up the legs he was lowering into the water, and traveled off at a rate that must have required wings and legs both, while two more "dogs of war" vainly barked in his rear.

Yet still they come, a few up the Bight, but most of them from the sea. Over the sand-banks and dunes they fly, black, thick, and swift, mass after mass. But nearly all are now drifting silently past, without deigning to look at the decoys ; for the tide has left the decoys aground, all except two or three which are still rocking in a few inches of water. Now and then a flock, drawn a little out of the regular line of travel from the sea by curiosity or sociability, comes over to take a look at the deceivers, but with little idea of stopping. Occasionally, a bird whirls plunging into the mud with a sullen thump, or comes struggling and flapping down at the crack of Belville's gun ; but the greater number pass by with inviolate broadcloth and dignity unlowered. Thus flock after flock drifts by out of reach. Strings of twenty, fifty, even a hundred, swing by just nicely out of reach, and without turning even to look at the decoys. Belville and Norton would now gladly have shot at the lately despised curlew, but no more were flying. All were feeding, and they could be seen along the shores, ambling over the mud-flats by the hundred, along with willet, sandpipers, dowitchers, snipe, and plover. And there were also brant, waddling along the outer edge of the mud, looking large as turkeys in the mirage. These were the first that had been seen to touch ground voluntarily. Before long, nothing was on the wing but the tireless gull and the ever-hungry pelican and fish-hawk. The flight had ceased, and there was nothing for the sportsmen to do but leave.

"It needs a regular sink-box for this sort of thing," said Belville, as they started to gather their traps. "But then we had good enough sport."

"Splendid, I call it," said Norton, who was delighted with his first experience of California shooting.

The sun was fast sinking into the west, when a light buggy containing two ladies stopped on the high *mesa*, or table-land, back of San Diego. One of them drew from her pocket a strong opera-glass and looked out upon the smooth face of the bay.

"Yes, there they are!" she exclaimed, turning it upon two small dots just coming out of the Spanish Bight. "I can see Charley plainly, and the Doctor is rowing with his back this way."

"Do let's stop and look at the sunset," said the other. "I have never seen the sun set on such a smooth sea and in such a clear air as that yonder. I have seen him go down in a wild whirl of boiling waves or slowly drowning in a bath of fog. I have have seen him rise with the pale glare that foretells a stormy day, or with the fierce glassy face of a hot morning. But this will be new as well as lovely."

Long fleecy streams of cloud spanned the western horizon like a golden suspensio: -bridge, while an outward-bound steamer, with her dark hull and rigging clearly cut upon the lake of crimson fire beneath, was trailing her sooty banner against the brilliant background. Over the placid face of the still ocean the light shot landward in a long lane of carmine and gold, down which the steamer with her long smoky trail on the sky, making a filagree of ruby and jet, seemed drifting into a haven of fire. Sixty miles to the eastward, the snowy crown of Cuyamaca shone with a golden glow ; the castellated crags of El Cajou and other rocky peaks were purplish gray ; the dark green vests of the chapparal-clad mountains turned gradually into a deep blue. The mountains of Mexico seemed to be swimming in a soft blue haze, and the bold rocky islands of the Pacific loomed higher and darker against the glowing south-west.

"They are nearly across the bay now, and will be at the hotel before us unless we hurry," said the lady with the glass. This was Miss Laura Wilbur, a young lady of about twenty, to whom Norton was engaged, who had come on from Boston to California partly to see the country, but principally to contribute to the recovery of her lover by giving him encouragement and cheer in his temporary banishment from home and friends—a most commendable plan, which those who send friends away for their health are too apt to neglect.

She was accompanied by Miss Eveline Norton, the only sister of Charles Norton, who had no duties at home to interfere with her joining her brother in his sunny retreat. She was slightly older than Miss Wilbur, "enough older," she said, "to matronize the party," and was possessed of the same delicate, intellectual beauty that characterized her brother, which was not in her case marred by the marks of disease.

Both these young ladies were strong and active, fond of such out-door sports as are accessible to a city life—boating, lawn tennis, and archery. In the latter field they had long been famous among the fair toxophilites of "The Hub," and had carried away in successive years the highest prizes and honors that their club had contended for. It was no small part of the pleasure they anticipated from their Californian trip, that they were to try whether their prowess with the bow upon the greensward could be turned to practical account upon real game in the forest. But they had not thought of indulging in a prolonged "hunt," until Doctor Belville had persuaded Mr. Norton that the ladies could easily go with them, and that their participation in his amusements would be a good thing for him. They had brought with them a complete outfit of bows, arrows, and other essentials, and were to share the sport with their brother and his friend, whose return from the first day's hunt they were now awaiting.

"What a beautiful site for a city!" said Norton as the returning boat approached San Diego, which the sun now deluged with soft light as it lay sloping toward the bay. "And what large buildings for such a far-off place!"

"Few cities in the world have had finer prospects than San Diego, and few could have existed so long upon deferred hopes. Time was when the Texas Pacific Railroad was actually building, and several miles were graded, capitalists by the score and the hundred arrived on every steamer, and men had to form lines at the real-estate offices. But "Black Friday" and the subsequent hard times brought about a collapse in the railroad finances and let the bottom out of everything. Few cities of its size west of the Alleghanies can boast as much culture, intelligence, and refinement as San Diego, and its people are a marvel to-day for their courage and unwavering faith in their future."

"You talk as if you owned real estate there," said Norton.

"Not an inch. But then I admire pluck wherever I see it, even though it may be kicking against the pricks."

The light in the lofty light-house of Point Loma twinkled like a star in the afterglow of the departed sun; the sea-gull folded his wing and settled upon the smooth water; the cry of the brant died away and the dark flocks rode silent on the distant water; in quiet dignity the pelican sat meditatively on the glassy surface of the bay, and his heavy *chug* into the water was heard no more. The shags and divers drifted silent on the flowing tide; the whistling wings of the fast-scudding buffel-heads ceased, and the distant Table Mountain of Mexico faded into the dim line of the surrounding mountains as the boat grated on the sandy shore by the town.

Leaping from the boat, the hungry sportsmen collected their game and their traps, and having arranged for these to follow them, they made their way to the hotel, where they were joyfully received by the young ladies. Over a good supper they recounted their experiences of the day, and afterwards, Belville considerately strolled off with his cigar, leaving Norton behind to talk of his friends at home, and to the more tender joys of communion with the friends that had come with him.

CHAPTER II.

FIRST GLIMPSE OF INLAND SHOOTING.

TO bump the reader over the long corduroy road of description leading to the various causes, emotions, propensities, tendencies, and motives which lead to a sneeze, is considered by some evidence of rare talent. It constitutes, they say, " fine character-drawing," " subtle analysis of human nature," " exquisite portrayal," and so on.

But there are also many who deem these tedious analyses boresome, even in a novel. And if a bore in a novel, it would be doubly so in a work which is purely descriptive, and in which the part that the novel-reader might foolishly mistake for the body of the work is only a faint thread inwoven to break the monotony and to fill the " chinks."

Many of the connecting links in the chain of events will therefore be omitted : why our *dramatis personæ* did this or that, or why they went here or there. And if any reader does not like the thread of romance on which are strung the pearls of sport and adventure, let him be comforted by the thought that it occupies far less space than in many sporting works is devoted to getting the hunters waked, dressed, fed, armed, " liquored up," and into the field.

It was the last week of February, and Belville and

Norton with the two ladies were whirling in a light, open, two-horse wagon over the strips of plain that in the fair valley El Cajou lie along the bottom of the San Diego River, fifteen miles east of San Diego Bay. Belville and Norton were provided with their shot-guns ; but the ladies were indulged in their desire to try if they could turn to practical use the skill they had acquired as archers over the tented lawns of Boston, and had brought their bows and a plentiful supply of arrows. Along the edge toward the river were small ponds, fringed with high weeds and grass. As the wagon drew near one of these, Belville stopped the horses and said to Miss Norton, as he assisted her to alight:

"Now, Miss Diana, there is a splendid chance to try the virtues of the weapon of the gods. There are some ducks in that pond, and if you keep around to the right and get into that little gully, and then stoop low until you get behind those high weeds, you will be sure of a good shot. But be careful not to let them see you. In the meantime I will slip around on the opposite side and hide behind that little bush to congratulate any that may chance to escape the deadly arrow."

Through the fringe of weeds that lined the pond some small dark objects were seen, some in motion, others at rest. In a few moments Belville was lying flat and motionless on the greensward behind the little bush, and Miss Wilbur with bow and arrows was fast nearing the edge of the pond. Forgetting the Doctor's instructions, she raised her head too quickly and too high, and in an instant there was a vigorous "*quack, quack, quack,*" mingled with the heavy beat of rapid wings, as about twenty mallards sprang into the air, in a bustling confusion of long necks of burnished green, gray mottled backs, white-banded dark green tails, and wings flashing with a broad band of golden green on a background of brownish gray. Loosed from her trembling hand, her arrow flashed harmlessly below the flock, and quivered in the bank on the opposite side of the pond. Away went the ducks slanting swiftly upward, but also onward, and directly toward Belville's hiding-place. When they were nearly over it a shaft of flame shot up, and two ducks wilted and came whirling down with a heavy thump. As the rest climbed skyward with a sudden dash of throbbing wings, another line of fire streamed up, and another duck relaxed his hold on air and sank like a plummet. As Belville picked up the ducks he saw Laura Wilbur fast emptying her quiver at something in the water, and when she had finished he went to her.

"I have shot one, too! I have shot a duck!" she exclaimed gleefully as he approached. He looked where she excitedly pointed, and there, near the side of the pond opposite Laura, lay a mud-hen impaled by an arrow, while the feather ends of about a dozen more arrows were just visible above the water around the supposed duck. Belville would not spoil her pleasure by telling her it was not a duck; but a feeling of deep disappointment stole over her as she contrasted its dull, dark feathers and miserable little body with the golden sheen of the green necks and heads, the cinnamon gloss of the breasts, the richly mottled backs, and large plump bodies of the mallards that Belville had brought down. And stronger yet was the contrast between the stupid action of the bird that sat and let a dozen arrows cleave the water around it, with the behavior of the mallards that sprang into the air at the first alarm and soared rapidly away at such a rapid pace. And to see one thing hit while at rest and another tripped in its whizzing career on high convinced her more than ever that she had not brought down the right kind of game.

"I'm slightly afraid, Miss Wilbur, that you will have to condescend to the vulgar gun if you want much success," said Belville, with a sympathetic smile.

"Oh, I prefer the bow, still," she answered decidedly.

"It is more poetic, I know," responded Belville, "and I admit there is a delightful flavor of antiquity about it. But like the aureole of sentiment with which we encircle the head of the noble savage, it is much better for all practical purposes to contemplate in books and on the lawn than in the field. Although a splendid thing for target-shooting and lawn amusement, and even very good for some kinds of game, it is hardly the thing for much success in general shooting in these days."

"That is because everything is scared nearly to death by the noisy and destructive gun," retorted Laura.

"Be it so. I regret that myself, and should enjoy hunting more if the gun had never been invented. But it has been invented, and has had its effect in making game both scarcer and wilder; and I adapt myself to the world as it is and not as I would like to have it. Some good shooting can still be had with the bow, and I should like to use it myself a little. Plenty of rabbits, some squirrels, mountain quails, a few valley quails, and a few ducks can be easily shot with it here. But the greater part of American game, and far the nobler part, must now be taken on the wing, which cannot be accomplished to any extent with the bow. Such birds as robins, larks, woodpeckers, and in my opinion even doves, it is a shame to shoot with anything, either at rest or on the wing."

During this conversation Belville and Laura had made their way back to the wagon with their game, which they displayed to their companions. Taking their seats they proceeded on their way. As they drove along, a large hare slipped out of a bush by the roadside, and cantering along with a few high and graceful leaps, stopped about thirty yards to one side of the road, and rising up on its hind legs, with its long ears pointed toward the zenith, turned its sparkling black eyes upon the party.

"Now, Miss Wilbur," said Belville, "please try my gun on that fellow. The horses will stand and you can shoot right out of the wagon."

"Oh! I'm afraid. Evy, you try it first."

Miss Norton took the gun and raised it. As the gun came up in line with the hare, the animal started on an easy canter, but on a straight-away course; and she caught a glimpse along the barrels of long ears, brown-and-yellowish coat, and flickering black tail, skipping over the golden ranks of the violets, the blue-stars and fern-like carpet of the alfileria, the thick mats of pinks and the white and azure bells of the shooting stars. Almost unconsciously she pulled the trigger. She felt a slight shock, and a faint vision of rolling clouds, with a brownish yellow acrobat tumbling somersaults over the spangled earth beneath, rose for a second before her sight. And in that second an entirely new set of feelings sprang at a bound from some hitherto unknown corner of her soul.

"That is splendid! isn't it?" she exclaimed.

"You will get to think so if you try it awhile," said Belville, as he jumped from the wagon to pick up the hare, returning with which he added: "But it is fair to tell you that all shooting, even in as easy a country to hunt as this, is not as simple as that. However, you will here find plenty that is easy enough."

In a few moments more, some small, gray birds were seen gliding over the sod to one side, at which Belville again stopped the wagon, and offering the gun to Laura, said: "Now it is your turn, Miss Wilbur. There are some plover, and you cannot get close enough with the bow. Take the gun and walk up to them as fast as you can, and don't let them run away from you."

She took the gun, after she had been assisted out of the wagon, and walked to within sixty yards of the birds, when they began to glide away. With soft, mellow whistle and thin trim legs moving so fast as to be nearly invisible, they slipped over the velvet sward several yards at a time, stopping occasionally to turn their little beaded eyes upon the strange apparition, then moving swiftly on again as the gun was raised.

"I told you they would run away from you," said Belville as he came up on foot. "You must walk fast and shoot the minute they stop. Raise the gun quickly, and the instant you see it in line with them, pull the trigger."

She started again on a half-run, but getting too close to them before she knew it, the little things with light and graceful wing swung themselves into the air making some musical observations as they went. Laura stopped and fired, but the charge only shivered a little mound of violets a few feet behind them.

"You see it is not quite as easy as giving an opinion on the financial question," said Belville. "And these are very easy birds to shoot, too."

"I should like to learn how to do it. But I suppose like everything else it needs a teacher."

"You can teach yourself quite well for ordinary shooting. Practice is the main thing."

"But there is nothing like a teacher. Mr. Norton taught me to use the bow at the target, and I soon—"

"Sent a shaft home into your teacher's heart?" said Belville, with a quizzical side glance at Laura.

She stood for a second, startled at the easy impertinence of the remark, but quickly answered: "It takes something stronger than an arrow to reach a man's heart."

"And therefore you wish to learn to use the gun?"

"You seem well skilled in chaffing."

"But are there not a few *grains* even among chaff?"

"There, they have lit again," said Laura, not appearing to notice the last remark; but pointing away over the Turkey carpet of purple, gold, white, crimson, and blue, to a broad patch of pink that thickly covered part of a slope of glowing green. "It is too far to walk. Let's ride," she added, as her companion started to go on foot.

"As you wish," he replied. "I will try and give you a shot out of the wagon, but you must shoot the moment it stops, please, or they will begin to run again, and you might miss them running as well as flying."

He drove rapidly toward the birds on a slanting course until within thirty yards of them, and then suddenly stopping, said, "Now shoot!" Laura pointed the gun until their little thin legs, flickering with speed like wheel-spokes, carried the game well out of reach, and then fired. The smoke came rolling back into the faces of the occupants of the wagon, and when it cleared away nothing was in sight.

"I hit them all, didn't I?" she inquired quite innocently.

"I knew you were hoodwinking me. You played it quite well, too," said Belville.

"What do you mean?"

"Why, I see you are an old hand at the business. But really, I would advise you not to give full scope to your skill here, for it is customary among California sportsmen to leave a bird or two in a flock." So saying, he jumped out and went over to where she had shot at the birds.

"Pshaw! I wasn't quick enough. That provoking gopher has got them all!" he exclaimed, looking into an owl's hole in the ground. He reached in and drew out two or three owl-feathers, and bringing them to the wagon said, " Here's something, though, for a trophy."

"Why!   Do gophers catch birds?"

"They 'go for' everything that comes along.   The next time we must hurry and get ahead of him."

"It's too bad, I declare!" said Miss Norton, sympathizing with Laura's defeat.

"Oh, that's a very reasonable contribution from one of her standing toward keeping up the gopher family. Some folks contribute half a dozen orange-trees or a dozen apple-trees every season. But there is a pheasant! Now, Norton, you can take a turn," said Bellville, pointing to a long-geared thing like a cross between a ruffled grouse and a weather-cock that was scudding along the edge of the plain near some brush. Driving rapidly up, they got within easy shot just as with nimble leg it was running around a patch of prickly-pear. Norton fired and knocked over a " road-runner," " paisano," or " chaparal cock," as they are called—an insignificant bird seldom shot in California, though not at all bad eating.

"I haven't seen a pheasant since I was a boy," said Norton, surveying it proudly. " But isn't it smaller than our Eastern bird?"

"Y-e-s—a trifle. But what it lacks in quantity it makes up in quality," was the reply. "Ah! there are some more plover," added Belville, after a short circuit that brought them around to the very same flock Laura had shot at before, and which had lit only a few rods ahead of the old place in a piece of low ground. "I'm almost afraid to trust you with these, but if you will promise to leave two I will lend you the gun," he said to Laura.

"Maybe I will leave them all," she answered, with a laugh.

"Well, I don't care," he said; "only please don't leave them long enough for the gopher."

She got out with Norton, and this time, crouching behind a little elevation of ground, approached quite close to the plover. Then rising up she fired, and two lay stretched upon the sod.

"Get them quick! Look out for the gopher!" called Belville.

She hesitated a moment, as if expecting to see a gopher come out. But seeing no hole at hand, she picked them up, saying, as she brought them to the wagon: "What little beauties! Are these like Eastern plover?"

"Not exactly," said Belville, as he whipped up again. "Most all southern California birds vary a little from their Eastern relatives, and it is interesting to note the differences. Do you see that meadow-lark warbling his spring song from that bush to the right that hangs so full of scarlet bells? You see his breast, like an island of jet in a pond of gold, is the same as that of the Eastern bird. So, too, is his coat of russet and black, and his modest cap and tail. But you might watch him a year, and you would never hear a note from him like that of the Eastern lark—the '*k-wank—krrrrrr*,' so often heard as he flirts his tail on the haycock or smoothly shaven face of the June meadow of New Jersey or Illinois. And the sweet and penetrating '*tee-ah-tee-ah-tee*' that lengthens out the summer evenings at your home are never heard here. In its place is only a '*k-chee-ah—wottle-wottle-wottle*,' fuller and richer in tone, as you can notice, but to my ear most ineffably stupid in meaning."

"I must say I don't admire the words, though the *timbre* is certainly very fine," said Miss Norton.

"The golden rays that the yellow-hammer or high-holder showers on the air as he rises and dips in his flight are here darkened into orange; but in all else the plumage is the same as that of the Eastern bird. But the '*witcha-witcha-witcha-witcha,*' like the distant whetting of a mower's scythe, is gone, and in its place there is an occasional '*ka-wicka,*' sounded only once. The sweet low notes, impossible to imitate, which they make in their social meetings on some high limb in the fall of the year, are never heard here. The rich, fluty '*cloi-cloi-cloi-cloi-cloi,*' rapidly repeated, is also gone, and instead, there is only a dull '*krrrr,*' much like the woodpecker's tattoo, only made with the throat instead of with the bill."

"You know that sound, don't you?" he added, as a "*woooo-woo-woo*" sounded from the timber along the river.

"Oh yes. That's the dove. There go two more," she answered, as two birds with whistling wing and long tails swept by with the swiftness of an arrow.

"Yes," she added, as they passed, "they are just the same here as at home. And what is that beautiful blue bird on this live oak ahead of us?"

"The prince of rascals, the bluejay. He's not quite so gaudy a scamp as his Eastern cousin. His colors are more subdued and arranged in a style less *bizarre*. No jaunty top-knot adorns his head, and gone is the jangling note, the only discord in the Eastern woods. But the same mischievous eye, you see, looks out from beneath his dark blue hood; and you can scarce conceive the villainy hidden beneath that indigo coat and gentle-looking breast. He has the most delicate ear for the cackle of a hen, the acutest perception of the direction of her nest, and the neatest bill for drilling the shell and absorbing the contents. The ingenuity he exhibits in picking each green apple, apricot and pear, just enough to insure its destruction, and then skipping gayly to the next one, so that every meal he takes costs a hundred apples or peaches, would do credit to an ancient Vandal."

"Are you sure he is not after worms?" suggested Norton.

"Sh—sh! don't breathe such a thing aloud here in California," said Belville in a serious and impressive whisper. "They will take you for that 'spare-the-birds' man who figures so regularly in the papers every three months. If they do, nothing in the world could prevent the immediate elevation of your substantiality by a lasso. I could myself cheerfully assist at the asphyxiation of that individual. He's worked so long that he needs rest."

CHAPTER III

COURSING HARES.

MINER'S RANCH in El Cajon is now a thing of the past. But the time was when twenty-five or thirty guests gathered around its ample board, lounged under its capacious porches, and laughed at the jokes of its jovial proprietor. And at the time our friends came to El Cajon, " Miner's" was at the climax of its prosperity. The winter sun rose soft and clear, as it nearly always does in this fair climate, and the boarders sat sunning themselves on the porch or in the hammocks. Nearly all were people of culture and means, and many of a high grade of education and standing in society; but nearly every one was a representative of some popular ailment, or the wife or husband of some one that was. Here was that ubiquitous nuisance whose "blood don't circulate," the everlasting bore whose "liver is out of order;" here also where the damsel with "nervous debility," the man whose "food don't assimilate," the lady whose "blood is too thin," the youth who has "outgrown his strength," and the rest.

Though the seal of the great destroyer was set more or less deeply upon many a cheek, and each one could see it plainly enough in his neighbor, scarcely one had consumption, in his own opinion. One had only "a little bronchial catarrh;" another admitted " a slight pulmonary difficulty;" a third confessed to "a nervous cough;" a fourth had a cold he had "come down to throw off;" and a fashionable shoddyite went so far as to admit that her doctor had found "two buckles" on her lungs, which, as Belville whispered to Laura, accounted for the "tightness" of the cough of which she complained. But little did any of them dream that the rocket was burned out, and that their life was only the useless stick traveling a little farther on with its original momentum.

And there they nearly all sit, and sit, and sit, and grumble and grow worse. Two or three take horses and go hunting every day, bringing home enough game, even though they are invalids, to abundantly supply the table. These are the only ones that seem to be recovering. And yet when they advise the others to get a gun and horse, how strange the answers! One says it will "use up his strength." He looks upon strength as so much wine in a bottle—every drop used gone forever. Another says he "gets all the exercise he wants coughing." Another says he "don't like California game; it's *flat*, like California fruit" (he has the fashionable "lingo" about California productions quite pat). Another says game is "not sufficiently nutritious," and "wants *beef*." And similar are the reasons of the rest.

Alas for them! The rolling green plains, the flowery hills, the tree-filled cañons of the land are, for most of them, full of life and health and enjoyment. Amusement with rifle, gun, and long bow lies abundant on every side, if they would only take it. But they are lost when they step off the brick pavement; they have never breathed anything but the dusty air of business; their ears are tuned only to the measure of the dance or the click of the billiard-ball; and their eyes know no beauty except in the human face or on the walls of the drawing-room or " Academy of Arts." What wonder that such should pine away with *ennui*, lose heart and appetite, become morose and discontented, and grow worse, even in the best of climates!   Yet such is the average invalid, and such his fate, wherever he goes.

Five horses stood saddled at the gate, and two lithe greyhounds, named Flirt and Flash, were racing about in a frenzied anticipation.   In a few moments Norton and Laura, Belville and Miss Norton, with Miner on the other horse, were mounted and cantering over the heavy greensward of alfileria, whose fern-like leaves were almost hidden in broad patches by a wasteful prodigality of golden violets, which, unlike the common wild violet, are here as fragrant as the garden variety.   Great beds of pinks and jump-ups lay along the slopes, and over all the shooting star, or American cowslip, hung its blue and snowy bells.

They turned down along the edge of the meadow by the river bottom, and inside of the outer line of weeds that lined it, keeping their eyes open for the four-footed game they sought.

" Hurrah! there she goes!" yelled Miner presently, dashing ahead as a hare sprang from a clump of green weeds and started for the hills nearly half a mile away, and the two dogs burst from a trot into a full run. The hare was some fifty yards ahead of the hounds, running with a few rapid strokes of its little feet, then throwing itself in the air with a lofty arching skip.   It

carried its ears well forward and danced along as if it
feared no danger, its black eyes sparkling and its glossy
coat shining like that of a deer in the morning sun.
But as the dogs gained upon it its actions changed in
a twinkling. It laid back its long ears, stretched out its
long body beyond its former length, and skimmed over
the ground like a low-flying grouse. The dogs, too, let
out an extra length, and their long legs glimmered
over the checkered sod like wheel-spokes; while the
horses settled down at once to business, and hugged the
spangled carpet of the plain at their keenest gallop.

Swiftly the hare scuds on, gaining at every jump for
over two hundred yards; the violets, pinks, and snowy
bells flying from the horses feet close behind the dogs;
Belville yelling with excitement; Norton hatless and holding to the horn of the saddle for safety; Laura terrified at
the unusal speed, but too excited to drop behind; and
Miner and Eveline, who was a bold rider, tearing
along ahead of them all. Now the hare twists and
goes down a slope, and the dogs begin to gain. Closer
and closer they come to him, Flirt ahead and Flash but a
yard behind, and fast the thundering hoofs close in behind the dogs. Still shorter grows the space between
dogs and hare, and Flirt is almost within a yard of it;
when, with a dart as quick as that of a humming-bird, it
switches off almost at a right angle, and leads up a slope
to one side, and heads again for the river bottom. Flash
nearly tumbles over Flirt as she tries to turn, and the
horses nearly tumble over the dogs, while the hare, with
bobbing black tail and ears laid back, spins up the slope
and vanishes over a rise of ground, just as dogs and

horses get fairly headed in the right direction and settle down again to work.

Two seconds bring them in sight of the hare, tearing down the next slope for the high weeds in the river bottom, three or four hundred yards away. Again the violets and bluebells fly from beneath the rushing hoofs, and yells of triumph ring out on the fragrant air as the distance again shortens between hare and hounds on the downhill run; for downhill the dogs have the advantage, and the hare is tiring, besides. Flirt soon closes in, and her white teeth glisten in the sun as she reaches out to collect the personal assets of the failing fugitive. But not yet is he ready to assign, nor shall Flirt be his assignee. He will run his own business a while longer and go into bankruptcy only on his own petition, and not on that of his eager creditors. So, with a sudden twist he dodges the panting mouth behind him and wheels off at a tangent to the left. But Flash, not so close this time as before, loses little time in turning, and, while Flirt is recovering herself, dashes straight ahead for the hare. Swiftly he gains on the weary runaway, but another twist throws him off, while Flirt, having to a still greater degree the advantage that Flash just had—not being too close—comes flying down behind in a straight line for the quarry.

Now do thy best, gay Flirt, or thou art beaten! Right well she knows it; her lithe body opens out another section like a telescope; the distance between her and the hare swiftly shortens; yells again rise from the exultant crowd behind. But all too soon their glee and cries of victory. For the hare, too, draws on its last resources, telescopes out still longer than before, flattens itself to the ground in a desperate burst of energy, and in another second the high stiff weeds of the river bottom close over it just as the jaws of Flirt snap vainly behind.

" Too bad !" exclaimed Belville, as they reined up their panting horses.

"Too good, *I* think," said Laura. "What more could the death of the poor thing that earned its life so well have added to our pleasure ? I'm sure I've never enjoyed anything so much as that race, even though unsuccessful."

" I stand corrected," said Belville frankly. " Yours is the true sentiment. The chase and its associations are everything ; the mere bagging of the game is nothing. That is one reason why I should enjoy hunting with the bow more than with the gun. But while I abominate above all things the monstrous heresy that the principal use of game is to eat, I must admit that I am so far earthly as to have a trifling weakness for seeing something overhauled occasionally."

" Flash don't seem to be of much use to-day," said Norton, looking at the dog, which was lounging along the open ground two or three hundred yards to the right of the " cavalry," and nearly one hundred yards behind their line, while Flirt was actively rummaging the weeds along the edge of the open ground.

" Everything has it uses," replied Miner. " An old tin kettle may adorn a tail, if it can't point a moral. And even that lazy dog may yet come handy."

There was a bustling noise in the weeds, a flicker

of brown scudding through the thick mat of dark green, and away skipped a big hare over the open plain, driven out by Flirt from within the weeds. It headed for the hills, six or seven hundred yards away.

"And now look at Flirt; what ails the dog? It seems now as if *she* didn't care a fig for hares either," cried one of the party, as she ran along behind the hare on an apathetic gallop, losing ground at every jump, while the hare, with ears erect and with high elastic bounds, seemed to be only playing in its swift career.

"Let them manage it. They've hunted this ground before," said Miner, as Belville in his impatience tried to urge Flirt on. And before he had fairly finished the sentence, a long-drawn streak of glossy darkness, with a slim tail projecting behind, came flying along the ground from the right, headed for a point some distance ahead of the hare. The hare, too, saw it, reefed in its ears, lengthened out, flattened down more to the ground, and skimmed the violets at a furious pace. Flirt now hastened her feet and traveled along quite briskly, but on a line that would carry her some distance to the left of the hare; while in the mean time the two lines that formed the courses of the hare and of Flash were fast closing into the apex of a long narrow "V." Too much so to suit Mr. Hare; for his bright black eye showed him that the two lines might soon meet, and in his inner consciousness he felt a possibility of his line merging in the other. So he concluded to shift his line to more pleasant places, and darted off to the left, so as to leave Flash on a straight line behind him.

Whether Flirt had been anticipating some such movement or not we will not say, but in a twinkling she had changed her course and was rapidly flitting along the ground on the line of another " V" and aimed well ahead of the fugitive. The idea of " merging" again suggested itself to the hare, and he wheeled away to the right again so as to leave Flirt behind him, while at the movement Flash went spinning along on another cut-off. As the hare tried to evade this by another twist he found Flirt's propinquity getting somewhat annoying, and endeavoring to escape that, he found Flash also getting too familiar on the other side. So he stopped suddenly short, doubled on his track, and turned directly back on his course, leaving both dogs a dozen yards behind in trying to turn with him. Right in among the clattering hoofs of the cavalcade he ran, whipped unscathed through the medley of legs as the horses tried to check their momentum, and by the time the dogs had got past the horses, there was nothing in sight but a distant bit of bobbing brown, fast fading toward the dim line of weeds.

"Wasn't that splendid!" exclaimed both the ladies, almost out of breath with hard riding.

"Well, I must confess I would have liked it better if they had caught him after such a scientific maneuver as they made. I like to see brains successful," said Belville.

"Well, so do I," said Laura. "Even if it is a 'hare brain'—for the hare showed intelligence too."

"It's very seldom a hare does that," said Miner. "Not once in fifty times. But I must admit that I like to see one get away in that style."

"And I'll stick to it that I like to see something caught occasionally," said Belville.

Norton was tired with the hard riding, and so were the dogs with running; so the riders dismounted and sat down on a sunny bank of flowers to rest.

"You spoke of the heresy of thinking the principal use of game is to eat. Why do you want to catch it, then?" asked Laura of Belville.

"Well, I don't, unless it is done skillfully. I wouldn't give a cent to shoot at a hare with a shot-gun as you did yesterday. I would only shoot at one with a rifle, and only when running crosswise at that. Although I cannot hit more than one in three, I enjoy it far more than if it were no trick to hit them all. Yet, at the same time, I do want to hit one third of them at least. And so I like to see a dog catch one occasionally, though I appreciate a skillful escape still more."

"I think all your ideas are slightly advanced," said Miner. "I feel somewhat that way myself; although I must say that a few years of dry ranching makes the idea of meat most tyrannically predominant over all finer feelings."

"You have a beautiful ranch, I think," said Miss Norton.

"Yes indeed. It is fairly stuffed with beauty. So much so that at times I fear it will burst."

"Why, what do you mean by that?" asked Laura.

"Burst *me*, I mean. Beauty is a little unsubstantial for a steady diet. It's thinner nutriment than rabbit. But we interrupted the Doctor's remarks about the uses of game," said Miner.

"My views are those of the minority of sportsmen,"

continued Belville. "But that minority is fast increasing, and in a few years will be the majority. I think that game was made, *first*, to hunt; *second*, to find; *third*, to look at; *fourth*, to shoot *at*; *fifth*, to hit; *sixth*, *and last*, to eat."

"That is exactly the reverse of the common idea," said Miner.

"I know it," said Belville. "And that is why the game is being swept from the land. It is the idolatrous homage that is paid to the palate as the principal and most righteous claimant upon the game of the country that now compels a man who would seek the medicine of the field and stream, the best medicine in the world for some kinds of ailments, to go so far from home and friends to find it. It seems to be generally conceded that the palate of the man who is too lazy or stupid to hunt his own game must be as tenderly cared for as any of our personal rights. And from all this comes the atrocious heresy that the first and most important, instead of the last and worst, use of game is to eat it. But a better day is already dawning."

"But why has not the man who is unable to hunt as good a right to get game in his way as you have in your way?" asked Miss Norton.

"That is the common argument, I know, and it seems very plausible. But the answer is more than plausible— it is undeniable. There is not game enough, and there never can be enough, for one fourth of the people. It is game for a few, or game for none—game under close restrictions, or no game at all. That is the question, and there is no avoiding it. With other animal food it is different. Fish can be bred, but game cannot."

By this time the party were well rested and ready to remount and return to the house, which they reached in time for dinner.

CHAPTER IV

THE VALLEY QUAIL OF CALIFORNIA.

EARLY in the morning of the next hunting day the enthusiastic quartet of Nimrods and Dianas were seated in their familiar vehicle, appropriately armed for the sport they were after. In a country so full of game, they had not driven far when they suddenly noticed dark objects energetically darting and gliding swiftly over the emerald-dotted ground, as the wagon rolled into a little valley that lay between two low ranges of hills. See how they vanish down the green vistas among the sycamores, skim the sod in the arcades of elders, and dart among the bushes and up the velvet slopes that lead toward the hills. Here, there, and all over, by twos, fours, dozens, and scores, they dodged, rustled, and disappeared from view. And look at old Prince, who hangs fifty or sixty yards behind the wagon, with nose high upraised, tail nearly rigid, and countenance as serious as that of an incubating owl, waddling along as if the pinks and violets were New Jersey sand-burrs. What sound is this that now rings from the hillside, shining with the orange glow of innumerable poppies, where the fecilias are just lighting their soft purple lamps of spring, and the *orthocarpus* is kindling its crimson fire along the ground, where the olive green of the *ramiria* is lovingly embraced by the rich pink of the wild pea, and the dark, glossy green of the sumac is twined with the lighter green leaves and the white showery blossoms of the chilicayote, or the golden bells of the wild honeysuckle ? It sounds like " o-*hi*-o, o-*hi*-o, o-*hi*-o," o-*hi*-o, blown from a silver flute. And it is answered from the opposite hills, from up the valley, and from all sides, until the whole region is filled with calls for " Ohio."

" Now," said Belville, as he tied the horses, " if you will please follow me you will see something quite novel, and a sight that few Eastern people would believe in without they saw it. You need not try to follow me all the time ; but after I first start the game, sit down on a rock until I get them scattered."

" They followed him as he led the way some fifty yards up the sloping hillside, when suddenly from the ramiria and wild buckwheat, a few yards ahead, came a sharp metallic-toned " *whit-whit, whit-whit*," followed by a muffled " *k-wook k-wookook, k-wook k-wookook, kwook k-wook, k-wookook*," from dozens of little throats. To the surprise of the rest, Belville tied Prince to a bush, beside which the dog was already standing like a statue.

" In the East," he explained, " a dog is absolutely necessary to hunt quails with any success at all, but here they run so fast that they will spoil a dog, unless he is kept back until they are thoroughly scattered and scared, so as to make them hide and lie closely. In the upper part of the State they often lie quite well, but here they will not until thoroughly scared and hustled. One can get here all the shooting he needs without any dog at all, but to see the dog work is for me nearly one half of the pleasure, although these birds are so plenty and so strong of scent that it does not call for as much care on a dog's part to find them as it does to find the Eastern bird."

Meanwhile the cries of "*whit-whit*" and "*k-wook-ook k-wook-ook*" had ceased. But after rapidly walking some fifty yards farther, they were heard again. At this, Belville, instead of going slowly or waiting to see something, started on the full run toward the sound.

What a change! A dark blue cloud roared upward from the low brush and flowers ahead of Belville, but out of shot, swept swiftly over some two hundred yards of space, and sank from sight in the shrubbery. Belville fired both barrels of his gun, but nothing "tarried."

"I could have hit so big a mark myself," said Laura to Norton.

"I shot at a bigger mark than you thought, and hit it —*space*," said Belville, who had overheard her. "I don't want to stop now to pick up any, even if they should rise within shot."

He did not wait for an answer, but started again on a run to the place where the quail had settled in the low bushes. Before he reached it the swarming cloud again rose well out of shot, and thundered along the ground; but this time it was more widely scattered than before. As Belville fired his gun over the flock it broke still more, and settled some two hundred yards farther on, but this time scattered over a circle of nearly one hundred yards in diameter. Again he charged, loading as he went; again the cloud rose and broke at the first shot into two or three smaller flocks, and these in turn broke up at the report of the second barrel; and in widely scattered bands of from five to twenty or thirty, with some single birds and pairs, they went whizzing here and there, and lit all over five or six acres of rolling hills some two hundred and fifty yards ahead.

"Now you can come on," called Belville to the rest of his party.

"I guess they will lie now," he added, as they came up. "You see, a person who did not know how to handle these birds would have hard work to get good shooting. Even the experienced Eastern sportsman is apt to vote them a fraud at the first interview or so. Sometimes, especially in summer or fall, one can get close enough for a shot into the flock. But now nearly all the flocks are so wild that the birds must be taken singly and on the wing, as indeed all birds should be taken for good sport. And this can be done only by getting them well scattered and scared, so that they will lie and hide."

They had been walking ahead while they conversed; but now they were suddenly interrupted by a whizzing and a "*chip-chip-chip*," and looking up saw a bluish bird that had started from a twining creeper with scarlet trumpets fly rapidly off. From the bushes all around a dozen swift-whirling companions rose, with mottled waistcoats of white and cinnamon flashing below dark gray-blue coats, little black and white heads, black throats within white collars, and long jaunty black plumes hanging forward over their bills, all in clear relief against the horizon, some darting straight ahead with defiant "*chip-chip-chip*," others twisting to either side.

Belville's gun was quickly at his shoulder; a puff of feathers flew at the report, and the stricken bird went plunging downward amid the buzz of his companions on every side and the roar of hundreds more beyond. Soon all were down again, covering the slopes and the heads of the little ravines over a space about two hundred yards in diameter.

"Pretty wild," said Belville, "but I guess they will be sure to lie now."

Meanwhile, brilliant passages of canine melody were coming from the bush where Prince had been tied, but no attention was paid to them.

"Now, Norton," said Belville, "you may try your gun, and Miss Wilbur may take mine, and I will keep in the background for a while and go after Prince."

Norton and Laura moved on a few yards, and half a dozen birds, each with a saucy "*chip-chip-chip*," sprang whizzing from the blooming ground about ten feet in front of them. One curled around Norton's head with his mottled breast flashing in the sun, while the thunder and smoke of Norton's gun roared and rolled at a safe distance in his rear. Laura had watched the birds between the hammers of her gun until a dozen rose at the sound of Norton's first barrel. When she turned her attention to them, they were ensconced in safety in the green pockets of a little ravine two hundred yards away.

"You're too slow, Laura. You must shoot qui—"

Whizz! buzz! "*chip-chip-chip!*" went three or four more, and bang! went Norton's second barrel before he fairly saw anything. Laura, however, improved upon her first attempt so far as to fire just as they were about to light one hundred and fifty yards away.

"Too slow yet, Laura," he said, and then in turn again seriously impaired the symmetry of a bursting plume of the *yucca*, as another pair of birds darted from the father side of it.

"It seems about as effective as your shooting," she replied, with a light laugh.

"Well, I was exci—"

Again he was interrupted by the obstreperous wings and chirping impudence of twenty or more birds bursting from every shrub, within five steps of the spot he had reached in advancing. His gun went off again before he knew it, and the second barrel tunneled the smoke of the first; while Laura pointed her gun from one bird to another, unable to decide which to fire at, until they lit about a hundred and fifty yards away.

The wild medley of cries and whizzing wings now increased as they advanced farther into the center of the ground where the flock had lit. On every side, from almost every bush, before and after the crack of the gun, while with trembling hands they hurried fresh cartridges into the heated chambers, birds were darting, whizzing, calling, buzzing, going up hill, down hill, crossing, quartering, or curling around behind them; some scudding like hares a few yards along the ground before bursting into flight; others rising almost perpendicularly a few feet before spinning away; others still shooting off on a low upward slant from the ground, but all departing with equal speed.

The guns flamed and roared. Miss Norton now took the gun from Laura, and succeeded in improving on the latter's shooting by firing about as the birds passed the one-hundredth yard instead of the hundred and fiftieth; while Norton scattered leaves of green, pink, purple, orange, crimson, or gold behind the birds before they fairly cleared the cover.

Hurrah! At last a bird whirls over at the flash of his gun! He runs quickly; it is only a few feet away, and he is soon there, just in time to see a dark object flash along the gaudy earth and disappear in a twinkling. You must drop them dead, Norton; for you might as well try to catch a flash of lightning as a wounded quail that has its legs all right.

"I'm completely demoralized," said Norton, as Belville came up, with Prince walking stiff-legged behind him. "Do you think such exercise good for me, Doctor? I'm all out of breath," he added, wiping his brow, which for the first time in many a month was wet with healthful perspiration. His face glowed with unwonted color, his breath came fast, and his heart throbbed with an energy long unknown to it.

"So long as it comes only from pleasant excitement, it is the best medicine you could have. You will eat more and digest better to-day when we go back to the house than you have done for a long time. If it were work or alarm that wearied or excited you, it would be vastly different. But, you see, you have walked scarcely a quarter of a mile, and that very slowly. I did all the work. You have had only the excitement and amusement, mixed with just exercise enough. And that is all an invalid should have—little work, much amusement. You should never venture out hunting without a buggy or saddle-horse, and should never hunt these quails without a companion to break and scatter the flock; which is sometimes quite a lively task, though it is not always necessary to run as I did. You can often scatter them on horseback. Now you can sit down on this stone and I will take a turn."

Belville again tied Prince to a bush, and went on alone, while the rest remained behind and watched him. The bewildering intensity of the rush and buzz in which Norton had become so demoralized was over. But birds were rising still at almost every step as Belville went on, and somber lines of blue were spinning through the air all the time, a fresh bird starting before the previous one disappeared.

Belville, though a good shot, was out of practice; and however well a person may understand hunting and shooting, and however well he may shoot with slower game, he must keep the very highest polish on his skill if he would successfully trip these dark, swift-flying fellows. For, remember that they rise at only about six or seven yards, and are not pointed by a dog in the method of hunting now described. They stand shot well, too, and they will keep up like hope in the bosom of a spinster. No more gamey bird flies than the California quail, and he dies game to the last. Unless fairly struck with the center of the charge, and that too at close distance, they are quite apt to win the victory even over the tremendous odds of the double gun in skillful hands. And though Belville had long hunted quails, he had not yet learned what it takes many so long to learn—to load for these quail with *very fine* shot, not less than No. 10, and heavy charges of powder; so that the air in the bird's course shall be filled with flying missiles, all at the highest attainable velocity.

And therefore it was that, as Belville went on firing at every eight or ten steps, many birds spun away, leaving the spectators gazing in wonder at the cloud of feathers floating back on the air. Some went for two hundred yards or more zig-zagging up and down in alternate yielding to death and victory over it, and finally descended with a plunge and a bounce upon the ground. Others towered swiftly upward with their gay plumes in sharp relief against the sky, set their little wings for a moment, and descended with a whirl down the side of a ravine, where it would bother one to find them; or, if there were much prickly-pear or other cactus convenient, they seemed to take especial care to select an impenetrable clump of it for their last resting-place. Some ran into clumps of cactus with their last breath, sat coolly down in it just beyond reach, and, while the little crested heads drooped in death, cast on the hunter a look that said, as plainly as words: " No, you don't, Mr. Smarty." Others descended out of a thick shower of feathers, and, recovering, went glimmering through the bushes on foot at a speed Belville could scarcely follow, even on open ground. There were some that unloaded a handful of feathers at the crack of the gun, and seemed to travel all the easier for it. And even when killed they kicked, fluttered, bounced, and rolled along the ground and down the slopes, as if determined not to yield; and one fluttered out of his captor's very pocket and went towering upward, after he was thought to be dead.

Quite as remarkable as anything about the practiced quail-shot of Southern California is his skill in picking up dead birds. Owing to the confusion, the swift running of the birds, the excitement—often too much for a dog to stand—and the frequent lack of water, without which on a warm day a dog can do little work, the quail-hunter of this section often does not use a dog even to retrieve dead birds, but prefers to pick them up as well as find them himself. Well developed must be his bump of locality, keen his eye, and quick his judgment, or else in the maze of green, yellow, red, blue, white, and pink, with birds buzzing and "*chip-ing*" on every side, and with no time to lose, he will never pick up two thirds of the birds he kills. But Belville had shot many a quail before in this county, and whenever a bird fell he went straight to the spot where it was.

Suddenly he stopped, came back to the party, and said : "It is too bad to cripple so many. I'd rather not shoot at all. But I've got a little slow from being out of practice and let them get too far off before shooting. It is almost time to let Prince loose, anyhow. Perhaps, now, you think there are no more birds on this ground that you have been over."

"I don't see how there can be, after all that got out of it," said Norton.

"Well, we'll inspect it. We will go around to the leeward of it, so as to have the dog's nose against the wind."

Prince suspended the few last bars of the variations he was brilliantly improvizing upon his original touching theme, and when he was untied his tail nearly thrashed his sides with joy. His master made him march behind until he reached the windward side of the ground where the birds had been first thoroughly scattered, and then, with the words " Hie on !" sent him out ahead. With nose nearly even with the general level of the bushes, and lashing his tail, he threaded the cover with the ease of a snake. Scarcely had he wound his way from side to side for fifty yards, when his tail began to slacken speed. His legs improved upon the example of his tail, and his tail set the legs a still better example; the rivalry continuing until the whole animal was anchored like a rock.

As the hunters came up beside him, he turned his head a bit and cast an inquiring and anxious eye upon his master, his nose twitched a little at the corners of its channels, his chops seemed fairly to water with expectation, and his tail quivered faintly at the tip with the effort to hold it rigid.

"You take first shot now. The bird is not over ten feet from his nose, probably in that little bush," said Belville.

Norton's heart suddenly felt like a shuttle between his hair and his boots. But he advanced, smiling and confident, into the arena. When one step ahead of Prince, he heard a quick rustle in a bush of ramiria, a defiant "*chip-chip-chip-chip*," a dark flash was dimly seen along the ground through the variegated undergrowth, and a quail suddenly burst into flight, with Norton's shot mowing the scarlet bells from a creeping vine twined around a buckwheat bush just behind it. But before the swift-scudding streak had lengthened another yard ahead, Belville's gun came up, and as the flame and smoke leaped out, a puff of feathers appeared to take the place of the bird. Prince lay down until the guns were loaded, and then at the word walked in, picked up the bird by the wing and brought it to his master.

How unlike any Eastern game-bird is this odd little combination of bluish slate, black, cinnamon, and white, with its long natty black plume! Yet the short, thick, curved bill, the full swelling breast, and graceful form would all show it to be unmistakably a quail, even if we had not witnessed its gamey behavior. Who that has not seen for himself could realize the great numbers in which the birds are often found, and the brain-befuddling extravagance of their whizzing presence, when one is in the midst of a large, scattered flock? And yet, if the reader will pause and reflect for a moment, he will see that what appears like a " California yarn" of stupendous size may be even below the actual truth. Consider that these birds are far beyond the orbit of the market-shooters, the " big-bag" louts often miscalled sportsmen, and the netter and trapper ; that they do not suffer from cold winters or wet breeding-seasons, the " dry year" only suspending their breeding without destroying the old birds. Remember, too, that in the breeding season they are equally at home in the garden or the wildest cañon, the depths of the ravine or the high hill-top ; equally happy among rocks or brush, along steep hillsides or in the long grass or tangled underbrush of river and creek bottoms. In timber or out of timber, by water or miles from water, four thousand feet or one foot above sea-level, all to them are the same. Then remember that they raise twelve or fifteen young, and sometimes nest twice in a season ; that in the fall the separate bevies run together and form in packs like pinnated grouse ; and that even these packs sometimes run together. So that sometimes all the birds bred on one, two, or three thousand acres of ground, or even more, may be found in a single band ; and when thus banded they are nearly always found in the little valleys, and no longer in the hills where most of them were bred.

The shooting soon changed character after Prince was introduced. Instead of a bird in almost every bush there were now not more than one in fifteen or twenty yards. But the birds lay much closer than before, and the shooting was more like Eastern quail or pinnated-grouse shooting. Old Prince wound to and fro on a slow trot, with his head and nose plainly visible above the brush. Every few minutes he stopped and stood, a statue such as the sculptor's art never yet portrayed, as his delicate nose detected, by that subtle scent unknown to man, when he approached some little plumed rogue ensconced in the dense wealth of flower-twined ramiria, sage, buckwheat, or sumac, unconscious of being seen. But though it is far easier to shoot when one knows exactly whence the bird will spring, they were still far too quick for the tyro. And though Belville gave them the first shot every time, neither Norton, with his nervous expedition in unloading, nor the ladies, with their dilatory fumbling of the gun until the bird was gone, could lower the nodding plume of a single one. But Belville sent them whirling at nearly every shot, and in a short time had a bagful.

"I have enough now," he said, "but if you don't feel too tired you can keep on and practice. We can find birds at this rate for two or three hours yet, and a man low enough down to shoot for count could kill over a hundred yet before night."

They were all ready to leave off the sport, however, both Norton and the ladies feeling somewhat wearied with exercise and excitement, and regaining their wagon they drove gayly back, reaching home as twilight was beginning to descend, after a sunset of surpassing beauty.

CHAPTER V

THREE or four miles above Miner's is a small laguna, with a bank some twenty feet high on one side and open flats on the other side and at each end. This was known to Belville as a capital hunting-ground; and, desirous of taking his friends there, he got them started at an early day. As they drove up in sight of the laguna, its smooth face was seen to be dotted with small dark bodies.

"Pretty liberally sprinkled with mud-hens," said Belville; "still there are some ducks there. And, as sure as I live, there is a flock of geese on that flat!" he added, pointing to a distant line of dark gray birds standing on the green sod across the pond. "If I can borrow that horse of that fellow I'll try a charge on them. It's the only way to get a shot."

So saying, he hailed a young Mexican who was coming behind them on horseback, and, pointing to the geese, asked him in villainous Spanish to lend him the horse.

The Mexican dismounted with a smile, perhaps at the Spanish, perhaps at the geese, possibly at neither. We shall see. Belville mounted and ambled down to within two hundred yards of the geese, on the windward side. Then, on a gentle canter, he rode on a slanting course toward one side of the flock.   He did not look at them at all until he got within about one hundred yards, when he suddenly wheeled the horse and charged directly at them on a full run.   They waddled and looked, and looked and waddled, until the "cavalry" got within sixty yards, when they concluded it was about time to clear the track.   Being compelled, however, to rise against the wind—geese *can* rise down wind, but *prefer* up wind— the cavalry, in its rapid career, was within thirty-five yards before the heavy birds got fairly started from the ground.   The confused bustling huddle of black necks, white collars, dark gray backs, together with the sound of heavily beating wings and the rapidly recurring "*onk-k-wonk—onk-wonk—honk—k-wonk-onk*," caused the horse, a mere colt, to sheer a little.   But the target was so large that a snap-shot, the only kind possible from a run-ning horse, could hardly miss it, and with the report of the first barrel two geese sunk heavily to the sod.

So did Belville at about the same instant.   As though a keg of powder had exploded beneath him he left the saddle, as the horse, springing high in air, struck ground stiff-legged and with arching back.   Belville sat for a moment, half dazed by the jar, but finding no bones broken, picked himself up, took an affectionate gaze at his swiftly retiring charger, and indulged in some highly philosophical observations upon mustangs and their skill in the art of "bucking."

He did not smile very much as he approached the wagon and thanked the owner of the horse.   But the owner did—a smile fully as deep as politeness demanded. Then be borrowed a bunch of matches and some tobacco of Belville, and hade him good-by in a tone and with a smile that said, as plainly as words, " If my horse can be of any service to you next time, he is entirely yours."

At one end of the pond a little arm ran up containing a few bunches of rushes, on the bank of which one of Miner's boarders had built a little hut of brush close by the edge—a place where many a duck had been shot by a lady.

" Now if one of the ladies will go and sit in that little blind and wait, patient and motionless, until they light close enough," said Belville, " I will go and drive up some ducks. And you, Mr. Norton, I will drop over there between this pond and that other little one beyond. Then do you please lie flat on your back in that little gully, and don't move until the ducks get right over you.

Laura took the blind and Miss Norton remained in the wagon. A number of flocks of ducks had been started on the wing by Belville's shot at the geese, but had settled again at the upper end of the pond. As the wagon drove along the shore they rose, some mounting high at once, others skimming low for some distance, but all in one flapping, quacking, squealing mob. In a few seconds they were divided off into flocks. The big mallards with long projecting green necks and heads, cinnamon breasts, and whitish-gray " underclothes " swung high in air and marched away. The sprigtail trailed for a few moments his plumed rudders along the sky, and left for more retired parts. But the widgeon in large flocks whistled their way on high a few times around the pond, and then, setting their wings, went hissing down the air toward the little pond beyond the big one.

As they passed over where Norton lay, they shot upward at the flame of his gun as if they had struck an incline of lubricated ice; but one at the rear of the flock eliminated two or three feathers and started downward at about the same angle the others took in going up. Down to within three feet of the ground he came, then rose again, gyrated, twisted and alighted for repairs, just as Norton again took a hand in and composed his anxiety with the second barrel.

Meanwhile a flock of teal, after scudding up and down the pond a few times and executing some handsome curves at each end, wheeled into the arm of the pond where Laura was posted, and settled in the water about thirty yards from her little hut. She could see their little beaded eyes, the green spots on the wings of the gray teal, and the blue bands on the wings of the cinnamon teal, all shining in the sun, and she saw them wiggle their tails, lower their black bills, and swim closer together. She trembled with anxiety and exultation as the thought crossed her mind that she might get them all at one shot. And as she put the gun through a little opening and fired too high, as almost every tyro will do at such times, she never dreamed of the possibility of getting less than half. But when the smoke cleared away she saw the rear of the flock just swinging at a rapid pace around a bunch of rushes, and the water where they had sat bore not a single feather.

Norton got back into his place just as a flock of spoon-bills came curving down to light in the pond behind him. On they came in solid array, and his expectations embarked at once in a balloon. So did his judgment. The first barrel rang out, and the solid ranks scattered for a second, rose and closed up again in solid mass just as he pulled the second trigger full at the thickest part. Not a feather, not a twist or "wabble" in the flight of a single bird! Norton turned around and watched them. He could hardly believe his eyes as he saw them curve, sail down in orderly array, and light with unruffled plumes in the distant pond.

He had little time to meditate on the causes, however, for Belville was soon around to the pond with the wagon, and started up that same flock and several flocks of widgeon, beside. They came along, some over Norton, others, remembering the place of their late scare, sheering off, others turning off to leave these quarters entirely. As a flock of widgeon passed whistling over him, he raised his gun too soon, and they climbed and sheered out of reach; but a flock of teal close behind them came whizzing on in level flight, and too swiftly to change their course enough to escape the gun. They sheered and huddled just as Norton caught along the barrels a fair sight on the center of the thickest bunch. Four wilted and whirled downward at the report; another lowered from the flock, and scudding downward toward the pond, splashed dead into the water at its edge, while a sixth mounted high in air, hung there a moment as if in doubt as to which element he belonged, and then decided in favor of earth.

The spoon-bills, after circling two or three times, putting on a great amount of style, slid down the air on a winding course and lit within about twenty yards of Laura's blind. They looked ineffably stupid, with their big shovel bills, but as Laura began to move her gun they began to swim suspiciously away. Suddenly they rose, but at the same instant she *happened* to shoot, and two of them fell flat as a pun in the humorous column of a weekly newspaper.

A flock of cinnamon teal were about to settle at the same moment, but changed their minds so expeditiously that Laura knocked down the roof-tree of her house in trying to get a flying shot at them. Before she had time to fix it another flock rounded the bunch of rushes, flying low along the water, and were almost upon her before they sheered and rose—a medley of shining cinnamon jackets and flashing wings of gray and blue. As she quickly raised the gun and looked along the barrel, she saw, or thought she saw, the whole flock directly in line, and with a smile of satisfaction pulled the trigger. The smile was instantly swamped in a quagmire of wonder, and to this day she can't understand how she missed those ducks.

" The big ducks are all leaving," said Belville, driving up. " Let's go up to the Monte and lunch, and when we come back we will visit the small ponds and sloughs where they have gone."

Two miles over rolling green sod brought them to the gate of the Monte, a long, narrow park of level, timbered ground between two ranges of hills, on the one side high, ragged, and rocky, on the other side lower, smoother, and blazing with all the colors of the rainbow, over a groundwork of soft, warm green. They rode along beneath old sycamores heavily festooned with grape-vines, now bright with new life, past thick jungles of wild rose and sweetbrier, by great beds of mustard whose rank green was now waving in a yellow sea of bloom, and heavy green elders just opening their snowy millinery, until they reached a grove of aged live-oaks that might have been monarchs when Charlemagne was a baby. And beyond they found on one side the river whirling its glittering mica sands, while the hill, covered with boulders beneath which sprang an abundance of lace-gold, silver-cotton, and other ferns, narrowed in on the other.

Across the river rose Mt. Cajon, a stupendous wall of granite nearly three thousand feet high, steep as the Palisades, born of agony, nurtured by convulsion, and baptized out of chaos. Here and there, through the chinks in the wild mass of immense boulders that covered its grizzly crest, the lilac or mauzanita struggled, and here and there a scrubby tree fought for a foothold in some of the rifts of the great sheer wall; but all else was gray, impassive granite. Far above the towering head of the mountain some dark birds were winding with outstretched, motionless wing in graceful curves through the soft blue air.

" How beautifully those eagles sail !" said Laura.

" Quite a natural mistake," said Belville.

" What do you mean ? Are they not eagles?"

" I'm a little afraid your knowledge of eagles has been derived from poetry," said Belville. " Except in poetry and tinsel rhetoric the eagle is only a great overgrown booby of a hawk, the clumsiest and most ignoble of his tribe. I've seen a hare outwit him by twisting on the open plain, and have found him dead by the side of a miserable sheep-stealing coyote whose poisoned vitals he had been eating. No other hawk eats anything but his own game. And besides, no eagle ever sails with half the grace of those unpoetical things that are curling with such majestic sweep above us."

"What are they, then?" she asked, with an air of mingled disappointment and skepticism.

"The Californians, who love to dignify all of the productions of their native State with imposing names, call them vultures; but they are in fact buzzards differing from the common buzzard only in color and size, being the largest bird in the world next to the condor of the Andes. But of all birds that fly their motions are the most beautiful and—"

"They are not either. I don't like them a bit," said Laura, dropping her shining eyes upon his and trying to look indignant.

"You change your opinion suddenly. A rose by any other name should smell as sweet."

"Indeed it does not, though. I'll stand by the eagle, and won't hear him insulted—the bird of Jove and America! I'm shocked at you," she retorted, with a pretty pout. "One or two critics like you could spoil the romance of all creation."

"I know," he said, "that to substitute a buzzard for the eagle in a poem would be to dig the poem's grave. I know, too, that he is indispensable to the callow city scribbler who takes a summer trip to the mountains or the northern lakes. The eagle on the blasted pine or spreading his great vans on heaven's breeze is invaluable to the literary upholsterer who has never seen any thing of nature except through others' eyes. But when—"

A mellow "*O-hi-o, O-hi-o, O-hi-o*," ringing from a distant opening in the hills, interrupted him.

"I can't stand that!" said Belville. "Let's go and enliven them a little."

"I'm a little tired with riding and hunting ducks," said Norton, "and it may be too far for me."

"Perhaps the ladies will go, then?"

Laura answered first, saying that she would go, and Miss Norton said she would stay and get the lunch ready. So Belville and Miss Wilbur started for the quail.

It took but a few moments to break and scatter the flock, as on the day before.

"Now, Miss Wilbur," said Belville, "I really don't care whether we get a bird or not, but it will be a splendid chance for you to practice, since you seem so anxious to learn."

"I should be delighted to try. It's fun to see them fly and shoot at them, even if you hit none."

"Then keep a little ahead of me, please, and when a bird rises try and see him along that strip between the barrels of the gun, and the instant you do see him, pull the trigger. This flock is not so big, and therefore not so bewildering as the first one you saw, which was of extraordinary size even for this country."

As Laura moved ahead, a bird sprang up, with a saucy "*chip, chip, chip*," from a bush almost beneath her feet. As she raised her gun at this one, another bustled out of a bush to her left with such vigor that she abandoned the first and turned her gun on the second. While doing so she heard a rustle and a squeal in a bush to her right, and a bird burst from it and scudded a few yards along the ground, almost as fast as if in flight, and then darted away on the wing just as she raised her gun at it; and at the same instant four or five more, buzzing and squealing as they flew from a bush to her right, completed her confusion.

"Mercy!" she exclaimed, as soon as she could catch the breath she had held all this time. "I'm too nervous. I'm trembling like a leaf!"

"So is every one at first that has any fine sensibility. But you mustn't allow other birds to distract your attention. Keep your attention on the first one you raise the gun at, and shoot at that one even if it does get too far away; and don't shoot until you get the gun well aimed."

Another bird rose at her first step forward. As the gun came to a level, she caught over its end a faint glimpse of a dark blue object swiftly skimming the top of the brush. A strange feeling tingled like an electric shock through her whole frame; she was scarcely conscious of touching the trigger; yet a shaft of flame shot out, and through the rolling smoke she dimly saw a cloud of fine feathers come drifting back upon the breeze, and the dark blue thing was gone.

"Isn't that just splendid!" she said, with sparkling eyes and rapid breath. "I never thought that shooting was so nice."

"Ah ha! Farewell now to peace of mind; farewell the dance, the piano, and the song; farewell the lamp-mat, the novel, and the tidy; farewell embroidered cats and decalcomanie vegetation !   You're gone now—lost, lost, lost '"

" Well, I'm awakened, surely, as you said I would be. If that s any specimen of the amusement, I'm a confirmed sportsman from now on "

" But it's only fair to tell you that you will have a long road to journey before you can do that often.   However, you will find pleasure enough in hitting one out of four."

" Oh yes, I'm sure that's enough ; for it's half the pleasure to be out of doors amid such charming scenery, and to see the birds fly and dart about so fast," she answered, walking on.   " I'm sure I shall learn to—"

Whizz! went another bird, and bang! went the gun harmlessly above it.   " *Chip, chip, chip,*" went another, as the shot from the second barrel shattered a wild cucumber hanging from a bush several feet behind it.

" Pshaw! I haven't quite mastered it yet, have I ?" she exclaimed ; then adding, as he reloaded for her, " I'm wasting your cartridges, too."

" I dote on their destruction," was the gallant reply. " But you must take it more easily.   Don't shoot until you see the bird between the barrels, and shoot a little ahead of birds flying crosswise."

Another quail darted from a bush to the right, skipped like a hare along the ground for a few yards, then burst into full flight with a " *chip, chip, chip,*" followed by the shot of Laura's first barrel far in his rear ; and *whizz! buzz!* " *chip, chip, chip,*" went a dozen more, drifting like meteors through the smoke of the gun, while Laura shifted her aim from one to the other, and finally shot at vacancy.

A few steps, and half a dozen more whisked out of the ramiria, radiating like the branches of a fan, and each made first-class time for a different point of the compass. She looked at them an instant in confusion, then raised the gun on one going straight away. It came full in range of a careering line of gray and blue, and almost automatically she pulled the trigger.

At the report, the bird rose upward; up, up, up it went, its little dark head and sable plume in clear outline against the sky; but now its wings beat slower and slower, it hung a moment on high, then drooped its little crested head, folded its fluttering wings, and dropped with a heavy thump to earth.

"Shot through the head! Fit emblem of many another crack-brain whose towering has only increased the violence of his fall," said Belville, as he picked up the bird and brought it to her.

"Oh, I feel so sorry for the poor little thing!" she said, with sad November morning in her expression. "But isn't this delightful?" she added a moment after, with a June noonday in its place.

Strange passion indeed! That even a woman should draw pleasure from the sufferings of poor little innocents! Yet what avail sentimental arguments against what is as fixed as the eternal hills? The taste is there, implanted by the Creator; not intended to lie dormant, for it is too intense to be given for nothing. The highest and noblest of our race have bowed to it, and each year the throng of votaries increases. And what, after all, *are* the arguments against it but the old plea of preferring the incidental before the essential? One might as well say that the pleasure of riding lay in the suffering of the horse that is compelled to travel against his will, as to say that the pain of bird or fish is anything but an unpleasant, although unavoidable, incident of hunting or fishing.

"You're doing remarkably well," said Bellville encouragingly. "Killing two birds the first day is rare even for a man."

"Oh, now you're flattering."

"May I never speak again if"— A bird here rose with noisy wing, curled to the left of Laura, and passed almost over Belville's head. As she raised the gun Belville was hidden by the barrels, and when she fired and took down her gun he lay flat upon the ground.

A shriek that might have waked the mummy of an Egyptian deaf-mute nearly froze the wine in the lunch-basket at the wagon. As the echo died away along the wall of Mount Cajon, Belville raised his head and said,

" Why, what's the matter?"

"Oh, Doctor! how could you scare me so?" she gasped.

"Scare you? Why, I only dropped out of your way, and stayed there, so as to give you a clear field for your second barrel: a thing one should always do when a bird comes near."

"You lay so long! I thought you were shot."

"Perhaps I did lie a little longer than was absolutely necessary. But I wanted to be sure the shot had got past. This San Diego powder is a little slow sometimes."

"I thought all powder was quick enough?" said she.

"Everything is slow in this country—life, death, railroads, debtors, and all, and the presumption is strongly in favor of the slowness of the powder," he replied.

CHAPTER VI.

HERE is a vast quadrangle of earthen wall and ruins, and our friends now stand musing in it. Who built and trod this long array of doorways, arches, galleries, and storied tiers of rooms, all now crumbling to decay? How quickly the past rises before the spectators as they gaze on the wreck of what was once the stateliest structure of California, and contemplate what has been spared by the Vandal hand that for a few paltry tiles has despoiled this noble shrine! These long colonnades and fretted arches, the long walls of adobe running in all directions, the rough mounds of earth that were once the walls of many houses, all speak of departed greatness. In one corner stands the massive church and tower inside of which, as in the olden days, is still the rudely-painted altar where thousands of dusky worshipers have bowed. High in the tower, where the cactus bristles from the rents of time, still hangs the bell that called to prayer the tenants of the fallen tombs in the graveyard below. But within and without all is now silent as the grave.

Sneer not, you who have "been abroad." When you contrast this relic with St. Peter's, remember that the hand that sprung those arches and that dome, that laid out those great walls, leveled those floors, and raised those colonnades so plumb, had no artisans to follow out its paper plans, and possessed few tools but those of the roughest sort; no nails, but only rawhide lashings; no wagons, carts—almost nothing but the raw material. There were no workmen but the wild and lazy Indians, the stupidest of their race, speaking a strange language, caring for nothing but food, and watchful of nothing but a chance to steal. From yonder mountain, thirty miles away and six thousand feet high, those beams were carried—yes, *carried*, on Indian shoulders; for there were then no wagons or teams, nor yokes of oxen to drag them.

Think of the toil, the patience, the nerve—no, the undying faith, for nothing else could have done it—that was necessary to superintend every inch of that massive work, from the digging of the dirt or hewing of the timber to the painting of the altar; and remember that the brain that directed it all was trained only to the work of the cloister and the confessional, and was thousands and thousands of miles from supplies or skilled help.

All now speaks only of death and decay. Yet there was a time when busy life streamed daily through these portals; when the dust of business whirled daily in these courts; when all these buildings were thronged with dusky artisans, vibrating between work, *atole*, and prayer; when thousands of Indians—not dragooned, for there were no soldiers to do it—bowed to the persuasive will of a single priest who had left home, friends, civilization, and comforts of every kind, for their sake alone; when thirty thousand cattle, ten thousand horses, and thousands of sheep roamed these rolling hills around us. Quietly this little world moved on, without feeling the jars that shook the greater sphere. They scarcely knew, until it was over, of the paltry scuffle for empire on the Atlantic coast; and when Napoleon was thundering at the doors of Europe the echoes died away thousands of miles from their peaceful hearths. They lived, built, worked, taught, prayed, and died, their lives one long, lingering summer day, until Mexican cupidity eclipsed its peaceful sun.

What sadness must have possessed the souls of the *padres* as they then hastened to put a barren sceptre into the hand of the secular invader, turned the Indians loose among the fattened herds, tore up the vineyards, threw down the wine-press, and dismantled the pictured shrines! Yet even sadder is the thought that this grand old ruin of the mission of San Luis Rey is, like all the missions of California, also doomed to destruction through apathy, stupidity, and Vandalism, aided by a bigotry that refuses to let others save what it will not or cannot save itself.

After passing over a few miles of smooth, rolling hills clad with wild oak, alfileria, clover, and mustard, our party of hunters descended into the fair valley of Santa Margarita, part of the princely estate of Don Juan Forster, and in a short time they reached the ranch-house itself.

This place is a relic of that golden age of California life which lay between the decline of the missions and the invasion of the Yankee. Here still stands the old ranch-house, a great quadrangle of *adobe*, built around a court-yard, the seat of a little empire of thirty square leagues of land, much of it the very best in Southern California. The great walls, nearly a yard thick, hint strongly of cool days in summer and warm nights in winter. The long massive beams, cut in the mountains thirty miles away; the rafters lashed with rawhide instead of being nailed; the old red tiles made by the mission Indians and held in place by their own weight —all speak of the difficulties of building in those days. Yet the whole is massive and strong, and will stand for many a year to come when far more costly structures are decayed. Here still, as in bygone days, may be heard the whizz of the *riata* thrown by the skillful hand; for here yet linger a very few of that almost extinct race, the old vaqueros of California—men who could, single-handed, ride down, lasso, and bind the wild bull of the hills on a mountain-side where a city rider would hardly dare to lead a horse.

Here, too, may still be seen another fast-fading relic, the hospitable old Spanish gentleman of the olden time. An Englishman by birth and a Spaniard by adoption, Don Juan Forster is well fitted to be the grandee that he has been and dispense the rare old hospitality to all the world that he has so long dispensed. Uniting the virtues of both races, without the vices of either—unless liberality be a vice—two generations have looked upon him with no feeling of envy, but only of friendly pride. And though, for the interests of the country, many will rejoice that his immense estate is thrown open to settlement, there are still many who will regret the loss of this grand memento of the olden time.

Despise not, my stylish friend, that olden time. The handsome rosewood and massive mahogany furniture of antique pattern, the laces and the linen of the fineness, solidity, and patterns of the past, and many other ancient household articles, show plainly that comfort and luxury were even then not strangers in this wild land.

But what if they were? What if the great *adobe* houses lacked the tinsel frippery of more pretentious mansions? Spend a few hot days in their cool recesses when your modern house of clear lumber, scroll-work, brackets and cornices is heated through by the sun, and you will begin to think it just possible that cheapness was not the sole motive in building of sun-dried mud. What if their tables lacked the fare that tickles the palate and makes the undertaker smile? They repaired their fleshly tenements with the solid oak and not the gilded pine; and they and their children show the difference. What if they lounged not on silken sofas or gazed on no costly daubs? They took their ease in the saddle, and their eyes rested daily on pictures that art can never degrade to canvas.

If they had no railroads, they could travel from San Diego to the farthest northern settlement without a cent —a proceeding that savors of bankruptcy in these enlightened days. They had no newspapers, but they knew not the torture of the column of bad puns, and cared nothing for the advent of triplets in Mr. Snipe's family in Texas, or for the abrogation of Barney Muldoon's optic in a Bowery row. They had no telegraphs, but also no mining-stock reports to steal away their brains and money; no imposing school-houses with big cupolas, but no bonds to swamp them with taxes; few novels or none, but also few lazy girls. They had no aristocratic pups, hammerless breech-loaders, or repeating rifles; but they could lasso the grizzly and drag him alive from his mountain home.

Rude was their system of justice; but they had no probate courts or public administrators. They had no doctors or lawyers; but then they died without expensive assistance, and their families got at least one per cent of the property they left. Living in true patriarchal style, surrounded by plenty of the solid necessaries of life, with plenty of servants that cost only their board, with nothing to do but look after their herds, roll *cigaritas*, attend fandangos and *meriendas*, and warble their beautiful language, they drifted down the stream of time without touching oar or rudder or striking sand-bars or snags.

That soft Arcadian day is gone. Its twilight still lingers in a few places, but its sun has set forever. Our countrymen came and were welcomed; for, contrary to the common belief, the majority of Californians were anxious for the change. We came with our usual Yankee conceit and our prejudice against everything that comported not with our notions of "progress"—all strengthened by the prejudice against Mexicans imbibed during the war with them. We came to load them with ruinous costs and atrocious lawyers' fees to maintain those vested rights of property which all nations respect; to squat on their ranches and live on their cattle; to pass laws to destroy their only industry, and, as time has proved, the best industry of this southern country. We came to lend them money at five per cent *a month*, and trap them into contracts to pay it for a long enough time to sweep away their homes with the mortgage. We came to turn up the parvenu proboscis at Indian-bred and Castilian-bred alike, and treated as "greasers" some who were our equals in every respect and the superiors of many of the upstart Americans who sneered at them.

I do not believe that justice has ever been done to the Spanish of California; and this is not the place to do it even if I were fully qualified for the task. But such ideas as are generally obtained from newspaper and magazine articles about Texas and New Mexico convey a very false idea of the Spanish of California. Their names are written high upon the roll of honor of the State; and they have been among the best and most honest of State and county officials, and the most incorruptible and impartial of judges. No more law-abiding or better citizens exist than the upper half of the Spanish, and it is difficult to see wherein the lower half are any worse than the lower half of American society. If they are, it is only because they have bettered the instruction of excellent and faithful teachers. Their "laziness," so much talked about, is precisely what that of the Western farmer would be if overwhelmed by a horde of Chinese, who should pass laws that virtually compelled him to abandon his way of making money and adopt theirs, of which he knew nothing, and which would barely make him a living. If their possessions are gradually slipping from them and their lands passing into the stranger's hand, it is due to the laws and the heavy taxes we have forced upon them much more than to either their own improvidence or want of thrift. And when more than half the Americans are going the same road, we might as well acknowledge that we do not know all about the best way to make a living in Southern California, and that the old inhabitants did know at least something of that art; for it is certain that they were nearly all wealthy and wanted nothing.

After their visit to the old mission our friends were glad to sit down under Don Juan Forster's great front porch and look down the valley toward the sea, just as the flood-tide of rosy mist began to flow in from the sinking sun, and the soft carpet of the high smooth hills to run through all shades of purple, green, and gold. The waves of light ran rippling over the rolling slopes of silvery-green wild oats; the emerald meadow in front was dotted with horses and cattle; the wild geese and brant in clamorous mobs were marching in from the coast; the wild ducks in whizzing flocks scudded up and down the valley; here and there a snipe was pitching and squeaking aloft; the sand-hill cranes, with dolorous "*gr-r-rooo, gr-r-rooo,*" were floating across the blue zenith; the white pelican, the egret, or the swan was winging its solemn way toward the Laguna; and from the cañons came the clear "*ohio, ohio*" of the valley quail.

"It seems like an enchanted land, does it not?" said Laura. "I don't wonder so many people fall in love with California."

"You are now seeing it at its best. There are times when it is different from this," said Don Juan, with a frankness that is too rare among the Californians when any question about California comes up. "We experience here three kinds of winter: First, the 'good' winter, when there is just about rain enough, and that properly distributed. Then vegetation is at its climax, crops are good, the sloughs and ponds have plenty of water, and geese and ducks, as well as other game, are plenty. Second, the 'medium' year, when there is not rain enough (or not properly distributed), to make much more than half a crop of grass and grain, but when there is still enough to feed all stock and cover most of the expenses of the settler. The first of these may be too wet for the very sick invalid, the second will be about right, and there is a third will suit him exactly if he wants only clear, warm weather and has no sympathy for a suffering land.

"But who with a sentient soul can behold the 'dry' or 'bad' winter and not feel sorrowful? Day after day and week after week the sun climbs the unclouded sky, sinks into his ocean bed of silver, carmine, and gold, and flames next morning at the eastern gate with as smiling a face as that of a just-accepted lover. At long intervals, as if in mockery of our hopes, a very few rain-drops patter gently on the roof. And once or twice there may be enough of a shower to tempt one to borrow an umbrella, but not long enough to make him yield to the temptation to keep it.

"But January treads on the heels of February, and February joins March in the long procession of bright days, with a smiling face above and sad and sickening faces below. Then yonder rolling hills of velvet green are brown and bare; the violets and the alfileria, called out by the first good rain, spirt, curl up and wither away, or seed out at an inch high; the earth yields no interest on the farmer's loan; the bee returns empty to his hive; the quail declines to mate; the hare retires like a monk to the cloisters of the rocks; and the goose returns disgusted to the north. Then the ewe deserts her new-born lamb, and the raven begins to feed on her even before she lies down to die. The ox or the horse staggers to the spring and is unable to return; bloated and weary, the overworked buzzards sit around on the corral fence; and still nature keeps up a steady dress-parade of fine weather, and the sun smiles on, smiles on, as bright and soft as if bound on an errand of mercy instead of an errand of death."

As he finished this doleful description, Don Juan shrugged his shoulders, with a gesture of resignation; and then, recovering his wonted demeanor, he rose, and with a smile excused himself to provide for the entertainment of his guests within.

"Many people are very much disappointed with California and do not like it," said Belville, after his host's departure. "It has been so absurdly overpraised by some writers who, not content with dipping their quills into the rainbow, must tear up the whole brilliant arch by the roots and splash it over their pages, that thousands have come here hoping to enjoy the felicities of heaven without the preliminary of dying. And nobody who has taken his ideas from these hyperdiabolical books—hyperbolical I mean, but it's all the same in this case—can feel anything but a bitter disappointment when he comes to California. All this has produced a reaction, until it is now the fashion to be quite as unjust on the other side."

"I don't think it fair to make California responsible for the imaginations of writers," said Laura.

"Of course no writer can guard against every misconception," said Belville. "But every writer is bound to know that certain mistakes will surely be made unless guarded against. And where a book is written expressly to induce immigration, as some have been, it is wicked not to provide against misconstruction, to say nothing of assertions positively false."

"But suppose you were writing up our hunting trip, you would not describe days of poor shooting, would you?"

"Such thing would not be a guide-book. Besides, *fully* detailed descriptions of hunting trips are always a bore, and every one of sense enough to read about such things at all knows that there are times and places in the best of hunting countries where the shooting is poor. If he should infer from anything I wrote about the hunting, scenery, or climate that he had better cut adrift from good moorings at home and anchor his bark in El Cajon, or any other place, as a farmer or fruit-grower, he could not blame me if he found himself mistaken. But if I allowed him to think that game grew on every bush— when, as you have seen, there are thousands of acres without a feather; or to think that he could get all the shooting he wanted in a short stroll on foot from any house—when, as you know, a buggy or saddle-horse is nearly as indispensable to comfort as the gun is to success; I should be doing wrong."

"Do you think any one would believe it, anyhow, if you should tell the plain, unvarnished truth?" asked Norton.

"Oh yes," said Belville. "The beauty of California

in spring is quite generally conceded even by those who dislike it most, and it is granted by all Californians that in a good year the southern part is the richest in flowers. It is also well known that California is one of the best, if not the very best, of states in the Union for game; although, except for quails and perhaps rabbits, the northern part is the best. It is generally known by all well informed on hunting matters that hundreds of farmers in the north have to employ 'goose cavalry,' or mounted men with guns, to keep the geese off their fields."

"And I should have to do so here if I raised wheat," said Don Juan, as he came out to invite the party indoors to take some wine, a beverage very different from the California wine so often seen East, which contains more headache than a green-hickory club.

"California is pretty well known, too, as the best of all the states for camping out, and the easiest and most comfortable generally for all out-of-door campaigning, especially for ladies, thousands of whom hunt, fish, and camp out every year," added Belville to Norton, as they left the porch.

CHAPTER VII.

THE next morning, under a sky of spotless blue, the wagon rattled down the valley toward the sea, with a jolly quartet on pleasure bent. The hills seemed to swim in a luminous mist of green, their round heads powdered with diamond and gold dust, their sides robed in the silvery green of the wild oats. The wealth of flowers our friends had seen in other valleys was missing here; but there was still exuberance enough, for the small blue stars of the alfileria twinkled from every slope, the scarlet of the cardinal flower gleamed here and there, the poppy blazed in small patches along the distant meadows, in places along the far-off hills glowed banks of violets or the orange-colored *toroso* flared in gaudy pride, while far up along the hill-tops the white and purple *yuccas* with their tall staffs and enormous plumes stood like sentinels of the land.

Along by little sloughs and ponds where cinnamon teal, green-wings, widgeon, and other ducks were diving, muddling, or floating; where great pelicans rode at anchor, and blue cranes and white egrets stood along the shore in solemn dignity and hungry hopefulness; past meadows where far-off troops of geese stood like ten-pins on the greensward, and brant were pitching and tumbling from on high with clanging cackle, they made their way.

. "Why don't you stop? I should think there was game enough here," said Norton.

"I'm bound for headquarters," was Belville's answer as he cracked his whip over the spinning team.

Suddenly he stopped, and pointing to three large white birds in a pond some three hundred yards away that to the rest of the party looked like pelicans, he took his favorite Winchester rifle, and jumping from the wagon, made a long detour to get behind a heavy fringe of rushes that grew along one side of the pond. This brought him to within fifty yards of the birds; but while he had been going around they had drifted away from where he had first caught sight of them, so that when he raised his head, a little too carelessly, to find them, they saw him first.

They rose with surprising ease and grace for birds so large, and floated upward against the rising breeze, while ball after ball from the swift-repeating rifle splashed the water and went singing gayly over the flowery meadow beyond. But at the fifth shot the hindmost bird wavered, and fell with heavy splash.

As the wagon drove up and they looked at the snowy plumage, the long neck, the black feet and bill, it needed little guessing to tell what it was.

"Why, it's a swan, isn't it!" exclaimed Laura. "How could you do such a wicked thing? Isn't the down soft and lovely! Can't I have it? I feel so sorry for the poor thing, so innocent and snowy. What a lovely trimming that down will make! I'm going to have it, am I not?"

"Of course," said Belville. "I only shot it for you."

"How can you lay the poor creature's death on me?" said she reproachfully. "But what lovely down, and so much of it!" she added, turning up the feathers; and then said, archly, "couldn't you get the other two?"

A few moments more brought them within sight of the sea. Long, lazy breakers were booming with perfunctory grumble upon the shore, and beyond them lay sleeping the deep, gentle monster, its soft blue face . reflecting the smiling vault above, more like a mill-pond on a still summer day than the mightiest of oceans.

And now the "*honk*" of the old gray goose, which they had heard at intervals ever since they reached the ranch, came ringing in from a hundred directions, until the deep, mellow tones mingled in one uproarious din. Hundreds of geese were rising here and there, hundreds were riding the light ripples of the bays and inlets, hundreds standing along the shores and on the flats and meadows.

Belville drove to a piece of low *mesa*, or table-land, on one side, where stood great flocks of geese that went waddling off a few steps and rose in flight as the wagon came on. Far off along the *mesa*, looking like bands of sheep, were flocks of sand-hill cranes. Along the sloughs ducks in varied flocks were whizzing, while gulls and numerous other sea-birds were flapping lazily about.

"We had better make a specialty of geese to-day," said Belville. "I'll take you to Temecula, a much better place for ducks, some other day. Now I want you to stay where I put you, please. Keep perfectly still when anything comes, and don't move a muscle until it is within good shot. Hide as close as you can, have plenty of patience, and don't shoot at anything unless you can see its eyes or hear its wings plainly. Stay in one place, and don't leave it because you think you see a better one somewhere else."

He then placed Norton in the grassy head of a little gulch into which the sun was shining warmly. Miss Norton he posted in a little clump of bushes in the head of another little gulch about two hundred yards farther on. He and Laura then went some three hundred yards beyond, to a large bush of the *Heteromeles arbutifolia* that stood at the head of another little grassy gulch.

"I'll stay here with you long enough to show you how, and then will go to another place," he said to his companion.

"It seems almost incredible that this is only the last week of February," said she, looking at the rank mat of alfileria that lay all around her with its little bluish blossoms and long pin-like seed.

A deep, silvery "*honk,*" so close that it thrilled her to the soul, startled her from her composure, and as she seized the gun a quick *wiff, wiff, wiff* of heavy wings in sheering flight told her that she had been seen. Before she could get into position to shoot, the geese were some eighty yards away and drifting off to one side.

Belville sat laughing and unconcerned.

"You see you've got something besides an ordinary goose to deal with," he said. "He who takes the *Anser Canadensis* for a fool is badly mistaken. Now, if you had been perfectly still with your hand on your gun and the gun in such position that you could raise it in a moment, that flock would have come directly over you. These are not at all like *Anser Humanus*. They are not at all susceptible, and are very shy of a lady."

"They don't look as if they had a bit of romance about them," Laura responded. "The human goose generally has too much."

"That is why he is so easy to capture, I suppose. But now crouch low and don't move. Look up there."

A long string of white birds with black-tipped wings were bearing down upon them from the north, not over twenty feet above the level of the ground. They seemed nearly as large as the gray goose, but flew with a more rapid wing and made a hoarse "*go-ak, go-ak!*" as they came along.

"Now let slip the dogs of war!" whispered Belville, as the birds were about twenty yards from the bush.

The gun flashed, there was a tremendous bustle and beating of wings and a wild array of flashing white and black in the air, and one of the flock with broken pinion came whirling down almost upon her head.

"What a beauty! What is it?" she exclaimed, as Belville caught it. "A white goose, isn't it?"

"That's the white goose, or white brant as they are sometimes called. That was splendidly done for your first attempt; but as these geese are not very good you had better reserve your energies for the others."

"Then why did you let me kill the poor thing?"

"To tell the truth, I did not think you would hit any."

"And you expected to have a good laugh at me?"

"No, I should have felt only sorry at the failure of so promising a disciple."

"And do you think me really promising? Shall I really learn to shoot?"

"If you continue as you have begun, you certainly will."

At this moment they heard the *bang!* of a gun from Norton's stand and a confused huddle of swerving geese above it, but never a sound of falling game. Away drifted the prey over where his sister was, and a report from her gun sent them all climbing heavenward.

"Miss Norton's gun is too lightly loaded, I'm afraid," said Belville. "But I was afraid to load her cartridges heavier, as she is not used to shooting. You have the heavier gun which does not kick so much."

A few minutes more and a V-shaped bunch of large dark birds with slowly moving wing and long necks outstretched came swinging down upon them with a clear, liquid-toned "*honk, honk!*"

"Don't move a muscle!" whispered Belville. "Now salute them!" he said, half a minute later, as he sprang to his feet and began to dispense hissing lead from his own rifle.

Dark and bewildering was the confusion of big bodies, huge wings, and outstretched necks into which Laura fired; but one only came down, and that one shot through with a ball from Belville's rifle.

"How could I have missed the rest?" she asked in wonder.

"Have you ever seen some fair enchantress shoot at a whole flock of the *Anser Humanus* without hitting any?"

"One generally hits them all," she answered defiantly.

"I stand corrected. But none were mortally wounded this time—feathers only ruffled a little."

"Proceed with your illustration."

"If she would take a dead aim on some particular one she might wing him."

"Even so.   I'll try and do it next time.

"It's the only safe rule in shooting at a flock of any kind to pick out a single bird. And with large birds this is indispensable.   Those geese were not over fifteen yards distant, and at that distance shot from that gun does not scatter six inches."

"Hadn't you better take the gun?   It's a pity to spoil your pleasure.   You could have easily shot two with it that time," said Laura.

"But I didn't come to procure nutriment, nor to make a big score to boast over. I detest hunting for either of such purposes.   Of course I like to get something, but I would rather shoot two geese flying with a rifle than ten with a shot-gun. The two are enough when you get them, and the skill required to get them with a rifle is five times that necessary with a shot-gun."

"Oh, I see! It's the case of bow *versus* gun in another shape.   I wish I had my bow with me."

"I think you will find the murderous gun requires skill enough at first to sufficiently amuse you. When you cloy on the ease of shooting with that, the rifle will then afford some scope to your desire to do something not too easy. When you get satiated with the ease of hitting with that again, you can fall back on the pistol. And behind them all as a last resort, when wearied with your own skill, stands the immortal long-bow."

"How sarcastic you are about the bow! It's a noble weapon," said she with an affected pettishness.

"So it is. Only too noble for common use, on flying game. See now yonder great birds that seem to be only floating in the air, whose clear penetrating cry we hear so far away. What could the bow do with them? I declare, they are coming this way, too! Here, let me put some long-range cartridges in your gun, for they are high up. Now keep still as death, and don't move even an eyelid until they are over us."

Louder and clearer came the *tremolo* of that piercing note the sand-hill crane sends from on high ; and swiftly the huge birds came sailing on, though to the eye their flight seems slow.

"Shoot at the leader," he whispered, as they swept by some fifty yards to the right and the same distance above the ground

At the report, one ashen-gray body, an awkward looking conglomeration of long neck and legs and great wings came whirling and flapping down· amid the ringing "*gr-r-r-r-o-o-o, gr-r-r-r-o-o-o !*" of its fast-scattering comrades. It landed on its feet and started off on a dignified walk.

As Belville and Laura ran up to it, it rose up, tall almost as a man, with the feathers on its head bristled up and its long dagger-like beak aimed at the party. Its eyes scintillated with strange fire and its whole aspect bespoke defiance.

"Keep back!" said Belville, "they're a dangerous kind of snipe. You keep him at bay until I can get a rope. He's only wing-tipped."

He ran back to the wagon and got a piece of rope, in

which he made a running noose, and coiling it like a *riata* threw it over the head of the bird.

"Now hold this," said he, handing the end to Laura, "and if he comes at you, run and keep your face away from him."

He then took some small cord, and going to the opposite side easily noosed the crane, when it drew the first cord tight. It was then the work of only a moment to muffle the great beak with a handkerchief and a buckskin glove, and to hobble the long legs, and the captive was safe.

"And now what will you do with your elephant?" said Belville.

Laura looked at the prisoner with admiration and pride; her dark eyes sparkled in the sun, and her cheeks were flushed as with wine. Belville thought he had never seen any one so handsome as she appeared at that moment.

"I'll keep him for you to take home, if you wish," Belville offered. "These birds make very gentle pets, and are cunning as can be. Such a dandy as that would make a rare sensation in Boston. We'll go into partnership with him immediately," he added, as he cut a stake and fastened the bird on the sod about twenty yards from their hiding-place, and then took off the muffling from his bill.

They sat there half an hour more, but nothing came near. A few flocks of geese and brant flapped lazily by out of reach. The captive decoy trilled out occasionally a cry to his distant friends on the *mesa*. Troops of geese and brant were seen standing on the grass far out of shot; and there was an occasional flash and smoke from the blinds where Norton and his sister were, but nothing falling. Belville seemed much more interested in talking to Laura than in watching for game, and was making some extravagant-sounding promises about getting her a shot at a deer, when a shrill "*gr-r-r-o-o-o !*" above made him drop a cigar he had just lit. A long string of cranes with stiffened wings outspread was sliding down the air directly toward the captive, who also was making some apparently very expressive remarks.

Unable to restrain her impatience, and deceived in distance by the immense size of the approaching birds, Laura fired before they got within sixty yards of her, and as they bounded upward and swerved to either side she sent the second barrel into the flapping mass of gray. Three balls from Belville's rifle spun whizzing among them, but not even a feather came as a result.

"You'd better take the gun and stay here alone," said Laura, "else we will get nothing at all. I'll go back to the wagon, where I will not disturb any one."

"Then I'll go too. I'll try and get you a shot out of the wagon. I don't know how it will work, for they are wild now, but early in the season a wagon can often be driven close enough for a shot. But, if we are not coming back here, as we probably shall not, we had better release this crane, and let him do the best he can without our protecting-care."

"We'll have to leave you here for the present," he said, as they passed Norton and his sister. "We are going to try for a shot from the wagon, and want it as light as possible for fast driving."

He took out the back seat and all superfluous loading, and drove out with Laura upon the long stretch of sod that sloped away to the sea. He swung around to the windward side of a large flock of geese, and started on a line that would carry him some thirty yards to one side of them.

"Now," said he, "keep your gun ready, but don't look at them at all until I slacken the speed of the wagon. Then shoot as quick as you can."

Looking straight ahead, yet watching from the corner of his eye, he sent the horses on a spinning trot. The great birds sat watching them until they had come within fifty yards. Then they began to waddle a little, and as Belville hurriedly stopped the wagon they rose in a clanging hubbub. Laura fired, but nothing stopped, and far and near the *mesa* resounded with their cries.

"The wind is not strong enough to make them rise toward us, as I had hoped," he said. "But we'll try that flock yonder."

He pointed to a row of distant heads that looked like a line of stakes just visible above the grass, and headed the wagon for it. "Try now and shoot without any stopping," he said.

The wagon whirled past the birds within forty yards of them, but the first shot went above and the second below this flock, which was one of gray brant. As they disappeared with a "*clank-a-lank! clank-lank!*" Laura said:

"Doctor, we shall go home without anything, at this rate. Let me drive and you shoot."

"Happy thought! I never yet saw a lady that couldn't

drive fast enough. But I'm afraid you'll go so fast you'll carry the shot a mile or so beyond. Perhaps I'd better shoot from here as soon as you start."

"Spare thy wit until afterward. I've driven in the city."

"So have I. I drove my mother nearly crazy," said he, as he handed her the reins, and she drove rapidly towards another flock of the great Canada geese.

Sweet delirium! who that has felt it does not enjoy it? If there be any pleasant road into the jaws of death, if ever there be a time when man feels a sweet resignation, it is when whirled along at a break-neck pace by some fair feminine driver who knows nothing of danger, and not much of driving except to apply the whip. So thought Belville as he was rattled, bumped, bounced, and banged in half a minute's time up to within thirty-five yards of the astonished geese. They rose in a cloud of black, gray, and white, the air thick with flapping pinions; and more by good fortune than otherwise, for it was impossible to take aim, the first barrel of Belville's gun rained its chilled shot into the very thickest part of the flock and sent four of them to earth, sprawling. Before he could pull the second trigger he was careering along beyond them, out of shot.

"Isn't this just ecstatic!" exclaimed the fair steed-compeller, as with Belville's aid she stopped the horses some distance beyond where the geese were.

"Y-e-h!" said he, catching his breath, "I'm not at all opposed to dying of ecstasy, and rather prefer that method of translation. But to tell the truth," he added in a serious whisper, "I am not exactly prepared. I should like to make a will first—"

"Why, that wasn't fast!" she exclaimed. Belville looked full in her eyes for a moment. With upturned face, smiling and sweet, she returned his gaze; and, with eyes full of inquiry and innocence, said:

" Did you *really* think that *fast?*"

" Oh no. But the geese seemed to think so, and it's a pity to deceive the poor innocent things."

" I'll try and drive a little slower, if you wish."

" For the sake of the geese, please make the effort as strenuous as possible. But be sure and don't let them know what you are driving at."

Half a mile over the carpet of alfileria brought them in sight of a flock of sand-hill cranes standing like so many sheep along a sunny slope of shimmering green. Laura took the reins, and the whip flashed over the horses' backs. The plain, so smooth and hard for ordinary driving, suddenly became like a corduroy road as they *ricochetted* over its gentle swells. Before Belville could say a word, the fast-galloping team had cleared a hundred yards; the cranes were getting restless, and the distance that yet lay between them and the wagon was glimmering fast away. Belville felt sweet resignation again stealing over him, and he cocked his gun to shoot. In a twinkling there was a bump, a crack, and a smash, and he was whirling in a headlong plunge to earth, with Laura following him with a death-like grip on the whip. The fore wheel on his side had shed its tire some yards behind and, striking the skull of a *functus officio* ox, had let Belville's corner of the wagon rather suddenly down.

He picked himself up, and gave a look at the flying

team with its three-wheeled attachment, and a lambent smile played over his scratched and grass-stained face as Laura rose, breathless but unhurt.

"What a narrow escape!" she gasped. "Thank Heaven that—"

"The lunch basket is safe. I took it out before we started," he interrupted gravely.

CHAPTER VIII.

NEW TACTICS.

"YOU positively shall kill a goose before you leave here," said Belville to Laura next morning. " You came pretty near to killing one yesterday, but to-day I'm bound you shall succeed—though not exactly in the way you tried it yesterday. We will drive up to the Laguna, a mile or so above the house, and try a trick on them. It's a mean one, I confess, but then what's to be done? To-night we will try and meet some by moonlight alone as they fly in to roost.   But to-day I propose to take advantage of their vanity."

So saying, he put into the wagon which he had obtained a large looking-glass that he had borrowed from the house, along with some strips of wood, some string, screws, and other things.   Arriving at the Laguna, he fastened the looking-glass in front of a little skiff that was there, so that it hung down to the water and concealed the boat completely.

He then fastened a piece of broken looking-glass to a split stick and lashed it to the boat, so that it projected sidewise from the bow and just beyond the line of the edge of the glass in front, giving to those in the boat a view of everything ahead.   Then, when all was ready, he and Laura pushed off, while Norton and his sister watched them from the shore.

" It will be some time before the geese come in, as they

are off feeding," said Belville. In the meantime we will let those swans take a look at themselves."

While approaching the Laguna they had seen four swans sailing on its smooth face, and Belville, placing Laura behind the glass, and getting on his knees and stooping low, sculled the boat with one hand out into the open water.

It was slow traveling, but the space that lay between them and the swans was gradually shortening. Laura and Belville could see the stately birds in the small piece of glass at the bow, looming up larger and larger on the shining water, moving to and fro, turning, floating and sailing with admirable ease and grace. Soon they began to stand out higher and higher from the water. And now their dark bills are plainly visible, and shine in the morning sun as they arch their proud necks and turn their eyes toward the boat.

"They're admiring themselves, or think they see friends," whispered Belville. "Let them look a while longer." And softly the boat drifted onward, while the swans closed up together and held a consultation about the approaching brethren in the glass.

"Now is your chance for edging!" whispered Belville. "They are close enough. Such lovely down, you know! Be sure and shoot straight; for it makes splendid trimming!"

She cocked the gun, and, as she raised it, there was a sudden *bang!* a scream, and four astonished swans rose from the water with skittering flight as a thousand bits of one of Don Juan Forster's mirrors flew over the water around

"Such lovely down!" said Belville, with a commiserating laugh.

"It was your fault," said Laura, with rueful face. "Look at that, too," she added, pointing to a hole in the center of the glass big enough to put her arm through.

"Why, that's just what I wanted. I was thinking about doing that myself."

"Doctor, I would like to ask one question, if not too impertinent."

"I burn to respond."

"It is this. Were you ever disconcerted?"

"Yes, once. A fashionable young mother once invited me to kiss her baby."

"Why, I never heard of such a thing!"

"Oh, it's very common. She didn't, of course, say it in that way. She only told the baby to 'give Dr. Belville a nice kiss.' But really that glass is better for having that hole in it. You can put the gun through it and get a shot at them before they fly, as they would do the instant you showed your head above the glass."

"But the swans are gone!" she said sorrowfully, as she pointed to four snowy flakes drifting seaward down the bright blue sky.

"But the geese will soon be here."

"And then I'll have to let Evy shoot. It would not be fair for me to do it all."

"As you will. But really the loss of the swans amounts to little. It is considered even by good sportsmen quite an achievement to get a swan. To my mind it is not a very illustrious achievement. I shot that one yesterday only because it was the first we had seen within shot, and the first I had got a chance at for two years. I could easily have brought my gun and killed one or two of these before they got out of reach. The swan is a rare, beautiful and harmless bird, but of little or no value to eat, being generally tough. What few there are should be spared. I hope to see the day when the man who delights to murder everything rare, the man who knocks over every egret or other beautiful bird, or kills any other harmless but worthless bird, will be choked off by the Society for the Prevention of Cruelty to Animals."

"Well, I think you are right. Of course I cared but little, after all, for the down, and the death of one of the beautiful things could have added nothing to the pleasure of—"

"Shooting a looking-glass? No, I doubt if it could. Well, let's go ashore and wait for the geese."

Laura was well chaffed by the Nortons, when she landed, for the extensive slaughter she had made—in looking-glass! and she laughed as heartily as the rest at her own expense.

An hour or more passed away with little but the lazy flap of some pelicans above the Laguna, the squeal of mud-hens in the rushes along the edge, the "*wauk*" of herons, the quack of a few mallards, and the whistle of a few passing widgeon; while the party, not caring to molest anything but geese, sat sunning themselves on the high green banks on the water's edge.

But hark! Pure, deep, and mellow rings out a welcome tone from yonder sky. Each pulse bounds faster as the penetrating note rolls in, soft and clear as that of a French horn, and each eye is turned toward where the verdant crest of a far-off range of hills fades into the blue beyond. Then comes a dark dotted line fast widening out, and beyond it is another and still another dim line just looming up from the blue depths beyond; while faster, clearer, and louder, comes the tumultuous clangor of trumpet-tones.

"Now, will you please hide in the head of that gulch ?" said Belville to Laura, "and do you, Norton, lie flat in that lot of sage beyond. They will swing over this high ground before they light in the Laguna."

He then put Miss Norton at the "port-hole" in the glass, and running the boat down along the outer edge of the reeds, he backed it out of sight into a small opening.

"We'll wait here," he said, "till a good flock lights out ahead of us, and then we will make a sally."

"Laura," said Norton, tarrying at the place where she was to stop, instead of going on to his own position, "I'm glad he took Evy in the boat."

"I told him to."

"Oh ! you did, eh ? And what did he say ?"

"He said he would, of course."

"Did he say it willingly ?"

"What a question, Charley ! Why ?"

"Well, to tell the truth, I think he is too much inclined to monopolize you."

"And you are a trifle jealous, you naughty boy ?"

"Oh no. Only I wouldn't encourage any such monopoly, if I were you. If he is going to accompany us on the whole tour, as we have arranged, it would be rather slow for Evy if he paid all his attention to you, and—"

"I see your meaning.   Don't be afraid, Charley, that I'll neglect you;" and she kissed him, and tapped his cheek with her hand in gentle reproach.   "Now, darling, you must get out of sight quick, for here come the birds, right toward us, too."

From an elevation of over one thousand feet there came, winding down in a curve half a mile long, a veritable battalion of large, dark gray birds with long, arrowy necks outstretched.   Swiftly, yet with majestic grace, they slid down the soft and sunlit air, not a wing moving, all silent as death, yet gliding swiftly down a gigantic spiral course which was winding unmistakably toward Laura.   Immovable as the rocks both she and Norton remained, until the soft hiss of sailing pinions was heard almost over them.   Then came an uproar of bang! whang! bang! bang! the *wiff, wiff, wiff!* of scores of heavy wings swiftly beating the air, the "*honk k-wonk, onk*" of dozens of trumpet-throats, and in a moment the birds were drifting swiftly away.

"Is it possible we didn't get any?" said Norton, scrutinizing the air in vain for even a feather.   "I didn't suppose we *could* miss such a crowd as that."

"I'm daily discovering that it's not the easiest thing in the world to hit even a large and slow-moving mark with the gun.   But the more I find this out, the more I love the gun," said Laura.

More geese were appearing in the distant sky, and soon another flock came curling down out of the blue.   Fully a thousand feet of descent, fully half a mile of curve, without a wing moving, and with a *swish!* plainly audible on shore, they settled in the center of the Laguna.   And scarce had they left the blue vault above, when another flock appeared far behind them.   But these birds are smaller and move with more rapid wing than the others, and utter a *"clank-lank! clank-lank!"* very different from the tones of the other flock.   Soon they are nearly over the edge of the water, and suddenly, as if caught in a whirlwind, they pitch, tumble, gyrate, and whirl in all sorts of motions downward, as swiftly as if struck dead in air.   Down, down they reel with obstreperous cackle, and just as Laura and Norton have about concluded that they are either very drunk or something worse, they catch themselves, fall into a long crescent line, glide smoothly down to the water, and settle beside the first that came.

"Those are the gray brant, a smaller kind of goose," said Belville to Evy.   "And now we'll start.   Put your artillery through that port-hole and keep it perfectly still, but have it so that you can easily pull it out and aim above the glass for the second shot.   Meanwhile I will row towards them."

They have not far to go before the eyes of the geese are almost visible.   A few strokes more are given, when the muffling that Belville has put on the oar to deaden the sound slips off.   The oar makes a dull noise as it rubs the oarlock behind; he stops it instantly, but yet too late, for the air throbs with the beat of powerful wings mingled with the excited cries of over a hundred throats.

"Too far!" said Belville, as his companion vainly fired. "These geese have been tried with boats before, and know right well the sound of an oar, you see; though I doubt if any one has tried the glass, as it is a trick that very few hunters know."

They retreated to the opening in the reeds and waited for another flock to light. Not long had they to wait; for beyond the rolling green in the southwest dark lines of clamorous birds already flecked the sky, and soon came winding down the air. A large flock lit some three hundred yards from the boat, and Belville started for it, his oars again being muffled. Softly the skiff moved on, the geese sitting passive and careless. Soon they turn their heads toward the on-coming boat, and a few move a little way toward it.

"Thirty yards more, and you can shoot," whispered Belville.

There was a soft rush of outspread wings, accompanied by a low, peculiar chirping note, as a flock of brant sped by some fifty yards above this spot, and the geese in front suddenly began to look suspicious.

" Those brant alarmed them," whispered Belville. "We must be very careful."

Slowly and softly he sculled along, and so carefully that he did not notice that the boat was swinging a little sideways with the rising breeze which struck on the back of the glass. In an instant fifty or more geese sprang flapping up from the water in front, all in a tumultuous huddle, while Evy vainly rained the shot from both barrels of her gun into the gray and white mass.

" Too far again !" said Belville. " They're a tough bird. Those others put them on their guard. I guess we'll have to give them up for this morning. But to-night I think we will hear something drop."

Old Phœbus had unhitched his wain, and Diana had

run the evening train high up in the eastern sky, when our friends again appeared upon the high ground along the Laguna.

"We needn't go far from the wagon," said Belville. "They will not be afraid of anything when it is dark."

He placed Norton near the wagon, taking out a seat for him to sit on. Eveline he posted one hundred yards farther on.

"Miss Wilbur had better stand about another hundred yards away, and I will go on to the bank of the Laguna," he said.

Soon the distant birds began to send in the deep-toned "*honk*," and the gray brant its cackling "*clank-lank;*" and very soon, from the dim obscurity around them, bloomed up into full view against the starry sky a dark, V-shaped line of dots that quickly changed into large bodies, not over thirty feet up, and almost directly over Eveline.

The liquid tones thrilled her like the sudden burst of a bugle-call close by. Her hands trembled as she raised her gun, and her heart throbbed wildly as along its barrels the silver moonlight showed, dimly painted on the blue above, a long black neck and head right in line with her aim. Quickly her tremulous finger touched the trigger; the circle of darkness around was for an instant illumined by a long jet of flame; and as the parted waves of darkness again closed in there was a confused *wiff*, *wiff*, *wiff*, a sound of something heavy falling at her feet, mingled with the silver-toned "*honk*," the clangorous discord of distant brant, the "*go-ak*" of snow-geese, and the dolorous "*gr-r-r-o-o-o*" of far-off traveling cranes.

A feeling such as she had never known stole over her as she picked up the heavy, dark gander from the sod, and said to herself,

"Ah! now I see why people are so crazy about hunting."

Shortly after, two long flashes darted up a hundred yards away, and the quick reports of the guns were followed by a heavy *whop, k-thump!* on the ground.

"Well done! Miss Laura," she heard in the voice of Belville, who was evidently close by Laura instead of where he said he was going. "That was a splendid shot. I never saw one learn so fast as you."

"There's nothing like a good teacher, you know," she replied.

"An apt scholar is better," he responded.

"Yes, better than a physician who neglects his patients to play with a gun."

"*Peccavi!* I would neglect more for so good a scholar."

"You would like more scholars, then?"

"No. One at a time is enough."

"Too many are dangerous, I suppose."

"Yes, very; even one is often fatal."

"I meant too many *guns*."

"Well, so did I."

Evy hardly heard this last remark, for the "*clank-lank*" of brant had come to be delightfully close, and in a moment a flock emerged from the darkness just ahead of her. As she was about to shoot, the fire from Norton's gun, streaming heavenward at another flock, caused her flock to swerve and huddle in the air, and she pulled the trigger fairly at the center of a black chaotic medley of throbbing wings and cackling throats. *Biff, whack, k-thump!* came down four on the grass, followed by a yell of applause from Norton and Belville, while the smile of the shooter nearly outshone the moon sailing among the fleecy billows of cloud. For half an hour more, flash after flash rent the stillness of the night, and many a heavy thump greeted the ear, until soon the cry of the last departing bird died away in the vault above, and the flight of birds had ceased for the night.

CHAPTER IX.

EASY WORK AT DUCK-SHOOTING.

THE next morning, our friends started again under the guidance of Belville, and were early whirling fast over the prairie-like *mesa* of the southeast corner of the great rancho, Santa Margarita. The land no longer heaves like great storm-waves with curling crests, but rolls before them like the ground-swell of the peaceful sea. The golden blossoms of the wild alfalfa begin to glow on every hand; the grayish-green stalks of the white sage, one of the finest honey-plants of the world, shoot up in myriads; the wild cucumber, with its drapery of light green and white, hangs from the dark and reddish green of the sumac; the purple flowers of the wild pea entwine in loving embrace the ramiria; the bunch-grass rears its slender blades among the thick mats of alfileria; and the starry eyes of the violet peer out from every opening.

Away this prairie stretches to the high bluffs of the Temecula River, where it is lost in the foot-hills of the dark, wavy mountains of Santa Rosa; and far ahead it rolls away into the green dales and oak-filled valleys of the rancho of Montserrate.

Swiftly our friends skimmed its northern boundary. Past hills where the wild lilac of California oppressed the air with its rich perfume; where the white blossoms of the tall *cercocarpus betulatifolius* rivaled the intensity of the lilac's pink; where the wild gooseberry stretched out its arms full-hung with long scarlet trumpets; where the bayonet reared its gaudy plumes, and even the dark, scraggly *adenostoma* of the chaparral smiled in its new spring suit,—they rolled along into the fair plain of the Vallecito, an emerald in a girdle of frowning rough hills. Then on through a gateway of rugged mountains, thick-studded with immense boulders, tangled with chaparral, dashed here and there with a struggling live-oak, they passed, until the great, snowy mountains of Grey-back and San Jacinto loomed like sheeted ghosts in the far-off blue; until, descending into the valley of Temecula and crossing a dashing creek of clear, cold water, they reached the end of a long slough.

"See there," said Laura, sorrowfully, "that spoils all our fun!"   As she spoke, she pointed to a sign-board on a post, which said in unmistakable English :

NO SHOOTING HERE!

"Well, I know better," said Belville. "There's just as good shooting here as I want, anyhow. Look at that bunch of cinnamon teal there, already. I'm going to let you do the shooting now, while I hold the horses. There's no hitching-place here, and it may be a bad country to borrow wagons in," he added, with a mischievous smile at Laura.

The slough before them was two or three miles long and only a few feet wide, with small, narrow ponds here and there, the banks of which were eight or ten feet high.

"But that notice means that we can't hunt here," insisted Laura.

"Well, I'm sorry to insinuate that the author of it tells a deliberate whopper," he answered, "for it is just the easiest place to hunt ducks that I know of, and that is just why I brought you here. There *are* a few places where a lady can hunt ducks."

"But it means there's no shooting *allowed*," said she.

"By all means let us shoot softly, then. There's a lot of cartridges in there loaded with the new Dittmar powder. It shoots in a whisper, but shoots just as strongly as the other."

"Doctor, I guess I'll have to give you up as—"

"Well, I can stand that; for so many young ladies have already done so that I am quite used to it."

Belville held the horses, while the other three, on foot, swung around over the smooth plain some two hundred yards, so as to approach the bank of the slough at right angles. They got to within fifteen yards of it before anything moved; when suddenly there was a splash, a funny sort of a "*quack, quack,*" and the air twenty yards ahead was full of little bodies of a shining cinnamon color, with whizzing wings of gray and sky-blue. Three barrels roared in succession, as they cleared the opposite bank, and two of the flock came tumbling on the greensward; and as the rest scattered in wild array, two more barrels materially accelerated their upward career.

"Only two, out of all that lot!" said Laura in a disappointed tone, as Belville drove up.

"Well," said he, encouragingly, "that's doing well enough for beginners. I've seen as many shots from old hands bring down nothing at all. But if each had taken aim at some one bird, or two, instead of firing at the flock, you would have done better."

The birds of California are not remarkable for beauty, but the little cinnamon teal has few peers among water-fowl. The wood-duck is gorgeous, but too gaudy; and the mallard is beautiful, but *bizarre*. But this little chap, with coat, vest, and pants of bright glossy cinnamon, and gray and sky-blue wings, whether he be gliding along the edge of the pond, springing aloft from danger on swift-flashing pinion, or lying lifeless upon the spangled sod, is the very embodiment of modest beauty and un-assuming elegance. Dull must be the soul of him who can pick up one of them without a feeling of self-re-proach. Yet who can stay his hand from the trigger, when he sees their little blue wings flashing?

The teal had flown on up the slough and lighted about five hundred yards off.

"Get into the wagon, please," said Belville. "We can drive to almost every pond here. We shall probably see more before we get far."

They drove along the bank of the slough for a little distance, when Belville, pointing to some ducks a hundred and fifty yards away, said, "I think you had better go as you did before, but when you get within shooting distance let two of you keep down while the other takes a shot at them in the water. Then the two can shoot as the birds rise. Those are sprig-tails, one of the finest kinds of duck."

So Laura and Norton went around out of sight, and came up to the edge of the water, stooping low as they approached. As Laura, who was to take the sitting shot, cautiously raised her head, a dozen or more large ducks with long gray necks, gray backs, white "aprons," and two long thin feathers streaming behind, sprang into the air at twenty-five yards' distance. Upward they mounted, with two barrels vainly roaring below them; then they turned away up the slough, while two more fruitless shots echoed along the dark green hills of Santa Rosa half a mile away. As they sailed off with their long forked rudders outspread, Norton looked regretfully after them, and remarked:

"There's considerable space outside of even a very big bird. I always had the idea that to hit a mark like that with a thing that scatters like a shot-gun was a mere boy's trick; but, judging from our experience on geese and on these fellows, we shall find it quite a man's trick before we learn it."

"Your teal are in that little pond above," said Belville, driving up again.

"I guess teal are our *forte*," said Laura. "Let's try them."

As they went up to where the teal were, Norton pointed to four or five of them in a bunch among some grass in the water. He fired, and brought down the whole bunch—consisting of half a dozen *turtles* on a dead stick, which went slipping into the water with a splash as the shot glanced harmlessly from their shells. At the same time, the air just beyond glistened with a flashing sheen of cinnamon and blue, as thirty or more teal started from behind a bunch of rushes.

Norton raised his gun again, caught along the barrels

a glimpse of red with glimmering spots of blue on either side, and pulled the trigger. Two of the flock sank, and as the rest radiated with a rush, the shot from his sister's gun spattered harmlessly along the water beyond them. Wheeling suddenly, they closed up their scattered ranks and started whizzing off in orderly array, when Laura's gun cracked, and the hindermost bird came gyrating to the ground.

"Hurrah! well done!" called Belville from the wagon. "If you had shot a little ahead of them you might have got more; but that was good enough, for it was a long shot," he added, driving to where they stood.

"Those sprig-tail lit not far from here," he said, as they got in the wagon.

"I think the teal afford ample scope to our talents," said Laura.

"I will put you, after a while, where you will have a chance at some under full headway. Sometimes, under those circumstances, it takes two persons to attend to one of them."

"One to hit if the other misses?"

"No. One to say 'here he comes,' another to say 'there he goes.'"

"Those are only spoonbills," said Belville, as they passed almost within shot of another flock of ducks.

"They don't act very spooney," said Norton, as the birds vacated their quarters with expeditious wing and vigorous quack. "Why didn't you stop?"

"They are not a highly desirable duck, and we will find plenty of a better kind."

"Nearly all Americans speak Spanish here, don't

they?" asked Miss Norton, seeing a Mexican pass by talking to an American. "I've noticed that several times."

"Yes. They do in all the Spanish-American countries," answers Belville. "They pride themselves very much on their accomplishments in that line. But it's generally of the quality of the German spoken by a young friend of mine who had been educated abroad. Coming down street with me one morning, and not knowing that I understood a word of the language, he said to a German friend whom we met, 'Gut morgen, mean hair; hast geheard daz die bank ist gebusted?'"

At this moment a flock of mallards rose from a pond just ahead with a great amount of bustle, their brilliant green heads and the blue and white of their throbbing wings shining bright in the noonday sun, and then sped away.

Belville handed the reins to Norton at the first sound, seized the gun, and, just as the ducks got fairly started on their straight-away course, tranquilized a heavy green-headed gentleman that was cheering on his laboring comrades with energetic *quacks*. Another one lit close by for repairs, a stray shot having "impaired his usefulness." Norton went to him to pick him up, taking the gun along by Belville's advice. As he approached the duck it rose with as vigorous quack as if nothing was the matter, and though its ascension was materially slower than before, Norton thought it rapid enough, and raised the gun. Instantly he saw along the barrel the white bands and delicate glossy green curl of the tail; he pulled the trigger, and the duck at last lay flat.

Driving on, they came in sight of a long narrow little

lagoon which was dotted with hundreds of ducks, some nearly black, some colored with white, blue, green, and cinnamon.

"There are some canvas-backs and red-heads," said Belville, pointing to some whitish-backed ducks with reddish necks. "And plenty of mallards too. Now we'll have some fun if we can only find good hiding-places. We can't very well drive them out of this, and they'll just fly from one end of the lagoon to the other. Now, Miss Laura, if you'll go around and hide behind that thing"—pointing to another board close to the water with "No shooting here" painted on it.

"But suppose the man comes?" she interrupted, looking at a distant house, evincing considerable hesitation about getting out.

"We'll ask him how he expects you to see it when you are behind it."

"But it is probably printed on both sides."

"Then get underneath it. That's where you want to be, anyhow. Tell him we don't read English edge-ways."

"But suppose he tries to teach me?"

"Oh, there's no danger. That sign is only to keep off a certain class who shoot rifle-balls anywhere and at anything without regard to cattle or horses being in range. They'll not bother us, you may depend."

Laura went to the sign-post and hid behind the brush and weeds at its base, but not without some reflections as to the possible consequences of the act. Norton remained at one end of the pond, while his sister went with Belville to the other. Then Belville began to drive back and forth to stir up the ducks in case they should light too far from any of the guns.

In a few moments there were about five hundred ducks in the air, and a hundred mud-hens skittering along the water, making as much fuss as if they also were in high demand at Delmonico's.

Away went the ducks to the upper end of the pond, curled around and upward like the thread of a screw, then turned and came swooping down along the water with their stiffened wings hissing with the speed; glancing up from the surface of the water like sunbeams, at the vain crack of Laura's gun; whizzing down to the other end of the pond, and bounding high in widespread confusion as Norton prematurely raised his gun; then gathering their scattered bands, turning, and rushing along on high back to the other end again.

Bang! whang! bang! went gun after gun, as the swift-rushing flocks went by. But not a splash was heard, and ducks were fast getting high instead of low. The mallards and canvas-backs soon set their shining sails for other waters and drifted swiftly away. The sprig-tails floated far away in the sky. The widgeon whistled his way to more congenial quarters. The spoonbill picked up his exorbitant bill and left, without waiting for a receipt. And the little cinnamon teal, tired of playing bobbin in that kind of a shuttle, finally faded beyond into the borders of another pond.

Tying the horses, Belville sent Norton to another pond, near by, to scare up the ducks, leaving the ladies at the first pond to scare them back again when they flew there. He then lay down in the long grass of a little swale midway between the two ponds. Flat on his back, with his gun beside him, he kept perfectly motionless as a flock of mallards started from the lower pond and came toward him. On they came like charging cavalry, their long necks stretched out and occasionally bobbing up and down. Now he hears the swift beat of their wings, and they are close upon him. Still he moves not. A second more, and they are almost over him; then he quickly sits up, and at his shot a duck, riddled through and through, comes plunging like a wet rag to earth. Swiftly, with pinions moving on the double-quick, the rest of the flock climb heavenward, when the second barrel cracks, and earthly cares outweigh the towering aspirations of another member of the band. Some canvas-backs, red-heads, and sprig-tails, that were coming swiftly on in the rear, sheer, tower, wheel, and whizz past out of shot; then close up again after passing him, and go gliding downward with hissing wings to the first pond.

No sooner had they reached it than the boom of Laura's gun sent them scrambling aloft in huddling confusion. Down they went to the other end, where the sight of Evy's hat, which was a little too conspicuous in color, sent them veering spirally upward; then, gathering their hosts into a serried mass, they went scudding back to the pond beyond Belville.

With a cautious side-glance, Belville had been watching a lone sprig-tail coming from the pond where Norton was, and, with its long pennant trailing in the breeze, it was now fast winnowing the air not far away. As he raised his gun, a yard ahead of it, a canvas-back—one of

the outriders of the flock coming from the other direction—came whizzing like a white meteor right across the
line of his sights, and—

He killed them both at one shot?

Nay, reader. That would have been a mere bungling
bit of good fortune. That might have been something
for a tyro to brag over; but the crack shot knows that
such a thing is more accidental than anything else. Belville did something far better. You may brag of springing two quails at once and cutting down one with each
barrel. You may boast of clipping the twittering wing of
one autumn woodcock in the tangled brush, then wheeling and dropping on one knee, and checking the upward-
wheeling career of another that started at the same time.
And you may still chuckle with pride as you recall the
time when in the darksome brake two booming brown
rapid-sailers, rising almost out of shot, came bouncing
and bounding to earth, one from each barrel, you scarcely
knew how, so quickly was it done. Your pride in all
these things is pardonable, for they require almost the
acme of skill with the gun, a skill unattainable by many,
rare even among the skillful.

But if thou hast never tried to stop two single birds
darting past each other at the rate of sixty miles an
hour, thou knowest little of double shots.

Amazing is the rapidity of a sportsman's thought at
such a moment. Only two or three times in his long field
experience had Belville seen this feat accomplished, and
only once before had he succeeded in doing it himself.
Yet, in an instant, he saw his opportunity, and saw that to

plished, and would only be to throw away the chance of making the finest of double shots. Quick as the thought itself the first barrel blazed out on a line a few feet ahead of the sprig-tail; almost before the victim of this shot had folded its sails, the gun was turned six feet ahead of the canvas-back, which was already a hundred feet past the other and darting skyward at that. At the report, the canvas-back came whirling down; the two ducks striking ground nearly a hundred yards apart.

"I guess we'll have to try the long slough again, or you will get no shooting," said Belville, as Norton came up, after waiting a long time for further game. "It must be well stocked by this time, as most of these ducks have gone down that way."

The party were soon driving back to the slough, where the high banks afforded them good rising shots, with nothing to do but to ride along until they came in sight of ducks far ahead, when they could get out and walk a few hundred feet around out of sight.

Many indeed were the bustling wings that sprang huddling upward, and few indeed the number that came to grief; yet, when they reached the end of the day, they felt prouder of the few ducks that lay in the bottom of the wagon, all shot on the wing, than if they had killed a wagon-load with sitting shots.

Evening closed in as they rolled down the dark shade of Tall Brook valley, and before long they stopped at Reche's apiary.

CHAPTER X.

"DON'T you think we could get a deer to-morrow?" asked Belville that night of Reche.

"I shouldn't wonder. There are two or three bucks in the hills below here, and they must be in good condition now," replied his host.

Full information was given, before they retired for the night, as to where the deer might be found, and by sunrise next morning the party had breakfasted and were in the saddle, winding through a grove of live-oaks that were pioneers of this land before Columbus set sail to discover it.

"Look at the robins!" exclaimed Miss Norton, as a dozen or more flew past.

"There are a few here in the spring," said Belville. "But though they seem to be exactly the same in plumage as our old Eastern songster of the orchard and the garden, yet one never hears the beautiful carol that sounds so cheery in the opening spring, back East. They are quite a silent bird, here, and even the single piping note is toned down to a husky squeak."

"But there is one of the birds of California that is handsomer and more gamey than his Eastern relative," he continued, pointing through an opening among the live-oak tops to a gigantic sycamore not far away, in whose upper branches thirty or forty large birds were sitting. "Suppose you try them, Norton. Just over yonder you will find a sandy creek-bed that will take you right to the tree. But be sure and keep out of their sight."

Norton disappeared, and in a few moments there was a great bustle and flapping of wings in the sycamore, and three or four birds sank with a great flutter when the report of the gun was heard.

Norton soon returned with beaming countenance, bringing in his hand four birds a little larger than common house-pigeons. Their color was a soft, glossy lavender, shading along the neck, wings, and breast into a metallic luster of changeable hue. Around the neck was a narrow white collar, and the deep lustrous eyes wore golden spectacles. The long bluish tail was broad and square at the end, like that of the tame pigeon, and the full strong breast, mild eye, tender bill, and pink legs and feet all showed unmistakably that it was a pigeon.

"The mountain pigeon, or ring-dove of California," said Reche, who had accompanied them. "They are driven from the high mountains now by the snow, and come into these lower valleys for acorns. Some winters they are very plenty in this grove, and others they are not."

"I should think the birds of California and their differences from Eastern birds would be an interesting study," said Miss Norton.

"So it would," said Belville. "But I am not much of a naturalist. Though I have shot thousands of quail, I could not describe one correctly without looking at it. My observation of birds is confined mostly to such of their habits as bear on hunting them. Still I have noticed many differences. There, now, is a thrush, that dark brown chap with snuff-colored vest, long curved bill, and long tail, that is whisking about under yonder bush. He has no music in his soul ; a stony '*chuck*' once in a while is his only note. He spends his life in hopping silently under bushes, never mounting to a tree-top to pour out his soul like the Eastern thrush. And yonder is a bird that looks very much like the Eastern blue-bird, though I doubt his relationship very much. He wears a pretty blue coat, but the soft purling note you hear from your bluebird in early spring is wanting, and there is nothing in its place. He cares nothing for your bird-houses or boxes, and is an unfriendly chap, generally. And there is a king-bird, that brown-backed, straw-breasted thing going ' *ch-caa, ch-caa, ch-ca-cha-cha-cha-caa.*' Different, you see, from the Eastern bird, both in color and note, yet of about the same flight, action, and habits, and quite as fond of bees."

"What quantities of quails !" exclaimed Laura, as flock after flock rose from their path. "How delightful it must be to live among so many birds !"

Reche smiled and gazed away on the distant hills. He had been raising fruit long enough to have his admiration of "harmless birds" slightly modified.

"Isn't that a deer?" he said at length, pointing to a distant ridge, as they came to a place that gave a view of the distant hills.

"Where, where?" exclaimed Norton and the ladies, who saw nothing but rolling ridges covered with grass, flowers, white sage, ramiria, sumac, and green bushes.

"Do you see yonder small, shining, dark spot by the side of that big green bush about six or seven hundred yards away?" said Belville, pointing to the bush.

As usually happens at first, the ladies and Norton began to look for *a deer*, and not, as they were instructed, for a "small, dark, shiny spot." Consequently they saw nothing. But Belville's knowledge of deer was not derived from pictures; so it was with all confidence that he drew his glass and turned it on the spot.

"That is just what it is," he said in a moment. "It's a fine buck, too. He is sunning himself. Let's drop out of sight and hold a council of war."

Through the glass the ladies could at last make out the outlines of a deer, but were much disappointed at its seeming so small. They did not consider it at all satisfactory.

"You will think him sufficiently big if we can get close enough to him," said Belville. "And now, which way will he be likely to run if started by some one going up the point of the ridge?" he asked of Reche.

"He'll either cut across the next gulch for that rocky hill beyond, or will run along the back of the ridge and aim for the live-oak cañon of Montserrate," Reche replied. "Or he may slope off up the gulch on this side."

"Then," said Belville, "do you go to the point of the ridge and try him, while we go around to where we will stand a good chance of being run over in case he slips through your fingers."

"Mercy!" exclaimed Laura, "I don't want to be run over!"

" It's the nicest fun in the world," said Belville. "He'll jump clear over without touching you, and all there is to do is to hold the gun perpendicular and pull the trigger the instant you find your sunlight shut off."

Belville took them around to the gulch that lay on their side of the ridge.

"You, Norton, had better stay in this gulch, as you have the best gun for buck-shot," said Belville, as he tied the horses in a little hollow. " I'll leave the ladies on top of the ridge, and go myself to the gulch beyond."

He then took the ladies about a hundred yards up a gentle slope to a large bright sumac-bush on the top of the ridge, and, telling them to keep behind the bush and to be both quiet and patient, he went down the next slope to the gulch about one hundred yards farther on.

Ten minutes passed away, and then, sharp and clear along the hills, rang the report of a rifle from the direction of the deer, causing a flutter in the nerves of the ladies and a lively activity in Norton's pulse.

In a few seconds a faint *bump, bump* was heard in the direction of the shot ; which soon became plainer, more distinct, and unmistakably closer. *Bump, bump, bump,* it came, like a wooden maul striking hard ground, at short intervals. Then the ladies saw over the bushes, some distance down the ridge before them, a dark object rising and falling, keeping time to the bumping noise, which was steadily growing louder. Soon they could clearly see an animal with glistening gray coat and thick dark neck, black forehead, long mulish gray ears, gray nose, black muzzle, shining dark eyes, and two thick, stubbed, velvet-covered horns, nearly black, with four trim slender legs, all grouped close together under the body, as it curved upwards—and *Cervus macrotis*, the deer of Southern California, was in plain sight and within easy shot !

This deer is commonly called the " black-tail " from the fact that its tail is nearly black on the upper side. But, according to Judge Caton, of the Illinois Supreme bench, probably the best authority on deer in America, it is a variety of the mule-deer of the Rocky Mountain basin; while the black-tail is not found in Southern California at all.   This is a smaller deer than the common mule-deer—though some of the males attain great size—and is shorter-bodied and shorter-legged than either that or the Virginia or common deer of the East.

But what this deer lacks in size he makes up in activity; and the peculiar gait of the mule-deer, most highly developed in this variety, the spectators could now plainly see.   There was no gentle canter, no rapid run, no hugging the earth like a greyhound, nor anything indicative of effort to absorb space.   Nevertheless the noble fellow bounded—not ran, as though the ground were India rubber and his legs steel springs, his four feet grouped close together, all striking the hard ground at one blow and glancing from the touch like the *ricochet* of a cannon-ball.   And yet there seemed to be no more effort, no more energy expended, than in the motion of a birch canoe over a stormy lake.

But oh, how deceitful that billowy flight to him who views it through the sights of a rifle !   Talk not of your snap-shooting or your double shots with the shot-gun !

Away with the mechanical smashing of glass balls practically at rest as they pause on the turn in the air, and at a distance so short that a mere boy could hit them with a putty-blower if they were actually at rest! Boast not of shooting pigeons tossed from a trap to nearly always the same point of space, or of your shooting with a rifle at a fixed mark at known distances and under almost unchanging conditions; or of your skill with the rifle on the common Virginia deer when running. Until you have tried *this* surging beauty you know little of rifle-shooting. The big mule-deer jumps high enough. So does the Virginia deer when there is anything to cross, and he rises quite high even in his gentle canter. But the rise of either is nothing to the upward glance of this compact magazine of condensed energy when the four feet all strike the ground at one blow with full force. The height of this rise is not fully appreciated, even by those most familiar with it. Much as we had admired it, wondered at it, and been deceived by it, we never fully realized what it was until we saw a half-grown fawn playing before some dogs. A fence, shoulder high, was in its course, and it skipped over it three or four times with scarcely a perceptibly higher rise and no more perceptible effort than when bounding along the level ground; although we stood not fifty yards away, watching it with special reference to these points.

Though by no means its only style of showing its heels, this is the gait it generally takes when started; and up hill, down hill, through brush, over brush, among huge boulders, rocks, shingle, or anything else, it holds this tiresome gait with such astonishing speed and endurance that it is always worth half a day's work just to see one run.

Vainly you hold the sights of the rifle on its body, unless extremely close. Aim at it when in the air, and your bullet whizzes through the space it has just left, three feet or more above. Aim at it when it touches ground, and your bullet has a clear field away below the gathered legs, for it stays on the ground no longer than a sunbeam on a wave. The forward motion is alone sufficient, if the deer is at any considerable distance, to leave the ball singing across his wake, unless aimed well ahead. And this, combined with the rise and fall, would make this deer the hardest of all big game to hit with a single ball, even on open level ground. One can easily imagine, then, what it must be on the rough brushy ground upon which this game is generally found, when at one jump it clears fifteen feet, at the next ten, at the next perhaps eighteen, and at the next twelve; now describing a high narrow arch in air, now a long sweeping curve more deceptively high. Cry not *Eureka!* if you happen to catch the first one or two at the first or second shot. Wait until you have shot at a few hundred, and then we shall be happy to hear from you—provided you have kept the reckoning of expended bullets by something besides the deer you bring home.

What wonder, then, that despite the rapid *staccato* fire and the hissing lead from Belville's Winchester rifle in the next gulch, the buck comes dancing gayly onward, as unconcerned as a careless man about a note his indorsing friend has been compelled to pay. On he comes, with louder and closer *bump, bump, bump,* smash of brush and scattering of flowers, annihilating at every bound five or six yards of the distance between him and the ladies. What wonder that their hands shake and their hearts throb faster and faster, that Laura forgets to shoot, and a charge of buckshot from Eveline's gun goes far above the glossy gray pelt, as the deer descends from a lofty spring.

You thought this deer didn't know how to run, did you? Behold him, then, as he wheels like a flash from the smoke of the gun. No longer the glossy fur shines undulating above the brush, but the gait is changed in a twinkling into a low scudding movement as, his head laid well back, with the pace of a racer the deer cleaves the low brush like a shot.

Straight toward Norton he shoots, bridges at a bound the deep broad gully at the bottom of the gulch, flirts off at a tangent as he sees Norton, dashes headlong into a deep branch gully as the latter's gun bellows vainly above, clatters up the narrow rocky bottom as if it were a race-track, skips out at the other end and resumes his *ricochet* gait with one of Reche's celebrated five-hundred-yard shots tearing up the dirt about fifty feet below and behind, and the buckshot from Norton's second barrel pattering harmlessly around him, stops on top of the ridge, gives a complacent wiggle of his stubby little paint-brush of a tail, and then strikes into a trot and disappears down the next slope, with jacket inviolate.

And this you call sport? I imagine some one asking. Perhaps not. To some, sport is only the securing of game. For such the "wild Western" tale lies ready and the reeking page of the African or Indian book, and in proper time the market, unfortunately, will again be open.

But there are others to whom sport is sometimes the getting *away* instead of the getting of game, or gratification of the almighty palate or of the stupid pride of the hunter for "count." Of such were the party of Nimrods whose doings are here chronicled; and they returned home, well satisfied with their day's work, even though no trophy crowned their efforts.

CHAPTER XI.

THE MOUNTAIN TROUT.

THE blaze of orange, blue, carmine, and pink is nearly burned out along the southern slopes; the golden glow of the *actinolepis* drowns out the last remnant of the violets and shooting stars along the plains; the pin-like seeds of the alfileria are beginning to pale and curl in spots; an ashen tint begins to creep along the brow of the wild-oat hills; the haze poured through the valleys by the sinking sun takes a tinge of deeper crimson; the granite castles of the hills shine at evening with a darker purple; the brooding call of the quail rings from hillside and valley; the mocking-bird's flood-tide of song begins to ebb; the bright steel-blue body and orange wings of the great beetle gleam here and there in the warmer sun, and the great miller booms at evening like a humming-bird around the honeysuckle. Yes, summer is approaching.

Like a great whale among his billows, Smith's Mountain rolls above the wavy land, and in the jaws of one of the great cañons that cleave its sides our friends have camped. A mile high, the mountain towers above them, its base a mass of boulder and shingle, its breast a carpet of waving wild oats, its shoulders orchards of green oaks with alfileria and silvery foxtail glowing beneath them, its head a forest of dark pine and fir. Through a vast rift, descending nearly four thousand feet in three miles, now tearing madly down short rapids, now sleeping in a basin guarded by huge boulders, now swirling gently between steep-curving banks, and again plunging down in a foaming cascade, comes from near the mountain's crest a clear crystal stream of ice-cold water, one of the very few living streams in all this county, and the only one containing trout large enough to be worth catching. Along the dank side of the giant walls of the rift hang in long green fringes the bright maiden-hair; gold, silver-lace, and other ferns spring on all sides in luxuriant waste beneath the boulders; the stately alders, great trees here, shoot up their glistening brown trunks and shining foliage in all directions; the old sycamores are festooned with grape-vines, and some of the live-oaks are hoary with mossy beards. Far above, the ring-doves are drifting across the great chasm; the linnet's warble rises above even the roar of waters; the quail's clear pipe rings along the mountain side, and the bluejay, the high-holder, and other woodpeckers flash here and there through the green shades.

Belville, in planning the day's fishing, had intended to go up-stream with Laura while he sent the other two down-stream. But while he was cutting a pole for Eve-line, Laura went with Norton, who called her to go with him when he went to cut a pole for her. So it happened that Belville and Eveline went together.

"Do you see those heavy boulders around yonder pool?" said Belville, after he had fixed the line for his companion. "You had better slip quietly behind that largest one and drop your line gently over it into the water, and keep yourself out of sight. These trout are not difficult to catch. One needs only to keep out of sight, put the bait on properly, and get them hooked. To get them fastened on the hook is the only thing about it requiring any skill. You can lift them directly out without any playing, for they are not large enough or gamey enough to require that."

She followed his directions, and he went with her behind the boulder. Scarcely had her line touched the water when there was a jerk on it. In a second more a four-ounce trout was struggling in the air with desperate vigor.

"Swing him in quick!" said Belville.

As she did so, the fish wriggled off the hook and landed on the sloping bank between two boulders. She made a spring and attempted to grab her prey; but the fish bounced so high at every flop, and flopped so fast, that it was rapidly nearing the water's edge, when she suddenly threw herself flat upon it.

"I declare!" exclaimed Belville with admiration, "you are more game than the fish. Most ladies would have stood still and warbled their heart-rending lamentations and let him proceed on his flopping career. It's a pretty good fish, too, for this brook. There are not many large ones here, few being over eight inches long. They are different from the Eastern trout, and not near so gamey." He held up the fish, while she inspected carefully and with pride its dark-green back and its sides like tarnished silver spotted with black.

"Not so handsome, either," he continued, "as the crimson-speckled beauty of the Eastern brooks, being rather more like chubs both in action and taste; but they are trout, nevertheless, and though they are deficient in avoirdupois, which to some minds is the chief criterion in judging of fish, this is trout-fishing all the same."

"Oh, I think," said Evy, "just to sit beside this boiling whirl of waters amid such dark and solemn shades, after a few weeks on the dry plains and along the open hills of this country, would be in itself a pleasure, even without any fish."

"You will be still more of that opinion when we go to the trout-streams of San Bernardino County. But there are more in here. Try it again."

Again she cautiously dropped the hook. Soon there was a gentle tremor at the line, a cautious nibble such as ye country verdant, pluming himself on his acuteness, first takes when he reaches Wall Street with the proceeds of the ancestral farm. Then came a bolder bite, such as ye aforesaid taketh when he turns a few pennies on the first venture and credits it to his own superior sagacity. She gave a pull on the line, and the fish came whirling up through the water and the air, dropped struggling on the boulder, bounced high from it again with a vigorous flop, and fell back into the dark water.

"I am afraid you didn't hook him right. You must give a quick, short jerk, so as to fasten him before you pull him out," said Belville.

"I thought catching fish was like catching men," said Evy, demurely. "They shouldn't be hooked too quickly, but played a little first."

"But some men are so eager that they don't need

playing at all, either before or after being hooked; and these fish are just like them—anxious and verdant."

"Just the kind I like, then, for I never can catch any others."

"Which—fish or men?"

"Fish, of course," said she, with a laugh, as she dropped her line again, while Belville pulled out a wriggling little trout which he tossed back into the water. She shortly followed suit and drew out one of nearly the same size. "The same fish, I declare!" she exclaimed. "If he's so determined to be caught let's accommodate him. He is not so *very*, very small," she said, looking at it critically with the fisherman's eye, which she was already fast developing.

"It is not the same one, although he's pretty small; but you should never fish for count," said Belville, sententiously.

"Go back then, and send thy big brother," said she, gayly, as she tossed it back and put in her line once more. Hardly had her bait struck the surface, when the line *swished* through the water, and out came a struggling, flopping beauty, almost ten inches long.

"Ha! ha! He sent his father instead of his brother," said Belville, helping it off the hook. "A nice one, too!—about a five-pounder."

"Five pounds! Oh, I'm so glad; for I have seen in some book that that was about the largest size they grow to."

"Yes, fully five pounds—fisherman's weight, of course. Avoirdupois, we might have to discount that possibly," said Belville. "Now here comes the brother on my hook," he added, pulling out another fair-sized fellow. "I wonder if his grand-daddy is still living? We must bag the family. It would be cruel to separate them."

"Yes, he's living, and at home, too," said Evy, as another five-pounder (fisherman's weight) came wriggling out. He fell on the boulder, flopped up between her hands into her face as she clutched at him, and landed in a small pool at one side which had an outlet into the larger one. In a moment she had one arm in the water to the elbow, trying hard to hold the slippery struggler.

"'Do what you don't dare to do,' says Emerson!"

"I never would have got him otherwise," she said, as she finally pulled out the fish and laid him high and dry.

"What Emerson said was sound philosophy that time, anyhow," said Belville.

Suddenly there arose a hubbub down the stream, such as jars the foundations of some mansion what time the first-born cuts its first tooth.

"Oh Charley, run quick! Oh! oh! oh! Look! look! Oh! I wish the Doctor was here to see it. Call him, Charley. Take him off! Oh! stop him! *Ain't* he a beauty?"

Belville hurried down, and found Laura holding a pole with a fish dancing in air, while Norton with the tips of his fingers was gingerly trying to unfasten it.

"You must learn to take off your own fish," said Belville, laughing, "or you will never become a fisherman."

"But it might bite," said Laura.

"Yes, that's so; they'll bite nearly as badly as a lamb."

"Is that a trout, Doctor?" she asked.

"Yes; a handsome ten-pounder."

"And is that very big?"

"Middling fair for this brook. They don't run over nine and a half here as a general thing."

"Doctor, does it *really* weigh ten pounds?" she asked, searching Belville's eyes with a half-doubting look, as she saw Norton smile.

"Well, I couldn't conscientiously recommend you to weigh it. The pocket scales lately invented are the greatest curse ever inflicted on fishermen. The invention strikes a deadly blow at the very root of the angler's happiness."

"And how much do you suppose it actually weighs?" she asked, with a pleading look in her deep dark eyes.

"If we had scales sufficiently delicate he might run as high as an ounce and eleven nineteenths, if he was first well fed with shot and weighed before he stopped kicking. But you know a trout never looks so big as when you first see him on the end of your line. You see, this fellow has grown small already," said he, tossing it back into the water. "We'll send him home, as his mother may be getting anxious. I see you haven't had very good luck. Come with me and I'll show you how to do it."

So Laura and the Doctor went up-stream to some untried pools above, while Norton stopped with his sister, who had followed Belville to the scene of excitement.

"Evy," said Norton, "don't you think he rather inclines to take Laura with him a trifle too much?"

"Well, he seems fond of her company. But what of it? You can't blame him for that. Following the rule of human nature, I of course ought to mind his being more attentive to her than to me. But I don't. I consider him only a kind of an agreeable flirt, and he likes her company best because she is more lively and prettier than I am."

"Well, I wish you could throw yourself a little more in their way. I don't like to have him monopolize her so much."

"Why, you surely are not afraid of him?"

"Not in the least; yet, to tell the truth, some how I don't like it. She seems to enjoy his company more than I care to have her. If he were not so indispensable to our trip I would gently drop him. But he knows all the country, and all about hunting, fishing, and camping; so that we can't get along without him at present. And he's such good company that, in fact, I don't want to lose him."

"I don't think anybody could shake Laura's attachment to you, Charley. And there's less danger from him than from any one I know. He's only a lighthearted fellow that cares for nothing but a little fun."

"What do you say to climbing the big Grayback of the San Bernardino range when we go up there fishing?" said Belville to Laura, after they were out of hearing of the others and had cast their lines. "It's the highest mountain of Southern California, and one of the highest —perhaps the very highest—in the United States, above the country around its base."

"Oh! I should love dearly to climb a mountain—if I only could," she added with a doubting accent.

"It is very easy. We can go almost the entire distance on horseback, and I believe a good mountain horse could make the top. It's really a noble mountain and well repays the toil."

"Let us try it then, by all means. I never have climbed anything higher than Mt. Holyoke, which is only a mole-hill by the side of this mountain."

"And Grayback is about as high again as this. But here's a bite on my line. Now will you please take hold of the pole, and when you feel a bite again give a quick but short and gentle jerk, a little sideways, so as to hook him. Then you can pull him out at your leisure."

There was another nibble soon, and in a second the hook was anchored in an alder branch about eight feet above the water, while the fish, describing a shining arc, fell back into the water.

Belville loosened the tangled line, and handed it back to her, with a caution about jerking too hard.

"Isn't it delightful to smell the water after being out on the dry plains and hills?" she said.

"Yes indeed; I could lie down on one of these boulders and dream the long summer away in perfect—"

There was another bite, another jerk, another shining arc, and a splashing back into the water; and as Belville made a grab at his arm when the hook stung through his coat like a hornet, his foot slipped on the wet boulder he was on, and the dark boiling water closed over him. The water was not deep, and he soon raised his head and quieted the apprehensions of his companion.

"You've hooked him at last!" said he as he caught his breath. "Now pull him out at your leisure."

CHAPTER XII.

THE SILVER TROUT AT HOME.

AND now where are we? On a low bank beside a rapid stream, the wind sighs soft music through the glistening leaves of the silver spruce above the camp, with giant walls about soaring up thousands of feet and robed in forests of sombre pine, scarred with tremendous gulches, bristling all over with primeval wildness. 'Tis the heart of the great mountains of San Bernardino, the home of silver trout.

Belville and Laura, both eager to climb the highest mountain of Southern California, had started at daybreak, each one on a good mountain horse and under the guidance of one of the very few settlers in these mountains, to climb the great Grayback. This mountain was until about two years ago deemed almost inaccessible, and but ten men by actual count had ever trod its top. Only five years have passed since its altitude was first taken by the government engineers, and it does not yet appear upon any map, the mountain on the maps at this point being San Bernardino, five miles to the west, and one of the shoulders of Grayback.

They were winding up a cattle-trail faintly marked along the mountain-side through thickets of lilac, past the red arms and bright green leaves of the manzanila, and the thorny embraces of the choke-cherry. Through groves of dark pine and under arcades of the mountain oak, the horses bore them steadily upward, until the spruce and fir that superseded the pine began to dwarf and grow awry. The Douglas squirrel that had succeeded the large gray squirrel of the lower altitudes was gone, and gone, too, the stub-tailed chipmunk, the bluejay, and other birds; nothing remained but a little dusky woodpecker and a tiny squirrel with a black stripe from his head to the tip of his tail, skipping from branch to branch like the ghost of an attenuated mouse. These soon vanished also, as the climbers ascended, and the manzanila, the lilac, and the oak, and even the scrubby chincapin had faded away. Snow-banks waist high began to appear; the soft crimson snow-plant reared its head from the ground, almost bare, and soon the last line of trees, dwarfed, crooked, and carved into fantastic shapes by the sand-blast, was reached and the bare reddish-gray scalp of the mountain was before them—a long ridge of partially disintegrated red granite, half covered with snow-banks.

"Your way is clear now," said the guide. "I'll go off on this other spur and see if I can sight a mountain sheep. It's only five hundred feet more to the top, and I'll meet you here when you come back."

"Pshaw!" said Belville, as they went on; "I'm afraid we are sold and haven't climbed a mountain at all. We haven't passed a single place where 'the slightest misstep would precipitate horse and rider thousands of feet into the abyss below.'"

"And there is also a painful dearth of '*thunder-splintered pinnacles*,'" added Laura.

"And the cliffs don't '*beetle*' nor the crags '*topple*' worth a cent," he replied. "And the eagle isn't on hand, either, to spread his great vans on the breeze. I'm really afraid it isn't a mountain at all."

"Oh! yes it is, too. It's all right; all right, for surely the sun '*glints*' on yonder peak," said Laura.

"Oh! I'm so glad. And, now I think of it, didn't we hear a brook '*brawl*' a while ago?"

"I thought I heard a rill ' *tinkle.*'"

"Yes, I heard a stream '*purl*,' too. But that is not enough. '*Brawling*' is absolutely indispensable to a mountain stream," said he.

"But those meadows we passed were certainly '*lush.*'"

"At any rate we can soon tell, for we must be almost in sight of the '*horrid crest.*'"

The top was soon reached, and, tying their horses to a rock, they sat down. Nearly all the great mountains of our country, and even of the world, rise from a region already elevated thousands of feet; so that the actual rise of the mountain is not great. Few indeed are the mountains that look down from an altitude of two miles; and Grayback, looking down from a height of eleven thousand five hundred feet upon a country less than a thousand feet above sea-level, is in fact a grander mountain than Pike's Peak and many others much higher.

And now with a glass they looked down upon a circle of two hundred miles in diameter—a wild and wasteful mass of beautiful confusion and imposing desolation, broken here and there at long intervals by a spot of green—the silvery thread of some stream or aqueduct, or the sheen of some rare laguna glittering like a diamond in the bosom of the plain. Where rests the eye upon a grander sight than great San Jacinto, heaving his giant bulk ten thousand feet in air at a single sweep? Yet there he stands just across the pass of San Gorgonio, eight thousand feet deep, curling up from the desert on the east, like a vast wind-swept wave, and tumbling in long lines of pine forests, blue foot-hills, and green valleys, away to the plains of San Jacinto and Temecula in the west. Dark rifts filled with boulders, pine, and snow-banks seam the great heaving sides; cañons and gulches untrod by man, the home of the grizzly bear and the panther, wind their great green arms upward toward the fir-plumed head of the mountain looming high in the southern sky.

Beyond stand the Cohuilla, Coyote, and Cuyamaca mountains, high watch-towers on the great chain of rugged guards that, fading far into Mexico, shut off the inhabitable part of San Diego from the fiery breath of the great furnace that yonder on the eastern side, a vast shimmering sea of sand, stretches far away to where Yuma lies broiling on its southern verge. To the southwest, the eye ranges over a billowy swell of hill and dale, table-lands and plains, mountains that in the East would be blazoned in song and story—all robed in russet yellow and bluish green. Westward, the great valley of San Bernardino merges in the far-off silver line that marks the peaceful sea, the dreary leagues of barrenness relieved by the refreshing oases of Riverside and San Bernardino, with their rich meadows, fair groves of orange and lemon, shining aqueducts, and embowered homes,—all witnesses to the wondrous power of water.

And there to the north-west another mountain rises from the plain far higher than any of the great mountains of our country, except Grayback and San Jacinto; and far above the sunlit clouds its head appears, an emerald islånd on a silver sea. This is Cocamunga, ten thousand feet in height. Just beyond, old Baldy tries to rival him, while over his base we catch a glimpse of the orange-groves of the far-off City of the Angels.

And what are those objects looming so dimly huge in the far-off north? Can they be the outposts of the Sierras? Even so; and there on the right are the mountains around Death Valley, and, far off in the east, the faint hazy blue of the mountains of Arizona.

This broad track of desolation to the north-east gleaming with withering grimness is the Mojave Desert, large as Massachusetts; and that one to the south-east is the terrible Colorado Desert, large as Connecticut and Rhode Island together. And those chaotic masses of weltering desolation that divide the two are not such mountains as welcome the parched and dying traveler. No streams or groves will the thirsty sufferer find there, but only dreariness doubly intensified by its vast extent.

Half an hour passed away while Belville was naming to Laura the various points and landmarks in sight, and at last, pointing down to the great waste of sand below, across which stretched the Southern Pacific Railroad bearing a locomotive at full speed, and looking like a cobweb with a gnat, he said:

"Miss Laura, as you see that desert, such is my life— a barren waste with but a single thread of hope reaching across it, and that, I fear, a very slight one."

"I'm very sorry to hear it. I had supposed your life must be a very happy one," said she after a pause.

"It was until I met you! Until then I had known nothing of love but a phosphorescent gleam or two, dying as soon as born."

She sat speechless for a moment, gazing upon the dreary expanse below with eye as vacant as the gray sand itself; and then, as the blood mounted swiftly into her cheeks, he looked full into her face and said :

"Miss Laura, are you surprised?"

"You know that I am engaged," she said softly.

"But is human love the growth of human will?" he answered quickly.

She sat silent and looked away to the blue wavy line of Arizona's hills.

"Miss Laura," said he, taking her hand in his, while her pulse bounded at the touch, "I loved you at the first sight, and for you alone I have staid away so long from my home, and remain now a willing prisoner."

"Oh! why did you? Why didn't you go sooner?" she asked most pleadingly, and turning her deep dark eyes upon his with a look earnest and sorrowful.

He gazed into them a moment, and said, "Do I divine the truth? You love me too?"

She was silent, and dropped her eyes to the ground; but there was a starry twinkle in them that was not the flash of indignation.

"Is it not so, Laura?" he said. "Is it not so? You love me too?"

"God knows how hard I have tried not to," she murmured at length.

"Oh thanks! sweet one, for that confession. I too have tried, but all in vain," he said with a long sigh of relief.

And now what will become of her poor invalid lover who lies eight thousand feet below, on a white boulder beside a foaming pool in the shade of the glistening leaves of the great alders, musing on his darkened life, and thinking of the only star that twinkles through the rifts of the heavy cloud that overcast his once brilliant sky?

There is a silvery flash in the boiling water where his line is whirling, a jerk, a tug, and up comes a struggling curve of opalescence, describing an arc in air as it slips back from the half-caught hook, and falls with a splash into the bubbling pool again. Does this remind him of any of the pearly hopes of life? He alone knows. But is there not a strange brilliancy in those sunken eyes that is not entirely the sparkle of assurance? And is not his face at times like an April day—half May, half March?

But quickly the clouds disappear again, and a June noonday spreads over his face as another gleam darts through the green water. *Swish!* goes the line, and a flashing fish comes flopping and wriggling out. What is there about the capture of that poor fish that can so chase the sadness from his heart? Not over ten inches long, its sides like mother-of-pearl with little stars of jet, its back a bright olive green, its head and mouth larger than those of the Eastern trout—it is the silver trout of California. Surely such a poor little innocent cannot so stir the life-blood of a full-grown man? He who has felt the electric tingle of a "bite" needs no answer. He who has not, and who weighs all pleasure on the dull scales of utility, cannot be answered. The only answer that can be made is that it is *trout-fishing*—inferior, indeed, to that of the East, but trout-fishing nevertheless.

It is not without full deliberation that I say it is inferior to the Eastern fishing, and I know that the statement will outrage the feelings of some Californians.

Almost as immense as the difference between what a Chinaman can live on when he pays for it himself and the amount he can hold when his employer pays for it, is the difference between these two trout. Like the warm hand-shake of the anxious candidate is the strike of the crimson-starred beauty of the Eastern brook, and vigorously he hugs the dark water. When he comes out at last, he flops and fights in death, and does not give up even in the creel. He steers clear of seductive bait. Although in his primeval innocence he may be caught by the rustic lout with cotton string and worm, yet he soon becomes wise, and it requires the cunning head and skillful hand to take him with success.

But tell me not in lying numbers that our trout is like to this. Like to the oystery palm of the defeated candidate is his grab at the hook, and he hugs the water more like a bag of shot than like a slippery beauty actively obstinate. He struggles and flops indeed on coming out, but it is more like the nervous energy of instinct than the desperate vigor that seems determined to conquer.

There are two varieties of this trout, though the difference is with much show of reason attributed to the different color of the bottom of the brook. Those found in white or light bottomed brooks, where the water looks green and the foam is snowy white, are said to be of a light pearly color, with light olive-green backs; while those found in dark-bottomed brooks have the color of tarnished silver on the sides and are quite dark on the back. Sometimes, however, the dark ones are found in the light-bottomed brooks. The flesh of these latter also has sometimes a reddish tinge, and they are therefore called by some the "salmon trout," while the other is the "silver trout."

It is barely possible that both theories are correct, that there are two varieties, differing slightly, and that their colors are also affected by the color of the bottom. In the brooks of San Bernardino County the silver trout is much the more abundant, and the brook bottoms are nearly all very light, and in places nearly white.

But there is no perceptible difference in the action of these fish on the hook. Both are decidedly deficient in the gaminess and wariness which give such a charm to the Eastern trout. Both can be caught in fair quantity by the tyro, and need comparatively little skill in either hooking or landing. But then they are trout, after all, and though not entitled to the throne are nevertheless of royal lineage. It is a dull soul that cannot enjoy the society of this little beauty or appreciate the wild splendors of his romantic home.

While Norton muses upon his gloomy prospects, as he sees them, a little comedy is going on behind his back that threatens his happiness more than he dreams of.

"How shall I tell Charley? I can't bear to tell him," said the faithless friend on whose devotion he had been so long meditating with pleasure, without whose companionship he would not have come so far from home, and without whom he would not stay, even now.

"You need not," replied the other false friend, whom he had chosen as a companion, physician, and guide to pleasure and health. "You need not. Let the poor fellow go down to his grave with all the comfort that you can give him."

"Mercy! Why, you don't think he's going to die?" she exclaimed with astonishment.

"I don't think it—I *know* it! I have watched him carefully, and have seen all along that the poor fellow is not long for this world; not long to be with us—or to part us!" said Belville, looking at Laura with mingled sympathy and tenderness—tenderness for her, and sympathy for their suffering friend whom he pitied while he robbed him of his love. "When he came last winter," he added, "he was in that condition where one wavers long upon the turning point, but where not to advance is most decidedly to fall back."

"O Doctor! I hope you are mistaken. I could not have him die; for I did love him, and I *do* love him! I cannot put the old love out of my heart, although a greater love has come into it."

"Well, he deserves your affection and mine, and we would not wound him. Let us smooth his downward pathway as much as we can. It would be a kindness to keep from him what would grieve him—perhaps hasten his death—and what is really not necessary for him to know."

Note—In laying the scene of the present chapter, the author has been moved by a desire to call attention to a noble and lofty mountain that has long been supposed almost inaccessible, but which is, in fact, one of the easiest to climb in California, and which commands a wider view than almost any mountain in the country.

A year ago I started for its top with two companions. Most discouraging accounts of its difficulties were given us from every quarter, and we could find but one man in San Bernardino who had ever climbed it, but plenty who had started and backed out. We had not gone a hundred miles to be deterred from at least making a desperate attempt. We climbed it on foot, camping for two nights in a beautiful meadow three thousand feet below the top. On our return we pronounced all the discouraging talk pure nonsense, and declared that a horse could be ridden by a lady to the very summit.

Our experience induced several other parties to try the ascent, and, as we predicted, some ladies actually went to the top. One comrade of mine, an old civil engineer, familiar with the highest mountains of Colorado, pronounced this the easiest mountain he had ever climbed, with the widest view from its top that he had ever seen.

To the U. S. survey Grayback is known as "Grizzly Peak." The official measurement of its height is 11,723 feet above sea-level, or about 11 000 feet above the desert and plains around. San Jacinto is 10,987 feet in height, while the desert, eight miles from its top, is only 725 feet high, and the San Jacinto plains are about the same.

CHAPTER XIII

THE GREAT AMERICAN TROUT-SWINE.

THE Indian, the Mexican, and the Spaniard long held this land of which we write, yet the game increased in their time rather than diminished. The antelope slept within sound of the fandango, the elk flourished among the ranchero's cattle, the trout flashed in the brook by the Indian's *rancheria*, and the deer drank by his *temescal*. Say not that these men knew nothing of the chase, or were too lazy to follow it for pleasure or for food. This can hardly be said of men who could outride the elk or the antelope on the plain, and lasso and bind the grizzly in his rugged hills. They were ardent enough hunters in their way. They lacked only the spirit of the Anglo-Saxons, who go to work at the game of a country like a drove of swine at a pile of grain, beginning at the top and trampling and destroying ten times what would suffice for their real wants.

Why is it that even here, in this far corner of our country, amid these beautiful and abundant streams, it is necessary to toil for miles over great boulder-washes, and penetrate the very heart of the mountain, to find plenty of trout? And why, even here, are they fast fading from the places that knew them? Let the great American trout-hog answer, for here he comes.

We see a rabbit-like complacency of countenance,

corn-silk locks, caterpillar mustache, butterfly necktie, *functus officio* paper collar, and lark-heeled boots. He has a small champagne basket strapped on his back, a quart oyster-can of grasshoppers and worms, a line with two or three hooks on a pole and half a dozen extra ones in his pocket, a soul that would rattle in a dried flea-skin, and an abysmal stomach that yearneth evermore for trout.

He has already over fifty trout in his basket—twice as many as any *man* should catch in one day; more than would satisfy the most exacting of his four-footed brethren. Yet he skips along from pool to pool and from riffle to riffle under the elastic impulse of the only love he ever felt, the love of a poor little trout, debased to the worst and last use to which game can be put—*cooking*. He tosses in his line with countenance eager as a cat's at a mouse's hole, and his face is radiant as a newly made bridegroom's when a little fish, a finger long, comes shimmering out of the water with feeble struggles.

But, surely, he will put that back?

Of course—back into the hole in the basket! Doth it not *count one ?*

Soon another comes out only a trifle larger. Too small yet even for him who was made only a little higher than the brutes, instead of (as has long been erroneously supposed) "a little lower than the angels." But not too small for this *porcus*. Joy elevates his snout as he slides the fish through the hole in his basket.

But what good is such a fingerling?

Go to! thou ignoramus! Doth it not *count ?* Are not its feeble bones tender? Will it not, in the frying-pan, sing celestial music to his soul? And so, the live-long day, he skips from pool to pool with tireless sole, as if the great problem of life were to see how many of these beautiful creatures could possibly be destroyed in one day. What to him is the *allegro* of the swift-rushing stream, the *maestoso* of the boiling pool, the *andante* of the wind in the pines above! He is deaf to all music but the sputtering expostulation of a poor little trout in the frying-pan.

What cares he for the ice-cold stream of crystal, dashing itself into sparkling spray as it leaps down that cliff from its high mountain home, then foaming away through long ranks of stately alders, whirling around white boulders, boiling in deep pools of green and white, glancing through narrows, shimmering over shallows, plunging down steep rocks! Excuse me; he does appreciate it, too. It's quite convenient to wash his fish, to water his horse, to make his coffee!

What to him are the stupendous slopes above, the turreted battlements and granite castles, floating like silver islands in the morning's dissolving clouds or burning with purple fire in the evening sun! Or the grand old forests, so refreshing to the denizen of the sun-baked plains; the pure, cool morning air or the view down the great falling valley as the sun floods it with his last beams! His eyes are blind to all but a "nicely browned" trout.

The morning passes, and he has *ninety* in his basket. He meets his comrade, who has about eighty. And now, surely, they are done; for the prince of swine could ask no more than this. And see, too, they are taking off their baskets and winding up their lines.

Yes, they are done. *Done with such slow work as this!* Not thus can proper homage be paid to the idols of the great American *porcus*—the palate, and the score! The stream shall be turned, for trout must be had quicker and with less work.

And now, mark how they dam up the stream and turn its current aside; and see the halo of delight that en-wreathes each snout when the old channel is nearly dry and the sordid fingers grab up the poor little flopping silver-sides! And see how they gloat over the struggling opalescence and writhing green in the basket, while their palates throb with joy as happy fancy hovers over the sizzling frying-pan! O Nature! why dost thou not whip such wretches around to thy kitchen door, instead of allowing them to root in thy drawing-rooms!

The next day Belville proposed a change of sporting grounds, and suggested various desirable places to try next. "The Santa Anna," said he, "just across this big mountain, is the best fishing-ground in the country; but for a change of scenery I think we had better go to the middle fork of Lytle Creek in the heart of the Cucamunga. We ought to go there, any way, if only for variety, and though trout are not nearly so plenty there as in the Santa Anna, we shall still find all we want."

"Anywhere that we can ride," said Norton, languidly. "I'm very much opposed to tramping among these boul-ders."

"Our horses can go anywhere, and when we get to Lytle Creek we can hire our things packed to our camp-ing-place. We'd better start early to-morrow morning."

"All right, then, if the ladies are willing," said Norton, as he stretched himself out for a nap on his bed of spruce boughs, and Belville started to the creek where Laura had gone to fish. He found her a little way above the camp, in the shade of the shining alders, leaning over a big white boulder, with her line and bait whirling in the foaming water below. As he approached her, there was a tug and a rush of the line as it tightened on the pole, a silvery gleam for an instant at the surface as the fair fisher raised the rod, and the bare hook came swinging out.

"A big fellow, that!" said Belville, just catching a glimpse of him as he came up. "You have too much slack in your line to hook him in such a small brook as this."

So saying, he took the pole and wound in half the line, and said, "Now slip around to the other side, keeping well out of sight, and rest your pole over that little boulder. Keep it stiff, and let the fish hook himself."

Monstrous as this may seem to many an angler, it is often the only way to hook these fish successfully. The best fisherman in these mountains generally uses a stiff pole with a very short line, which he pokes in between the rocks or trees and allows the fish to hook themselves. Unskillful and mechanical as it is, it has often to be resorted to where the trees, branches, and rocks are very numerous and close together.

Swinging around behind the boulders so as to keep out of sight, Laura went to the other side of the pool, and, stooping low as directed, she ran the rod through a broad open space and rested it over a low boulder. The line and hook whirled and danced upon the boiling white water, which rested not from its last tumble, but fumed and seethed in haste to reach the next fall. Around, on all sides, were the glossy brown trunks and shimmering green leaves of the alders, covering all with shade. Laura then sat down upon an almost pure white boulder, and, dipping her cup into the ice-cold water, which hissed and frothed like a soda fountain, she exclaimed:

"Fishing is splendid, isn't it; whether you catch anything or not?"

"Such fishing as this is. But when it comes to sitting on a stump by a mill-pond on a hot day for five hours without a bite, you—"

The line tightened with a jerk that twitched the rod off the boulder and elicited a dainty shriek from the fair angler that cut short Belville's remark. She recovered both herself and the pole in time to draw out the hook again bare of either bait or fish.

"You must pay strict attention, you see; fish incline to be slippery," said Belville. "I guess I shall have to give you another lesson."

He came and sat beside her and showed her how to hold the pole, and in a moment more there was another faint flash in the water and a quick heavy tug upon the line.

"He's fast. Now pull him out!"

She gave a pull, but found "pulling him *out*" quite another matter, for the fish dragged and jerked as though the best pulling might be on the other side. Summoning all her energies for the task, she gave the pole a mighty swing, and landed the hook in a bunch of drift six feet above the water, where it stuck in the crotch of an alder; while the struggling beam of silvery light that accompanied it to the surface shot down again in a shining curve to the bottom.

"I shall never learn it in the world!" said she in despair.

"You must pull more steadily and not with such a jerk. Try him again. These fish will bite a dozen times and sometimes take hold again after being dropped on shore and flopping back. Imitate their perseverance, and you will succeed."

The hook was soon rescued, baited, and whirling in the foam again. Soon there was a new tug at the line, and the hook under the impulse of her nervous arm went on another exploring tour among the leaves above. A small fish followed it about half way up and went wiggling and shimmering back to the pool below.

Belville again fixed the hook and laid his hand on the pole to steady it for her. It was not long before there was a heavy pull upon it, for these fish, like mining-stock gudgeons, often return to the hook while their jaws are yet bleeding from the former bite. Belville held the rod firmly until sure that the fish was fast; then steadily but rapidly he raised it and drew in a vigorously-flapping beauty a foot long, showering silvery rays from its thrashing sides of pearl.

"There are probably some more in there," he said, as he took it off. "Try it again."

A few minutes passed, when a faint "jiggle" on the line startled Laura from her composure, and in a twinkling a tiny little fish was hung up to dry on an alder limb.

"Is that the way you hang your victims?" said Belville, as he hauled it in and tossed it back into the next pool below. "You must positively be more gentle, or you will never catch a big one."

"I think I'll do pretty well if I catch a small one. I haven't caught even one yet on this trip."

"Except the big one you caught yesterday," said Belville, significantly.

"Why, I didn't fish yesterday."

"No. The fish did all the work himself, and, like these, hooked himself. But, Laura, it seems so like a dream to me; I can hardly realize it."

"Oh!" said she, coloring, as she saw his meaning. "Your simile is a bad one. People awake from dreams."

"But I never shall unless you wake me."

"Sleep on then, happy dreamer!"

"But you must be careful, too, not to wake your other dreamer."

"I dread that more than anything, for I do love Charley. It's an anomalous situation, I must confess, to love two persons at once. And yet I do really love Charley still, and could not bear to hurt his feelings."

"I can understand your feelings exactly, though, as you say, the situation is anomalous. I really feel all the more complimented by the strength of your regard for him. His condition relieves us from any trouble about breaking the news to him. You have only to soothe his declining days with your love, and—"

"What! play the hypocrite?"

"Confound it!" thought Belville, "I'm always spilling my words on one side or the other when I try to balance them."

"No," said he aloud, "that's not what I mean. You can still be as friendly to him as ever without being hypocritical."

"And leaving him to infer that I am still—"

"His own? Yes, if he chooses. Are you responsible for his inferences?" interrupted Belville.

"I call that hypocrisy."

"Possibly it is. But I think a deception is pardonable that is undertaken solely from kind motives. Were he to live an explanation would of course be necessary, but as it is——"

A sound of some one coming interrupted them, and in another moment Miss Norton joined them. She displayed a respectable string of fish with a proud smile that outshone the silvery sides of the prizes themselves, and said as she sat down:

"This is just delightful. What! only one? You have not been fishing much, I guess."

"Oh, she don't catch anything but big ones," said Belville, "and I'm not fishing at all."

"She's caught the biggest one yet, hasn't she?" said Evy, holding up admiringly the big fellow that Belville had landed. "I tried a big one down below here, but could not catch him."

"They're very easy. Only let them alone and they'll hook themselves. The larger they grow, the more they exhibit this tendency," said Belville, with face as sober as the pine-clad heights above.

"I guess I'll go back and stay with Charley," said Laura, "and leave you and the Doctor to catch fish enough for breakfast."

"What a false position I stand in!" she soliloquized, when alone. "May heaven help me! I do not mean to do wrong, yet how can I help loving both; loving one more than the other, yet loving the other too much to tell him what I should. Heaven forgive me if I am wrong. I do not mean to be."

"I'm so glad you have come, Laura," said Norton, with a smile, when she had reached the camp.

"I knew you would be lonely when Evy left, so I came right away."

"Yes, Laura, I was very lonely, as I always am without you. And I have something I am very anxious to tell you. Laura, I am dying!" He spoke in a deep, solemn tone, and fixed his dark, sunken eyes, burning with weird brilliancy, full upon hers.

"Why, Charley! How can you talk so?"

"Yes, Laura, dying. Dying by the day," he said with the same tone and look.

"Why Charley, you are looking better every day."

"Yes," said he, with a tinge of bitterness, "the sun and wind improve the color. But such skin-deep recovery does not deceive me in the least. The oil is burnt out and it is only the fast-charring wick you see, and soon its light will cease. Laura, there is just one thing left for me now; just one thing. It lies in your power, and in yours alone, to brighten the few days that yet remain for me."

"Charley, you have the 'hypo.' You are surely stronger than when you came here. Let's go fish a little, and that will cheer you up. To-morrow we start for the Cucamunga Mountains, and they say the scenery there is even finer than this. There is more variety there," said she; adding in a light gay voice, "and a little variety will send your spirits up, up, up!"

It produced no effect, however, and he continued in the same tone and with the same look :

"There is one thing, Laura, for which I have tried—oh! so hard—to live. Otherwise, I should willingly have staid at home and allowed death to work his will with me. But for your sake I have come here and tried to live. That hope has been vain, Laura, and already I feel rising fast around me the dark tide that will soon overwhelm me. Laura, must I die without seeing the dream of my life fulfilled ?"

"I hope not, Charley. I hope you will recover," she faltered.

"Laura, lay that out of the question. *I—know.* But whether I recover or not, why should we wait any longer? Why not unite now our hands as well as our hearts? And if I die—"

"Charley!" she exclaimed in a half scream, "how can you talk so? Don't! don't!"

"Well; if I *live*, then ?" said he, earnestly.

"I *hope* you will. I *know* you will," said she, brushing a tear from her bright eye.

"Then it will only anticipate what's to happen anyhow before a great while."

A low "yes" slipped out before she knew it. She

attempted to recall it; but a troop of strange feelings filled her breast, and embarrassment strangled the half-framed retraction before her tongue began to utter it.

"Then, Laura, let us be married when we get to San Bernardino!" said he, quickly.

Again she decided to tell the truth; but the fire of embarrassment withered the thought ere it could bloom into words.

"Why be in such haste, Charley?" she said at length, finding all other words stick on her tongue.

"Laura, can anything be haste for a dying man, for one who is doubly dying, dying for your love as well as—"

He left the sentence unfinished, but his thought was plainly interpreted by his agonized and pleading expression.

"But what will people say?"

"They will say you did right, of course. What else could they say?"

"Of course it would be right. I didn't mean that I mean, what will papa say? I shall have to speak to him about it first."

"I took care of that, and have his consent here in his last letter. He says you may do whatever you think best."

As a poor weary hare, cut off at every turn, sometimes sits bewildered nor again attempts to run, so Laura subsided into silence, which to her great relief was soon broken by the nimble tongue of Belville, who came in chattering to Miss Norton.

CHAPTER XIV.

IN THE HEART OF CUCAMUNGA.

NEARLY ten thousand feet above the San Bernardino plains, Cucamunga rears his dark green head, a pyramid of spruce and fir rising from long pine-clad shoulders, seeming when long cloud-banks lie along his breast a floating island on a sea of foam. On the south the rise is swift and unbroken, but on the north the mountain tumbles away in tremendous ravines, valleys, gulches, ridges, and smaller peaks. In the heart of this portion trickle from the snow-banks and the great reservoirs of the rocks the three forks of Lytle Creek, once the home of innumerable silver trout and still the home of enough for any one but the great American trout-porcus.

It was still early in the day when Belville drove his friends over a divide and down into the little place of Mrs. Glenn—a bright oasis in a wild rolling desert of granite, gravel, boulder, and hill, pine-clad heights, and foot-hills robed in chaparral, with the north fork of the creek sparkling through the long deep valley in the center.

"You will travel many thousand miles before you see another such cloud-cascade as that," said Belville, pointing upward toward the southern sky.

Driven by the sea-wind against the southern slope of

Cucamunga, miles of cloud had been carried up the slope far beyond their natural level, and, sweeping over the long shoulders of the mountain, came tumbling down again into the tremendous gorge of the creek. Great billowy masses flowed over the fir-clad crest of the vast wall, and down hundreds of feet they rolled over each other, till they reached the proper level. Then closing up in orderly array they resumed their northward march. Their backs of snowy white and edges of silver and pearl, where the sun struck through, lent a deeper shade to the serried ranks of pine or fir that showed here and there through the rifts of the great fleecy flood, and a darker tint to the soft blue sky out of which the snowy cascade seemed to come.

By noon the tourists, with their camp equipage packed on their horses, were making their way up the middle fork of the creek. Like all creeks in these mountains this one comes hissing down, an immense boulder-wash, with a fall of hundreds of feet to the mile, its course marked by a long line of green alders amid a wild chaos of boulder and gravel. Over all this the horses picked their cautious way at the rate of a mile and a half an hour. The cloud-cascade was no longer seen, and the sides of the great ravine shone clear and bright in the midday sun. The long white slides that furrowed the walls, the great boulders hanging along them, the dark pockets of serried pines that marked the heads of the gulches, the gray castles of granite that rose here and there from the forests of fir or spruce along the mountain-tops, were all now close around. Before them five vast pyramids of boulder, cliff, fir, and chaparral rose

thousands of feet on high, crowding together like a family of giants standing for a picture, and seeming to bar all farther progress, while to right, to left, behind, wheresoever one turned, great barriers shut out the world.

Four miles were passed and the stream rushed and roared more furiously, the boulders grew larger and whiter, the sand that covered the bottom and edges of the little pools became like snow, and the water seemed greener and colder. The fall was fast becoming so great, and driftwood and heavy boulders so numerous, that it was decided to stop; and soon a little alcove in the hills was found where some campers had been before and here the camp was pitched.

The creek at this point spread out in a succession of small pools of boiling green water over a white bottom. Short cascades plunged over the white rocks in the dense shade of the rank alders. Here was a part of the stream that the great American trout-porcus could not turn from its course—a place where no net or other device but the hook could be used; and consequently there was plenty of fish.

After luncheon Belville went to work to cut spruce boughs for bedding, while the ladies went to the brook to fish, and Norton lay down to rest after his tedious ride.

Laura took her seat upon a great boulder by the seething pool and dropped in her line. In a moment it was carried with a jerk to the bottom and a weight like ten pounds of iron held it there. She pulled hard and steadily, and the shining struggler came to the surface. Still harder, and he is in the air, dancing with all sorts of strange antics, and as the pole is swung in over the shore he hops up and down like a pea on a hot griddle. With a chuckle of exultation, the fair fisher maiden reaches out to take the fish with loose and careless hand; and then an interesting shriek rang up the dark pine-clad walls above, while pole, line, and fish fell upon the sand among the boulders, the fish dancing the line into a tangle.

The fish was still waltzing on its tail when Belville, nearly breaking his bones over the boulders, arrived on the spot, while Norton, roused from his rest, came panting and pale, scrambling along in the rear with the gun. Laura was examining with great solicitude a mark in her hand such as might have been made with a pin in the hands of a six-months-old baby.

"The dreadful thing stung me!" she exclaimed, as Belville began to laugh.

"Too bad, I declare! I left my instruments in the wagon. It may not prove fatal, though. Will you please allow me to look at it?"

She held out her hand with such a smile as one makes when conscious of doing something silly.

"Deep as the legal knowledge of a justice of the peace!" said Norton, as he examined the scar with an affectation of seriousness.

"An unfortunate simile," said Belville, "for such knowledge is generally fatal—to the party who ought to win."

"Do you think it will be necessary to resort to amputation, Doctor?" asked Norton.

"I can't answer for the consequences unless I do."

"I never can take off another of the horrid things," said Laura, provoked at their pleasantry.

"Then I'll stay and assist you," said Belville; and Norton went back to lie down again.

The fish were as greedy as a public administrator, and it was not long before there was another vigorous bite. The line swirled around in the water for a second, and then a three-inch fingerling hit Belville in one eye, as he was peering over a boulder by Laura's side.

"I beg your pardon. I didn't mean to do that," said she.

"Too bad to lose him! That was a ten-pounder at least, judging by the feeling of my eye. Let me know when you are ready to sling another. I don't object to catching fish in that way to please you; but it's sometimes convenient to have notice," said Belville, with a laugh, as he baited her hook for her.

She tossed in again and in a moment felt a quick twitch; one or two more twitches were followed by a tug, and shortly a beauty, almost white below and light green on the back, came lashing and thrashing up through the shade.

"Now take a short hold of the line—so—and catch the fish tightly—so—with the other hand. Their spines are not strong enough to hurt you if you grasp them firmly."

"That is the proper way to grasp any difficulty, I suppose," said she, as with velvety touch she proceeded to loosen the fish from the hook.

"I think the best way to avoid a difficulty is to dodge it," said Belville. "That's what that fish evidently thinks," he added as it flopped from her loose grasp and landed among the stones at her feet.

"Well, we have a new difficulty to practice on," said she in a low voice, looking around to see that no one was near.

"Eh? What is it?" said Belville in some alarm.

"Charley wants me to marry him as soon as possible."

"Saints defend us! I had not thought of that," said he, with much trepidation. "It will be apt to precipitate a crisis."

"He says he's sure he cannot live long, and begs me to make him happy as his wife during the brief time he has before him. What is the best thing to do?"

"The best thing to do! Why, of course you don't contemplate doing *that?*" said Belville in amazement.

"I would do anything in the world to make Charley happy. But marriage is not a thing to be entered into through pity; nor at all, without one loves the man better than any other. And I do not see that the situation is changed by the danger of his dying—except that it is worse."

"And suppose he should *not* die?" asked Belville after a thoughtful pause.

"I wouldn't have him die for the world."

"Of course not. Neither would I. But he speaks only too truly when he says he *is* dying. So you must act upon that assumption, although it is a sad and unpleasant one."

"Perhaps I can—"

"Sh—sh! Here he comes," interrupted Belville. And

sure enough, in a moment more Norton appeared with his pole and line.

"I felt too badly to sleep, and thought I would try a little fishing," he said, with a sigh and a deep sepulchral cough. He seemed very much out of breath, and took a seat on one boulder, leaning against another to rest before he cast in his line.

"I'll go back and finish cutting some bedding, and then I'll join you and catch some fish too," said Belville, starting back toward the camp.

A smile lit up the pale features of Norton as his line was carried with a rush under a boulder; he drew it out with a gleam of silver and green wriggling at the end; and as he took off his catch and put it into his basket a faint glow suffused his face and he seemed perceptibly refreshed.

"If I had only had more of such life as this, what a difference it might have made!" he said, sighing. Then he looked about him and exclaimed:

"What could be grander than these great hills, what softer and purer than this high, dry air, what sweeter than this icy water, what more comforting than these deep shades? I only wish I could live to enjoy it!"

"Oh, you will. I know you will," said Laura, looking encouragingly at him.

"Bury that hope, Laura!"

"I cannot. I cannot think of your dying. It's too dreadful—too dreadful!"

Laura, I once risked by life for you, and you promised me then that when the test came you would show that you could do anything for me. I am dying now as much for your love as for anything. It is a dreadful thing, I know, to ask one to marry a dying man, but if anything will save me—"

"Oh come, Charley, you must not talk so."

' Yes, I am sinking—every week—almost by the day. If you were in my place and could feel the change that is creeping over me—"

"But Charley—"

"Please don't deny me the last favor I shall ever ask you—"

"You must give me time, Charley. I shall have to think it over a little," she said at length in a hesitating tone.

"And meanwhile my brief days are passing. Time is too precious to wait. Let me have your promise to be my wife when we retun to San Bernardino."

" It will be time enough then to say."

" Well, I suppose I can wait till then. We shall be there in two days," he replied, casting in his line again.

"Isn't this delightful fishing?" she said as an eight-inch wiggler illumined the dark shade with his flashing sides, and came twisting out of the water.

" Yes indeed! It's not so wild and exciting as hunting, but softer and more tranquillizing. What a pity that such a place cannot be within reach of every overworked mortal," said Norton, as he pulled another fish out of the same hole.

And who that knows the influence of such recreation on both mind and body does not echo Norton's opinion? You, my scientific friends, who go forth with cunning tackle and gaudy flies to catch the wild and wary old warriors that still linger in the Eastern brooks, you who love the skillful arm, the rocket-like rush and strike, the struggle and the capture, despise not the simplicity of these little silvery cousins of *Salmo Fontinalis*. Gladly would I tell of wilder and larger fish, of deeper and wider pools, of vain casts and fruitless experiments with flies, of scientific drowning of fish that could not be pulled directly out, of broken lines and sulking five-pounders, if the facts would only bear me out. But my duty is to be true to nature, whether the picture be fine or not. Whether or not it be the proper thing to underrate and depreciate our own game is not the question with me. Northern California I hope can show larger and gamier fish than these, but Southern California can show nothing like the carmine-spotted prince of Eastern fish.

Yet, I must repeat, these are by no means to be despised. Their home is in nature's grandest houses, their reception-rooms furnished in a style no art can imitate, and on the walls hang pictures that confound the cunningest pencil. Lie for a few moments on the luxurious sofas of snowy rock fanned by the gentle air through the green alders, with the fragrance of the water stealing over your senses like a breeze over the flower-banks of Elysium, lulling you to repose, and see what feelings come over you. How fancy skips back over the milestones of the past and pauses at each stopping-place in your piscatorial life! Quickly before you come up the boyhood days when with up-rolled pants you waded the old country brook with " gig " in one hand and torch in the other, and the crunch of the iron teeth into a sucker scrambling over a riffle thrilled your soul with electric fire. You recall the smell of the sawdusted water below the old mill, and seem to see again the foam that runs away from the dark dripping wheel, the great pool below the dam where you used to gig the fish among the big stones when the opening of the gates stopped the sheet over the dam and left the surface of the water still. And there, too, is the old bridge in whose shades the sunfish used to lie, while stretched upon the boards above, and peering over the edge, you floated the bait toward him; and, on either side, the line of deep holes by the old stumps of overhanging trees where the cork disappeared ere the sinker reached the bottom, and the greedy chub or golden sunfish came flickering out. Can you forget those soft, warm nights when the "bob" jiggled on the bottom and the writhing eels, their teeth fastened in the linen thread, came squirming out and fell with a dull flop into the scow? Or how, in later days, the light skiff glided over the smooth face of some little lake, while a fair friend sat in the bow, the soft music of her words blending in your boyish ear with the stroke of your oars, and the glittering bait spinning just below the surface in the wake of the boat lured the ravenous pickerel from his shady lair? Swiftly memory calls back the time when the first bite of the speckled trout thrilled you and the bright days spent by the wild-rushing streams in the deep old woods or the dark mountain glen, with comrades whose mirth outblazed the camp-fire at night and outsung the winds by day. And when your soul is borne away on the flood of such recollections as these it tarries not to inspect with too critical eye the swelling springs from which it flows.

NOTE.—In the lower parts of these San Bernardino County streams are still a few trout of considerable size, but very scarce. Some are said to weigh five pounds ; but this is probably *fisherman's* weight. In the only parts where trout are plenty enough for pleasure even half-pound fish are rare ; and I have never seen one that would weigh a pound. Of course the large ones would fight pretty well, but I don't believe any of them are as gamey as the Eastern trout.

CHAPTER XV.

TROUT AND TROUBLE.

"Oh, what a tangled web we weave
When first we practice to deceive."

SOON after daylight the next morning, Belville and Laura went to the brook to get the morning fishing, which is always the best here. Eveline staid at camp to cook breakfast, and Norton was still king of the realm of dreams.

The fish were as ravenous as parishioners at a donation party where the parson's "spread" outvalues the donations, as they jumped, flashed, and darted at the bait. Laura had learned at last how to pull them out and take them off, and many a glimmering beauty found its way to her basket. Belville, throwing back all but the largest, soon had what even the great American trout-porcus would call "a nice mess." So he soon wound up his line, and having caught enough for the day, went up to the pool where Laura was and leaned over a boulder beside her.

"Any new developments in matrimonial prospects?" he asked.

"I don't know what I am to do," she answered. "He's so very urgent and seems to desire it so much. He is certainly failing, and I am afraid this distress of mind is making him worse."

"There is no mistake about his failing."

"Perhaps then— Oh, heavens! isn't it horrible!"

"What?"

"To even think of—doing such a thing—with such an expectation."

"But you surely don't intend—"

"What can I do? He's actually suffering about it. And his state of mind is pulling him down faster than disease. Oh! Heaven forgive my deception! Why didn't I tell him the truth when he first spoke of it?"

Her pole lay idle in the water, and a trout, after breakfasting on the hook beneath a boulder, was trying to work off indigestion by tearing around the bottom of the pool. The crags far above, lit up by the sun's rays softened by passing through thin clouds, shone like silver castles. Down the valley the cloud-cascade was rolling over in great fleecy billows with edges of gold and backs of pearl, with green islands of pine or spruce behind. Below, the manzanita spread its red arms and bright green leaves in the morning sun, and the lilac, still in bloom on the northern slopes, tinted the dark chaparral with its soft purple. Here and there were bushes hung full with golden bells, creepers with trumpets of scarlet and blue, vines festooned with orange and pink. The shades seemed deeper and more solemn, the boulders larger and whiter than ever. Yet Laura saw nothing of it all.

Belville sat staring at her and said not a word.

"I'll do as you say," she said at length.

"No. Do as you think best. I cannot advise you. Nothing will alter my affection, however you decide. I look upon it only as a delay, anyhow."

"Don't speak of such dreadful things," said she, quickly.

"But how are we to help it? There are times when we must reason coldly upon things against which the feelings rebel, and it seems to me this is one of those occasions," said Belville.

"I no longer know what is right and what is not. Why did I not tell him at first!" she repeated, in distress.

"Then why not tell him now?"

"I can't—I can't. He is suffering too much, poor fellow, and I can't bear to have him suffer. I love him yet, and if I had never met you—"

"He certainly is worthy of any woman's love, and I don't wonder you wish to smooth his pathway to the grave, whither he is so surely going. You are the best judge of what to do."

"I hardly see any way but to do as he wishes. But then comes in another dreadful feature of it all—to be the wife of one while my heart belongs to another.

> ' Oh, what a tangled web we weave
> When first we practice to deceive.'

May God forgive me ; I do it only for his good."

A cheery call to breakfast rang from the rocky wall behind them.

"Well, I'll leave my fate where it has always been—in your hands," said Belville with a sigh.

"It's safe enough, but I hate the idea most mightily," said Belville to himself. "I'd stake my reputation on her being a widow in three months at the farthest,

Otherwise, I should object most decidedly. The plaguy arrangement will cheat me out of her company, too, for most of that time. But objecting is an extremely delicate matter. However, mortality will soon eliminate him from the problem, and until then I suppose I'll have to consider it irreducible."

Breakfast passed quietly away, neither Belville nor Laura talking any more than was necessary. After breakfast Belville went to look after the horses, and then returned to the brook and stretched out for a nap on a huge boulder; for at this altitude and in this air one can sleep at any time. Eveline took her line and went up the brook, leaving Laura and Norton alone at camp.

What wonder that so many parties of ladies and gentlemen, the most refined in the land, go out to camp in California, though they know nothing of the pleasures of either hunting or fishing? What wonder that they thread the passes of the high mountains and spend days and weeks among the rugged hills or in the deep cañons? For where has nature made another such country for camping with so little work, so little discomfort, and so much to see; and where earth, air, and sky all combine to produce such a delightful indifference to the flight of time? Where is the land where one can dream time away with a sweeter *abandon* than here? To lie down in the cool night air with no tent but the starry blue or the glistening moonlit leaves of some royal oak, with no fear of rain or dew, unsung to rest by the tuneful Thomas or the festive mosquito, with no fear of the tarantulas, scorpions, rattlesnakes, and other horrors which the Californian rarely knows except in correspondence of Eastern papers written by the perfunctory hand of some quill-hack who has spent a few hours in Woodward's garden; to rise in the morning with the certainty of a bright day, finding the hare perhaps playing around you, the quail calling on every hand, the mountain ringdove drifting past, the squirrel's bushy tail whisking through the bushes, or the dove cooing in the trees by the spring—this, *this* is camping! The mountains are of course the best in summer, but even in the foot-hills and lowlands there is attraction enough to call out thousands every year for camping alone as well as for hunting and fishing.

Though there was little or no game where our friends now were, it was with no little regret that they packed up that afternoon and threaded their way back to where they had left the wagon, and got ready to start on the morrow for San Diego's lower hills and drier valleys, but no less healthful air.

"It's decided," Laura whispered to Belville, as he helped her off her horse, when they reached the wagon at Mrs. Glenn's. "It will be at San Bernardino."

CHAPTER XVI.

JUNE SHOOTING.

WHERE can one shoot in June without violating at least the law of propriety? you naturally ask. Even here. Perhaps no part of the country can show such a continuous round of shooting as this, there being no month when some kind of game is not in its prime here. May, June, and July are here the palmy days of the hares and rabbits. The young are full grown, and both old and young are fat, sleek, and lively. The rabbits of this country need no frost to put them in good condition, and the parasite of the Eastern bunny is rarely or never found among them.

But why sneer at the idea of shooting rabbits at any time? You may indeed have outgrown rabbit-shooting and concentrated your love upon nobler game. But can you forget the time when the flicker of a woolly tail through the frosted weeds of the old meadow, or the rustle of scampering feet over the dead leaves of the woods, swept like a thunder-storm through your boyish heart? Do you forget when it snowed in the evening and you rolled sleepless through the long, long night, waiting for the first scouts of dawn to appear? How you outstripped the daylight in getting up and out upon the snow! How the first glimpse of that four-dotted track thrilled your soul with a strange fire! How you followed it with tingling fingers and trembling knees along some bank, across the brook, and up the meadow fence; how the shivers danced along your back when it led into some brush and you circled the patch to see if it had gone out; how you followed it to the old rail-heap back of some one's barn, and felt a shower-bath of chills as, stooping down and looking in at one end of the heap, you saw a dark, fuzzy object through the opening! Can you ever forget how with trembling hand you cautiously pulled down the rails until at last the sheen of that little black eye beamed on your soul like a meteor? Can you forget how you carried that rabbit home by the legs, although you had a game-bag with you; how you hung him up and for a week went a dozen times a day to look at him, standing at all point of the compass so as to take in all his various splendors; how you thought over him at night and bored your father, uncle, and cousin about him by day; how at last he was served before you at table in becoming state, and with a thrill of pride you helped your mother to a piece; and how in spite of its rank taste you persuaded yourself that the dish was superb? Talk not of the first deer, the first bear. The glory of the first *anything* pales before the memory of the boy's first rabbit.

And what but a boy is the oldest sportsman when in the field—what but a boy slightly modified? And is it not the very life and soul of the field's attractions, that it does thus make us boys again? However this may be, I defy one in whom any love for the field has ever been fully awakened, and who values hunting not for the game but for the skill required to get it and the associations connected with it, to stroll with rifle, pistol, or bow at evening or early morning along the edge of the plains where rabbits and hares are plenty, where the walking is as dry as in your parlor, where he does not have to tear and swear his way through briers, brush, or long grass, where he is neither baked with heat nor benumbed with cold, and say that it is not first-class, scientific shooting and exciting sport. And even if a shot-gun be used, such a one will quickly admit a total eclipse of Eastern May or June shooting, which is reduced by comparison almost to zero!

Our party had camped at the Vallecito, between Temecula and Fall Brook, on their return to San Diego County, and, about an hour before sundown, started out from camp, Laura with bow and arrows, Norton and his sister with shot-guns, and Belville with his rifle.

A few traces of the tristful visage which Belville had worn at San Bernardino, while playing the part of impromptu groomsman at the wedding, still lingered under the mask of good-humor he had worn ever since; while Norton's face was bathed in a perpetual smile and beamed with joy; and he evidently had not failed enough in the last two days to prevent the short walk that is necessary to have good sport with rabbits in this locality, in places where they are plenty.

"Now, remember," said Belville, "that the larder is not suffering, and that we are out only for amusement. So don't shoot at anything unless it is running; with the exception of Miss Lau—excuse me, Mrs. Norton, —who of course will take sitting shots with the bow. And there is a chance for her already!"

He pointed as he spoke to a ball of brown fur between two low bushes of *chemisal* on the edge of the open ground, and some sixty yards away.

Laura walked to within twenty yards of the spot, and a head and a pair of ears suddenly appeared above the rest of the object, with black sparkling eyes turned inquiringly at her.

Tang! went the bowstring, and with a faint *chiff!* the arrow sheathed itself in the carpet of dry alfileria upon which the rabbit was sitting, a little on one side. She placed another arrow on the string, and as it hissed just over the rabbit's head, touching an ear as it passed, the ball of fur in a twinkling became instinct with life and took on an undulatory motion as it disappeared with a zigzag flash of white bobbing in its immediate rear. A ball from Belville's rifle tore up the dry dirt just behind as the rabbit passed an opening in the bushes, and Norton's gun sowed the seed of a black sage-bush about two feet above where Belville's bullet had struck.

"Well, there's another for you," said Norton, shortly, pointing to a little knoll about seventy yards away. As they went toward it a young hare darted out from behind a projecting tongue of *chemisal*, and, like a circus performer running into the ring with a half skip and jump, he hopped proudly and inquisitively out into the open, stopped not far off, reared up on his hind legs, and with long ears perpendicular, fore legs hanging at rest and hind legs ready for business, surveyed the party with his little black eyes flashing in the sun. Meanwhile, preparations for his annihilation were in progress.

"Let the bow have first shot; then we'll try him if he runs," said Belville.

With trembling hand Laura loosed an arrow from the string, but forgot about giving enough elevation. The shaft struck about three feet short, snaked its way through the light, dry grass, and glided out just in front of the living target. Quick as a bat he wheeled and dashed off in a twinkling, making for the brush some eighty yards away.

"Can't I hold far enough ahead of him?" exclaimed Belville, as the first bullet made the dirt fly behind him. He held about six feet ahead, and the next ball sent up a shower of dirt just in front of the scudding hare. Almost like the rebound of a sunbeam was the reversal of that swift engine, and back it went the other way with the shot-guns belching harmless thunder behind. Another ball from the fast-repeating Winchester struck just below the rabbit as it rose in its rapid course, and like a flash it shot away at another angle, with another ball hissing just over it. And now it was running on a quartering course, when the rifle, aimed some three feet ahead, cracked again, and a rolling somersault of yellow and brown took the place of the swift-darting hare, even before the *thud* of the ball came back to the ear.

Rabbits were as thick as friends in prosperity, and before the hunters got through the point of brush out of which this last hare had run, they started three more, one of which stopped just in time to catch a load of shot from Eveline's gun that would otherwise have gone behind him.

"Is that what you call shooting on the run?" said Belville.

"Yes; I shot on the run and hit it on the stop," she replied.

"I presume stoppers are your *forte*. But you did very well. Now, Mrs. Norton, your rabbit still stands on yonder knoll, idly waiting, and looks as if he needed the stimulus of a shaft in his ribs to put him in proper running order for the guns."

She walked up nearer to the rabbit and sent an arrow whisking just over its back into the weeds and grass beyond. It jumped, turned around, shook its head and pricked up its ears for some more music. *Twang!* went the string again, and with a dull *chug* the arrow anchored in its ribs.

"Beautifully done!" exclaimed Belville. "Isn't that far better than shooting it with a shot-gun?"

"I always told you the bow was the best," she responded.

"And I always admitted that it was for rabbits; especially in this country, where it is so easy to get sitting shots. These rabbits, too, unlike the Eastern hares, are worth something when killed. They are, as you already know, vastly ahead of the Eastern rabbit in flavor, and are quicker and more gamey in action. To get sitting shots at the Eastern rabbit at ten or twelve feet is very easy for one who knows where to look and has a sharp eye to see them in their forms. But these fellows you can seldom see in their forms, and when feeding or playing in the open it is hard to get a closer shot than fifteen or twenty yards unless they are running; and often you cannot get closer than thirty yards."

Some two hundred yards away from where they stood a pair of long ears now came into view, just over the edge of some *chemisal.*

"There's a chap we must keep out of sight of, and get behind so as to make him run on the open," said Belville. "Let's slip down this old road here and get behind that strip of brush and be as quiet as possible, keeping our heads down until we get close to him."

A few minutes brought them to about thirty yards in the rear of the animal.

"Now enliven him a little," said Belville to Mrs. Norton.

Twang! went the string, and *chiff!* went the shaft through the edge of the *chemisal,* close beside the hare. He stood not upon the order of his going, but started across the open with the speed of a rocket, and his pace was soon materially accelerated by a shower of dirt thrown up by a Winchester bullet, which fell a little short and bounded over him, and by a stray grain of fine shot from Norton's gun, which acted as a very efficient stimulus to his muscular system. Another bullet sang through the tip of his long ear, causing him to whirl partly about and hop along half dazed for a few yards, flopping his long ears and looking very foolish. But he immediately started out again, quietly, on tiptoe. Another bullet clipped a little unnecessary fur from under his belly as he rose in a spring, and in a twinkling he let out another length of his long body and darted away at right angles to his former course, with two more bullets whizzing vainly behind and above him.

Meanwhile another hare, standing erect on the open ground some two hundred yards away, had been calmly "taking in the show."

"Let me try that fellow as he stands," said Norton, who first caught sight of him. . Belville threw up the globe-sight and adjusted the peep-sight of his rifle to two hundred yards.

"Get the little ball square on the center," said Belville, as he handed the rifle to Norton. "You had better stoop down and rest it on your knee."

Norton did so, and at the report a puff of dust flew from the dry ground, fifty yards beyond the hare. Mr. Hare took down his ears and gathered up his hind legs with exemplary expedition; but before he had run fifty yards his curiosity overcame him, he suddenly stopped, took a look from a sitting position, and then raised himself on his hind legs, with his ears pointed towards the zenith.

Bang! went the rifle. The dust flew at that side of the hare that was towards the rifle; he jumped three feet heavenwards, and, turning in the air, landed on his back, struck in the neck by the glancing ball.

"A splendid shot, that!" said Belville, who would not spoil Norton's pleasure by telling him that the ball had first struck the ground—a fact which the smoke had kept Norton from noticing, although it was by no means a bad shot as it was.

The light of the fast-sinking sun turned into misty carmine as it poured along the great valley leading

up from the San Luis River ; the gray uniform of the
great host of giant boulders that stood guard along
the gateway through the high hills towards Temecula
changed into purple, and the dark-green of the chap-
arral-covered hills towards Montserrate shaded into
blue ; and with these changes of the face of nature
the rabbits and hares (to preserve throughout for
clearness this unscientific distinction) appeared more
and more numerous.   At single points along the edge
of the brush might be seen half a dozen at a time.

Here is one just stepped out of bed, still uncertain
whether it is yet time to get up.   He looks dubiously
around, then draws himself up until he looks like a
little ball of brown fur, and sits between two bushes
of white sage, looking out upon the world as unconcerned about you as an Eastern friend who owes you
money when you get buried in the wilds of California.   A wavy glimmer of brown with a flickering
attachment of white, fading in the sage almost before
it can be seen, is all that remains of the serene little
bunny if you approach a step or two closer.

Here is another, a callow youth of only a few weeks.
He is nearly full-grown, however, and very naturally
feels his importance.   As the party approaches, he
hops out farther on the open ground, sits up and
scratches one ear, neglects even the precaution to turn
his head towards the brush, and nibbles a little dry
alfileria.   He will prove an easy prey, this fellow.

Yes; to him who hunts only for nutriment.   But not
to those who care not for the contents of that little
brownish-gray fur coat, but give him heavy odds for

his little life. *Zip!* goes an arrow into the dry grass beside him, and swifter than "the rainbow's lovely form evanishing amid the storm" of shot, arrows, and bullets, he scuds into the brush.

But never mind. In a country where a rabbit-proof fence is often as necessary to a garden as is the soil one need not wait long at this time of day for a shot. Here is another already, an old and sage one. Wisdom sits enthroned upon his brow as he surveys the party, turns about and hops a step or two into the brush, pricks up his ears, and, like some other smart folks, watches the enemy from behind a blind of two or three sage-stalks which he imagines they cannot penetrate. He might have changed his opinion, perhaps, if he had had a chance, but the *chiff* of an arrow through the sage was followed too suddenly by an impairment of his abdominal functions to permit good brain-work, and he remained as firmly of the same opinion as man often does when floored by an opposing fact.

> "At eve the beetle boometh
> Athwart the thicket lone."

So doth the evening gun of the San Diego bugherder as he taketh in his daily rabbit. *Bang!* comes the echo of a gun from down a long cañon that leads to Montseratte. *Whang!* goes another off toward Fall Brook. The roar of another in the Vallecito itself rattles along its boulder-studded hills, and is answered by the boom of still another far away on the San Luis River.

"Thank God for the rabbits! I'd have been busted

long ago without 'em," an old settler once said as he rose from his matutinal mastication cf cotton-tails. The remark came from the depths of his heart, and can be fully appreciated only by the country resident of Southern California. The bee-keeper's staff of life, the stockman's relaxation from the arduous labors incidental to the deglutition of "jerky," the joy of the cactus *ranchero*, the mainstay of the tarweed or mustard ranch, the great relief of the soul that is weary of bacon or too poor to buy it—the cotton-tail of Southern California stands without a peer among the useful animals of this world.

After going on a hundred yards or so, as the hunters rounded a point of brush, a huge hare shot out with a rush from beyond it, and, turned from his straight-away course by an arrow striking ahead of him, he sped away directly across the face of the party. *Bang!* goes Norton's gun, but still he holds his rapid way. *Whang!* goes Eveline's, yet still that old hare's days go on, go on. *Crack!* goes the rifle, and the dirt flies just beneath him as he rises—a pretty good shot nevertheless, for no human skill can allow for that rapid rise and fall. *Bang!* goes another barrel of Norton's gun, and one hind leg dangles in the air. The rifle cracks again, and the dirt flies just over his back; again, and he spins over and over in a whirling somersault.

Note.—Since the wonderful discovery that glass balls may be hit with a rifle when *practically* at rest, and at a distance so short that a mere child could hit them if *really* at rest, such absurd ideas have grown up about rifle-shooting at moving marks that Belville's shooting at hares may to some seem to be very poor. But until some of the great rifle-shots dare to give an exhibition on balls tossed *across* the line instead of straight-away fire, and at fifteen *yards* instead of fifteen *feet*, it will not be considered necessary to show why Belville's shooting with all its misses was first-class.

CHAPTER XVII.

A JUNE BUCK.

THE next morning, just as the last star on the western verge had ceased its winking at the brightening east, Norton and Belville might have been seen winding up an ancient cattle-trail that led up the side of one of the boulder-bespattered hills that inclose the green amphitheater of the Vallecito. Norton soon discovered that there was plenty of room among the boulders, and here and there the gulches terminated in heavily lined pockets of dark chaparral.

The trail led to a little plateau filled with boulders, brush-patches, and strips of meadow-grass, breaking all along the edges into small benches with brush-filled gullies, and pockets between.

"There is a highly exuberant old buck up here somewhere," said Belville, pointing to a print of two sharp-toed hoofs in the hard ground of the trail. "This track was made last evening, and he is somewhere ahead of us. We must go up to that ridge before us and take a look."

They rode up to the top of the ridge, and, after tying the horses, climbed quietly to the top of a pile of granite rocks and peeped cautiously over. Belville took first a cursory glance over the several hundred acres of wavy ground that lay before and below; then, taking his opera-glass, he began a cautious survey of each particular part. Like all tyros, Norton gave a general glance at the whole, and not at once seeing anything that looked like a deer in a picture, concluded there was nothing there and began to look at the scenery.

Long and thoroughly Belville scanned the sides of every gulch and pocket, the sides and back of every ridge, and the broad top of every bench. And surely he must be looking for rabbits, or mice perhaps, by the way he examines every little spot of brown, yellow, gray, white, and even black. What have such spots to do with deer?

Ah! my friend, pictures of field-sports to the contrary notwithstanding, nothing in the whole line of hunting is more difficult, nothing in still-hunting is so important as to *see a deer before it sees you.*

And this is the hardest and slowest of all rules of hunting to get into the beginner's head; and even many successful hunters, by losing sight for a moment of its supreme importance, often, in a second of haste or carelessness, throw away the fruits of hours of patient toil.

Be not too ready, then, to blame Belville for wasting ten or fifteen minutes in scrutinizing objects that turned out to be stones, patches of bare ground, stubs of burnt chaparral, bits of dead brush, and so on.

And now what so suddenly catches his attention in yonder small patch of chaparral some three hundred yards away? Only a faint motion in a top of a bush; a bird, perhaps, or even the rising breeze. It will bear watching, nevertheless; and Belville knows that the bush is choke-cherry; rather stiff for either a bird or the faint morning breeze to stir, especially without stirring any other bushes.

It moves a few times and stops for several seconds. Then, again, a slow wavy motion and another pause. Yet there is nothing else to be seen even with the glass, and that brush is both low and thin. And now the top of the next bush moves with a twitch, and Belville whispers to Norton, "There he is, browsing in yonder brush. Now you stay right here, for if he runs he will be just as likely to run this way as any. When I signal to you from the rocks or whistle to you, do you take the horses and follow that trail. But don't leave here or show yourself until I do signal in some way." So saying, he pointed out the place where the brush was, backed off the ridge and disappeared.

With rapid but quiet tread of moccasined foot, Belville soon reached the base of a rocky ridge that ran out to within fifty yards of the place where the deer was, and some forty feet above him. Along the side of this ridge, out of sight of the deer, Belville slipped with cautious step, taking care not to snap the brittle brush that lay along his path. He soon reached a pile of rocks such as crowns the end of nearly all such ridges, peered cautiously over, and saw — nothing. Nothing but half an acre of blackish-green brush, the everlasting *Adenostoma fasciculata* of the Southern California hills and *mesas*, mingled with small patches of the sea-green lilac and the pea-green choke-cherry. This half-acre formed the top of a little bench which rolled into the main plateau in front, on the sides into chaparral-filled gulches, and behind into masses of frowning boulder chinked in with wild waving arms of the craggy *cercocarpus*. Away to the right he could see Norton's hat just over the rocks where he had left him; in the valley, a thousand feet below, he could see the distant bug-shepherd going from his rabbit breakfast to his apiary; around him the honey-bugs of the said shepherd were already humming at their morning toil; but of other sight or sound of life there was none.

And what, then, is the matter? Has Belville forgotten the very important point of locating the exact place where he saw the motion? No, he has doctored too many deer to make an error in marking so plain a symptom. Then the deer must have departed while he was coming around. Quite possible. Perhaps it heard, smelt, or saw him, and was sufficiently amused without his company. Possibly. But Belville evidently has another theory. It is just possible, you know, that a deer might stand still in that brush, thin as it appears, without your seeing him. And by the way Belville leans over the rock and looks he must think it highly probable that the deer is still there. He has lost too many good shots by the too hasty assumption that a deer had left the place where he had last seen it. So he stays and looks one, two, three, five minutes—and yet nothing moves.

And now, Doctor, why with all your experience *will*

you get up on that stone to sit down? Is not your present position behind it just as good to examine all the ground ahead? But how the deer-hunter loves a seat; especially after scrambling among San Diego's rugged hills! So he rises up to take a seat on the top stone, when a sudden *smash, bump!* is heard below and a bright yellowish-brown animal with graceful neck, long gray ears, white buttocks, and light trim legs gathered close beneath it, bursts upon his sight. With easy grace it rises, throwing itself above the brush at every bound, descending with a smash of brush and a resounding bump of its four stiff legs as they all strike the hard ground together, then bounding upward from the touch of the ground as though it were a spring-board, making it seem as though the great difficulty were to stay on the ground instead of in the air.

As Belville raises the rifle a most touching "*maa!*" comes from the brush; the bright brown animal stops a moment, turns around its gray head and black forehead and utters a husky but plaintive "*chaaa!*" in reply, then ricochets away, as Belville takes down his rifle again. For a moment the deer is nearly out of sight as it bumps along in its billowy flight down the slope; and then, again it comes into full view over a smooth open place in the plateau, bounding as high as if there were a fence every ten feet. In a moment it reaches the opposite side of the plateau, stops, and throws itself into the attitude of the artists' deer, and sends back a penetrating "*chaaa!*" to the heart-rending cry that follows it from the starting-place.

And now two little brown objects are dimly seen flickering like hares through the brush, and appear shortly out on the open ground. There they stand for a second, their bright little mottled coats shining in the just-rising sun, look inquiringly around and send forth another distressing "*maa!*" It is answered by a responsive cry from the old one on the other side, and with heads up, one on a trot, the other on a half-bound and half-canter, they cross the open ground and join the old dame, who sends forth another "*chaaa!*" and goes bounding away over the rocks and through the brush.

"What's the matter with you?" said Norton, as he came up with the horses in answer to Belville's signal.

"Fawns entirely too small to get along alone, and I wouldn't shoot," said Belville. "Look, here is that old buck's track again in the trail. He's gone down into the cañon yonder, for water probably, and the question now is whether he has come back yet. He certainly has not come back this way, and, as this track was made last night, it is not very likely he will return this way at all now. It would be of little use to follow this track, for it will lead too far and will become too hard to follow as soon as it leaves this old cattle-trail."

Half a mile beyond where they are standing, and several hundred feet below, is a basin in the rugged hills, a great hollow or pocket with sides of ragged chaparral, huddled boulders, and a few gnarled and scattered oaks. A small spring trickles from the rocks in a gulch, and around it a hundred quails, little and big, old and young are running, calling, and drinking. There is a sudden flutter among them, a scrambling, squealing, and running. Some fly up into the bushes, others hop upon stones or run up the slopes and under the bushes. But they all quickly stop and look behind with a low "*k-wook, k-wook, k-wook,*" and some steal timidly back again, as a huge deer steps to the spring and dips in his black nose. How quickly he drinks without stopping for breath or even to look about him—a thing the deer rarely neglects to do! He lingers not a moment after drinking, but walks away with that slow-looking, but really rapid gait that so often deceives the hunter. One hundred, two hundred, three hundred yards he goes, up one of the many old cattle-trails that lead to the spring. But not up the one he came down. He passed last night on yonder slope where the scrubby live-oaks have elbowed their way among the boulders, and to-day he will hie him to a cool sumac bush on the breezy heights a mile in the other direction.

And now he stops, nibbles off the tender leaves of a live-oak, then squares around and with up-raised head takes a long and careful look. His neck is thick and arched like that of the pictured war-horse, his coat has a tawny gloss, his forehead and nose are black, his branching horns are covered with dark brown velvet, his rump, round and bulging with fatness, is white behind, and in the center of the white is a little stubbed black tail which he wiggles with considerable complacency.

Satisfied with his inspection, he stamps a fly from

one of his trim gray legs, wiggles his paint-brush tail again, and walks on to another bush and takes a nip. He evidently does not care much about this particular bush, so he steps along to another, takes two or three bites from its tender twigs and leaves, then raises his head and takes a long look all round, takes another bite or two and another look, wiggles his tail again and moves on a few paces, then stops again and strikes an attitude.

He is evidently of the opinion that he is pretty smart. And he is quite correct, too, although he is appallingly ignorant of the limits of his knowledge—a failing which some people should be charitable enough to forgive.   Like old Wisdom, who discovers a trick or two in mining-stock swindling, he thinks because he can see a few hundred yards beyond his nose that he sees the whole horizon ; and consequently he does not observe a head rise slowly above the rocks on the high ground that forms the opposite side of the basin, some five or six hundred yards away.

"Do you see that chap yonder?" said Belville to Norton, pointing to what at that distance showed only a spot of brown through the bushes.   After a long and careful look through the glass, Norton concluded that he did.

"He's mighty small," said he.   "It looks like one of those fawns."

"Not quite as big as an elephant, but big enough to worry two stout men to put him on a horse," said Belville.

"Can you hit him from here?"

"No; nor any other man, except by accident. I shall make a surer thing of it than that, and if we lose him at all it will be through those natural difficulties that there is no avoiding, and not by deliberate folly. We'll wait here first and watch him, for he is not going to stay long where he is, and it would be nearly impossible to get a good shot at him there, anyhow. He is on an old cattle-trail, you see, and he will not lie down until he gets all the way to the top of the hill."

They stood and watched him through the glass and saw him lounge in elegant leisure up the hill, now stopping to bite off some leaves, or take a look at the scenery, to watch for danger, or to gratify that inordinate propensity a deer has for being as slow when you want him to hurry, and in a hurry when you want him to be slow. But on he went, along the brushy hill-side, now a dim moving glimpse of white, now of brown, now of both; but little of the head visible except when he stopped to browse and look around. Soon he reached the high ground on the same level where the hunters were, and disappeared in a little sag of brushy ground that led to an open plateau.

Quickly they mounted their horses and rode to within two hundred yards of where the deer had last been seen.

"We'll have to wait now for the breeze to turn," said Belville. "You see, the land-breeze is still blowing and we can't follow him in; for that will take our scent directly toward him. And if we swing around to the other end, we will not have time enough to work on him before the sea-breeze begins, which will also carry our scent to him. In the mean time I will go around to the side and climb that rocky ridge and look over into the flat."

He was gone nearly half an hour, but could see nothing. About an hour later the sea-breeze began to come in, and they rode among rocks and brush on their tough mountain-horses to where the deer had disappeared.

"You may keep on your horse for the present, while I go afoot," said Belville, handing his reins to Norton, after which he went some distance ahead. "Deer are not hunted enough here to make them watch their back track more than other directions. But you had better keep well behind, so as to be safe in case he should look back."

The track was plainly visible in the old trail, and Belville followed it some two hundred yards, when it was suddenly lost. He looked quickly from side to side, and then dropped suddenly on his hands and knees and executed a retrograde movement that would have done credit to a blind crab. After going in this manner a few yards he got up, and, slipping softly back to Norton, said:

"He came mighty near seeing me. He is up that gulch, but a little too far off for a sure shot, and he was moving, too. Now do you please go up this trail to where I rose up off my hands and knees, and lie down there behind that little bush; and don't move unless he comes near enough to shoot. If he runs

out you will get a shot, and I will swing far enough
around behind him to make him run this way if he
gets a chance to run at all."

Tying the horses, Belville started up a little gulch
next to the one in which he had seen the deer. A
cattle-trail led up the middle of it, where quiet walking was an easy matter. Reaching the head of the
gulch, he wound cautiously out of it and upon the
ridge that lay between him and the gulch where the
deer was hidden. Slowly and cautiously he raised
his head, while his heart throbbed and his hands
trembled; yet he saw no sign of venison. Higher and
higher he raised his head until more and more of the
bottom of the little gulch came in view. Yet all was
still. The *cercocarpus* looked darkly green as usual,
the sumac and *fusica* reared their arms full of glistening leaves, and the manzanita fairly smiled in the
warm sun. The other side of the gulch was bounded
by a barrier of boulders, and over their tops he saw
the silver face of the far-off Pacific, and the black
wavy hills, yellow slopes, and orchard-like oak groves
of Santa Rosa. On the right, nearly two thousand
feet below, lay the great gorge filled with green timber, where, like a shining serpent embroidered on green
velvet, the Santa Margarita winds its swift way to the
sea. Far off to the left the hills rolled away in great
ridges with bright green timbered cañons between,
and were lost in the high-frowning hills that gird the
rancho of Montserrate. Behind, the rugged chain on
which he stood stretched away, and far beyond lay
the brown plains of Temecula and San Jacinto; while

the far-off looming blue with cloudy crowns marked the sites of Grayback and San Jacinto.

Yes, all was there except the thing he wanted—a luxury that never fails in San Diego's bountiful stores of rock, brush, mountain, plain, and cañon.   Long and eagerly Belville gazed; but all was still, except the soft whispering of that unfailing daily breeze from the shining sea which makes summer in this southern land much less uncomfortable than in higher latitudes on the Atlantic coast.

In the bottom of the pocket into which he is looking is a large sumac with bright green leaves, full blown with blossoms of yellowish white.   The sea-breeze that here searches almost every cañon, gulch, and pocket breathes a grateful coolness through the verdant shades.   What a fine place to loaf away the longest day of the year, far above earthly cares and earth-born jars!

So Belville thinks, as he tries with his glass to pierce the heavy verdure; when a thrill of delight shivers through him as he catches a glimpse of brown at the bottom of the gulch.   He raises his rifle; but when he looks through the sight he finds the mark too dim and uncertain for a sure shot.   So he backs quietly out of his present position, shifts around some twenty yards to one side, and cautiously raises his head again in time to discover that he had come within an ace of shooting at a piece of brown rock in the bush.

He looks a little sharper and raises his head a little more, when a sudden crash of brush by the shady side of a big rock some thirty yards to one side of the bush reminds him of a highly important fact which he had in his haste overlooked—that deer do not always appreciate the hunter's kindness in selecting good places for them to lie down in, but sometimes prefer to make their own selection.

He also discovers another important fact—that deer do not always run just where you want them to ; an idiosyncrasy highly developed in the deer of Southern California. Thus, instead of running down the gulch so as to offer a good open shot, with a run past Norton in case he should escape Belville's rifle, the brown beauty now in question bounds up the hill among great boulders and bushes so thick that it would seem difficult even to walk among them. Yet little cares the buck for either ; rough ground is his delight ; he rises, falls with a crash and a bump, and swings again on high like a thing of air rather than of earth.

Bang ! goes the rifle as he sweeps through the shrubbery, and the ball, whizzing through the place he has just left, hisses harmlessly away over the great Temecula cañon far below. *Bang !* goes another shot aimed to catch him as he rises ; but he never rises twice alike, and as he clears a bush with slanting spring the ball splashes itself to pieces against a rock by his side. Vainly Belville tries to hold the rifle on the point where the buck will touch ground ; for now he springs fifteen feet ahead, sinking out of sight among the brush and rocks; now ten feet ahead and five to one side; now five feet ahead and five to the other side; now going down behind some rock, from the top of which the ball sings over the depths beyond; now flashing full on high with his whole shining body in the bright sun, clear above brush and rocks, falling as the ball spins over him, and glancing up again from the hard ground as he strikes —all the time fast nearing the top of the ridge. Over he goes in a high curve, clear-cut in outline against the western sky, a beautiful mark if it only stayed long enough. The rifle cracks as the figure clears the climax of its bound, a plain *whack!* is borne back on the ocean breeze, and a fore-leg dangles useless on the buck.

Thanks to the light moccasins, which never slip, Belville skipped along the tops of the boulders and reached the farther edge in about a minute. A wild mass of steep confusion, chaotic with rocks and scraggy brush, lay before him, and the buck—stopped? Yes, as the rocket when it is once fairly started stops when the stick breaks. Fast as before, but more erratic in his twist, he went down the rocky slope, smashing through brush like a circus rider through papered hoops, bounding as high as if he had gained another leg instead of losing one. *Bang! whang! bang! whang!* went the swift repeater with desperate energy. The bullets sank glancing from the rocks into the bluish-green abyss below, or spattered into leaden spray against their granite sides. *Bang! bang! bang!* in quick succession sounds the rifle ; and at last a faint *spat* is heard ; the bound changes to a lumbering canter ; the buck no longer clears the brush, but smashes headlong through it with his momentum ; he still steers clear of the rocks and bushes, crashing onward for several yards, when suddenly he lunges, staggers, rolls heavily through a bush, which is crushed beneath his weight, and the dust rises from his scuffling feet as he turns a somersault on the dry ground among the rocks.

CHAPTER XVIII.

CORRALING ANTELOPE.

A LAND bare and sere, swept by clouds of dust, oppressed with unrelieved heat, its weary existence enlivened only by hosts of tarantulas, centipedes, scorpions, fleas, snakes, and other reptiles and vermin —such is San Diego County in summer, according to the imaginations of many who have had no opportunity to know better, and according to the report of many who do know better but fear that the harbor of San Diego may some day take away a few dollars' worth of trade from some northern port.

Yet never was a falser picture drawn. The sun is indeed at times too loving, and at rare intervals the desert's breath overleaps its high mountain barriers and pays a visit to the coast. And the same is true of all Southern and of portions of Northern California. The dust on those very few roads that are much traveled with heavy teams is bad enough ; and bad enough are the fleas if you carpet your floor with cats and dogs. Tarantulas, centipedes, scorpions, and such like, may be found in the cabinet of the bug-hunter, and if you spend a season in camping and hunting you may see, perhaps, a dozen rattlesnakes— the only poisonous snakes here.

But for him who has nothing to do but make himself

comfortable and knows how to do it, there is hardly a part of the Union where the summer is more free from insect and reptile pests, from dust, heat, mud, rain, or other climatic discomforts, than the western half of San Diego. The desert is, of course, nearly intolerable with heat, but the mountains cut this off almost completely. Although there are three kinds of winter here, there is but one summer—a long chain of sapphires in settings of gold and ruby. Weeks glide into months and months roll into seasons, yet the long procession of cloudless days rolls on so swiftly and so smoothly that one forgets the day of the week and almost the month itself.

Come hither, my young friend who hast taken a few primary lessons in philosophy, and let me catechise thee.

What is the effect of air so dry that a piece of meat nearly an inch thick hung in the air will dry up and cure without salt or smoke?

The direct rays of the sun would be hot; the shade cool; and the evaporation of perspiration would be so rapid that the body would feel much cooler at the same temperature than in damper air. Like the gentle breeze or the well-plied fan, it produces faster evaporation on the skin.

Very good. And what would be the effect at night?

Rapid radiation of heat from the earth, and cool nights in consequence.

Suppose the heated air that rises from the land could not flow over eastward because of the hot deserts of this country and Arizona ; where would it go ?

To the west, out to sea.

And suppose it there met the cold current of air that, sweeping down the northern coast, makes San Francisco so cold in summer, and which passes this country several miles out at sea greatly modified by the difference in latitude.   What would be the effect ?

It would quickly cool and descend.

And from whence, then, would the vacuum caused by the rising of the air on land be filled?

By this same air that has thus flowed over and become suddenly cooled.

So that the daily sea-breeze which searches every nook and cranny of the hills, instead of being a damp sea *wind*, is what ?

The dry land-air, tumbling over seaward from above and coming back again on the same principle as the undertow on the shore.

Correct.   And that is why meat that would spoil in the driest part of Illinois will cure here on the coast almost as well as in the interior.   Then there would be a daily breeze of cool dry air from the sea, and a cool land-breeze descending from the mountains at night.   And now if ninety-nine per cent of the surface of the country were as dry as a fresh-baked brick, how about the malaria that is deemed inseparable from southern climates?

There could not be any.

And now you see how easily one can deduce the

summer climate from the unquestioned conditions. And such experience shows it to be, all these effects being heightened, of course, by the thinner air and better shade of the mountains.

But surely the land is dreary and bare; for no vegetation is possible under such a steady sun-bake?

Yes. The fern-like leaves and bright blue stars of the alfileria are gone, and dead and brown are the bright green clovers with their little golden and bluish-purple flowers. But in their places is a thick mat of hay and seed all ready for your horse, on which he can travel farther and keep fatter than on the best of high-priced timothy and oats. Gone, too, is the bright green grass that glowed along the sunny slopes, and in its place is the yellow glare of the ripened fox-tail, abundant and worthless. The bright scarlet of the *orthocarpus* is gone; the blaze of shooting stars, poppies, buttercups, and daisies has burnt out; and the glittering host of violets and pinks that lately spangled the land with such prodigal splendor have trailed their bright banners in the dust.

Some of our fair friends of a few months ago have changed to enemies. The *fecilias* that beamed with such wealth of purple are now hateful with fine dry "stickers;" the soft moss-like little creeper, so tenderly pink, is now too "stimulating" to sit down upon; the delicate little clover, that spread such a thick green carpet over meadow, plain, and hill, has sown its burry seeds by the myriad—the joy of your horse, but the terror of your blanket; and·the silken grass, that shone so bright beneath the aged oak along the mountain's breast, is now the hateful " tickle-grass" that hankers ever for your stockings.

But perhaps you think all color has faded from the land. You very natually forget that nature is prodigal of vegetation that would flourish best on the southern slope of old Pluto's ash-heap. With the exception of grass and small flowers, the land is nearly as green as ever. In the cañon and river bottom the sycamores, the oaks, the cottonwoods, willows, alders, and other deciduous trees, are all in the noon of life. Over their tops the rank grapevine clambers and hangs in showers of foliage, and around their trunks or over the piles of old gray rocks the poison oak — beautiful serpent — twines its shining green leaves, now rapidly turning to crimson. In thick-matted jungles the wild rose and sweet-brier, which are now in full bloom, line the paths through the creek bottoms; on the more open flats the elder's green wealth and berry clusters still shine on every hand; all over the low ground the wild gourd spreads it great green leaves; and on those lands that are low enough to be still wet the *agua mansa*, the *tule*, and a score of rank grasses and reeds are struggling to surpass each other.

The hills are less changed than the plains and cañons. The bayonet's proud plume of purple and white no longer waves. The myriads of colored creepers have shed their gaudy robes; the cardinal flower, the larkspur, the painted cup, the Indian pipe, and their thousand and one comrades have folded their starry flags. But the *fusica* is more green and shinnig than ever; the sumac is in its fullest glory of leaf and bloom; the wild gooseberry has indeed shed its crimson trumpet-flower, but its leaves and those of the currant are as bright as ever; the wild buckwheat shows it reddish snow on every hand; the cedary arms of the *baccharis* are tufted with white feathery plumes; the lilac, *manzanita*, cherry, *cercocarpus*, *chemisal*, and other chaparral bushes are all in the heyday of life; the tall stalks of the white sage are still bright with blossoms for the busy bee, and around the ever-green *ramiria*, the buckwheat, and other bushes, is twined in endless mazes the silken orange-colored floss of that fairest of parasites, the love-vine (*Cuscuta Californica*).

The quail that last winter was so wild now nods its black plume from the rock by the roadside, or leads its band of half-fledged young trotting swiftly along in front of your horse or scrambling up the rock pile by his side. The linnet and the lark still pour a flood of song, though it is a flood that is fast ebbing; the road-runner or chaparral cock scuds along the edges of the plains; the mocking-bird, humming-bird, oriole, swallow, and all birds except the robin, are still here at home in summer as in winter, and never leave for northern fields; ground-squirrels, about the size of eastern gray squirrels, run and scamper on every hand, very pleasant to look at if you are not in any agricultural or horticultural business; while at evening and morning rabbits and hares play around the brush more numerous than ever.

This much, not by way of praising the country—a business gladly left to those who live in this country from choice or own real estate here—but to show that the invalid who stays here for the summer, instead of fleeing as he would from Florida and most other sanitary retreats, is not such a " pluperfect pancake" as his wiser brethren might imagine.

It was not strange, then, that Norton said, as he and Belville with the two ladies early on the day following the capture of the buck rode down through the heavy oak grove of Montserrate, " I really believe we are going to enjoy the summer here as much as the winter."

They were bound for Miner's ranch again, where they were to prepare for a trip to the Cuyamaca Mountains. Over many a weary mile they rode; but the horses were good, the roads were hard and free from dust, and the breeze was in their faces nearly all the way. So they soon cleared the bouldered heights and oak-clad hills of Montserrate, the billowy slopes of the San Luis River, covered with sage and sumac, and the rolling plains of Buena Vista and San Marcos, passing the wheat-fields of San Bernardo and Poway and descending the Sycamore cañon of El Cajon just as the sun went down.

" Look at those goats! Are they wild ones?" exclaimed Mrs. Norton, as they went down the cañon.

Some three hundred yards away were eight or ten

light, trim little creatures, white beneath and half-way up the sides, and light cinnamon shade above. They were stringing along, one behind the other, up a gentle slope that broke away from the hills, apparently little concerned about the wagon, yet watching it as they advanced on a walk so swift it seemed a half-trot. A large one with two short curved horns led the line, and three little kids closed up the file.

"Antelope!" said Belville, reaching for his rifle.

"I didn't suppose there were any antelope in the country," said Norton.

"There are three or four bands still left in this part of this county, and this is one of them. California was once the leading country of the world for antelope, but the demands of the almighty palate has nearly closed them out. Still, for sport's sake, I must have one of them."

He took out his rifle, raised the sight, looked at the slowly-retreating antelope, and after a while said,

"If I shoot from here, the chances are all against touching them, for they are now over four hundred yards away. I stand little chance of getting closer, for it is too late to make the circuit that would be necessary. If I try to get closer by going toward them, they will be quite sure to run, and when they once start they will probably go several miles. They are not scared now, and if left alone will be very near here in the morning. So I will let them go till then."

So they continued on to Miner's, at which hospitable place they received a hearty welcome, and secured a good night's rest in preparation for the morrow's sport

At daylight the next morning they set out from Miner's, Norton and the ladies riding along for amusement, since they had no rifles and were told it was quite idle to take shot-guns. Miner, who was always ready to help his guests to have a good time, went along, taking two of his best *vaqueros*, or herdsmen to help "corral the band," as he and Belville said.

Over two or three dreary miles along the bluffs and over hills hideous with Turk's head, prickly-pear and *cholla* cactus, cobblestones and rough ground, the patient horses picked their way. All eyes were scouring the plains below, while far down along the river Belville, with Miner and his men, was searching the low slopes that ran away from the hills. Over an hour was thus spent before one of the men, pointing to the broad bottom of the valley, said,

"There they are !"

A mile away, five or six little whitish animals were descried, and with the aid of the glass a few more were discovered lying down.

"I don't believe I shall have to use the red flag at all, but can sneak on them down yonder *barranca*," said Belville.

"All right," said Miner. "They are not very wild, and are very little hunted nowadays. But to make sure, you had better go around about two miles and strike into the left branch of the *barranca*, for you cannot get into the other branch without passing over open ground where they may see you.—In the mean time we'll spread out and get on the courses they will be apt to take, if you should let any get away from you."

As Belville departed, one of the men started for a bush on a ridge a mile across the valley with a rifle that would occasionally hit a deer if the sights were not held too closely on it. Another took the center with a *riata*, or lasso, and a horse that would charge on anything he was turned at, from a cactus patch to a grizzly bear. Miner took one of the slopes on the hither side of the valley, armed with an American navy revolver warranted to overshoot an elephant at ten paces unless the shooter aimed at his toes. Norton and the ladies remained on the hill with the glass to see the fun. As the antelope were on the extreme end of their range, which ran from the Tia Juana River to El Cajon, about fifteen miles, and there were nothing but brushy hills to the north, in which these animals will not go, while Belville was to be on the east of them, there was almost a certainty that those on the hill would get a good view of the show, whatever it might be.

It took Belville over half an hour to get into the *barranca*, or gully, and when he had accomplished it he found the antelope had moved a hundred yards or more, and were now standing around a little knoll. He came cautiously a little way on to the open ground with a strip of red flannel tied to a stick, and, lying flat in a little depression in the ground, gave an upward flip of the rag. Several times he waved it at intervals of a few seconds, allowing it to remain in sight only an instant.

This performance he had read of and heard talked of by hunters; but as usual, both quills and tongues had omitted about the most important part of the instruction—to have plenty of patience. He had not waved the stick three minutes before it seemed half an hour, and he could not resist the temptation to take a cautious look—extremely cautious, he thought.

He took it, but it was at a dissolving view of an "arrangement in white and brown," lithe and easy in movement, *spirituelle* in grace, only cantering with gentle rolling gait, but vanishing—oh how fast!

He sprang to his feet and sent a bullet after them. In his haste he aimed at the bunch with the usual invariable result—a miss. Ball after ball went hissing among them or past them, or, glancing from the ground behind, went singing over them. But still they held the even tenor of their way, not like the high-bounding deer, but with low, easy canter, scarcely seeming to rise or fall, yet fast fading away.

They take the low open slope lying between the hill where the spectators are and the brushy middle of the valley. The horseman who had gone across the valley mounts, and, riding down the back side of the ridge out of sight, starts to head them off. Miner cocks his pistol, and rampant murder gleams in his usually mild eye. The man in the center begins to coil his *riata*, and to reflect on the possibility of lassoing two at one throw. Meanwhile the victims come rolling gracefully on into the very jaws of death.

Yes, here they come, the old buck ahead, the kids stringing along in the rear, not a bit in a hurry; running quite slowly, in fact. So thought Norton and the ladies as they watched them from the hill; but then they were not behind them, even with good horses, or they might possibly have thought otherwise. On they come, right toward the waiting murderers. If the other man with the rifle were only there too, to lie down in the path! But fortunately he is not, so that two shall escape to keep up the band; for Miner's pistol has only six shots, the lasso can catch only one, and there are nine in the band.

"*Whoop-ah!*" Now they go for them, one from each side, right for the leader of the band, the herdsman swinging the *riata* furiously around his head, and the horse snorting with joy at the prospect of roping something; for a good lasso-horse likes the fun as well as his rider.

And still the antelope come ambling on with the same easy grace, and without swerving to right or left. Alas! how can the poor things swerve, when to swerve is only certain death? Would you swerve, reader, with hanging on one side and shooting on the other? And how could they turn back, with a battery in their rear, the hills lined with frightful *cholla* cactus on one side, the middle of the valley nearly barricaded with the almost equally frightful prickly-pear cactus? With all deference to friend Miner's opinion, corraling antelope is, to say the least, a mean trick, and every one must feel his finer sensibilities outraged by such a gross advantage taken of such lovely and innocent creatures.   But still, here we are, and we must look.

Bang ! goes Miner's latest model American breech-loading navy revolver, and the ball aimed at the toes of the leading buck shivers the skull—of a Turk's head about two hundred yards up the slope and ten feet above the line of the buck.   *Wizzoo, wizzoo, wizzoo, wizzoo, wee-oo!* goes the *riata,* and the noose, shooting out some thirty feet, encircles with its deadly embrace the stubby tail of a terrified doe which, however, it does not detain long.

Both the horsemen get turned around in time to see the white rolling waves rippling away over a wide expanse of cobblestone and little mounds ; and the other horseman comes charging through the brush in the middle of the valley, reaching a bit of rising ground just in time to catch a glimpse of the fading white caps and say,

"Yes, that's 'em."

CHAPTER XIX.

MOUNTAIN GAME.

CAN this be in San Diego, this place where our friends are now camped? One whose observation was confined to a few miles along the coast, as is the case with nearly all visitors, would hardly think so. Around them stand trees as large as any seen in Eastern forests, pines with great thick trunks and stupendous cones, oaks that bear acorns thrice the size of any Eastern acorns, and other trees of various kinds, standing shoulder to shoulder as they have stood through long ages. Softly sighs a cooling breeze through the tree-tops and the dark arcades beneath. It is a hot day in the lowlands, warm even here out in the sun; but what do these wanderers know of heat, as they lie stretched out in hammocks beneath the shady trees, with a crystal spring of ice-cold water—so different from the flat warm stuff of the lowlands—trickling close at hand. Along its edge the ring-dove of the mountains bathes his coat of burnished lavender, then flits to the dead limb above and bobs his glossy head and white collared neck, and inspects the visitors with his golden eye. The bluejay and woodpeckers of varied hue flit here and there through the shades, while far above through the heavy screen of leaves one may see the black eagle (we have him at last!) wheeling his dark form against the blue dome.

And here, too, trailing his gray brush swiftly over some limb, up some trunk, or over the carpet of pine needles, is another dear companion of early days. Ah, thou dear old friend of childhood's happiest hours, though long since I ceased to enliven thy peaceful existence, I love thee yet. Who that has known thee in those bright days can ever forget thee? Who can forget those early morning hours when, with stealthy tread, straining eye, and listening ear, he threaded the old oak and hickory woods in constant hope of catching sight or sound of thee? Does not the heart bound again as memory hears the distant patter of the crumbs from thy lofty breakfast-table, the snapping of some distant branch beneath thy spring, thy rapid bark slow-sliding into a sleepy " *cha-a*," or the patter of thy swift-bounding feet over the dead leaves toward thy favorite tree?

Does not the life-tide start again as recollection sees the little strip of gray swift-flashing through the green shades above, dodging around the heavy trunk, flattened on some limb, rolled into a fuzzy ball among the highest leaves, or ensconced in some big crotch? And when did it ever burst into a wilder flood than when he flung his graceful form in headlong haste from tree to tree while you, trying to load that old single-barreled muzzle-loader as you ran, perspiring and burning with anxiety and afraid to take your eyes off the fast-scudding gray, stumbled and tumbled along below? Then you recall that great day, a land-mark on the journey of childhood, when you ran him into a hole, climbed the tree and stopped it with leaves, and ran home for an axe and a bag. You remember how your father and brother and the hired man came back to help and look, how the bag was fastened over the hole and the squirrel, smoked, punched, and scared by hammering outside, went with a bound into the bag. Do you not recall how you took him home and tried to get him into that revolving cage, how warm his teeth or claws felt when you tried to take hold of him, how you got him in at last, how he lingered there several days, uttering an occasional melancholy "*cha-a*," until one day he rolled up his bushy tail and died, and with quivering lip and flooded eyes you carried him out and buried him in the best little box you had?

Nor is this merry fellow to be despised even by the full-grown boy. Where finds the eye a prettier short-range target for the rifle, or one that takes more skill to hit, than that little head, seen against the sky over some high limb or darkly visible in some dusky crotch? Nor is he altogether unworthy of the shot-gun, when he runs up one long limb that reaches out toward another, bridging the space with crashing spring, and scuds as swiftly down that limb and up the next one almost as fast as one can follow from below.

"There's a fine chance for a lady to try the rifle," said Belville, pointing, as he lay smoking in his hammock, to a squirrel that with energetic twitch of his bushy tail was barking on a limb about sixty yards away. "Or you can try the head of that pigeon on that dead limb above the spring. Only we want nothing hit but the head. Body-shots dont coun't."

He set the globe-sight, and Mrs. Norton, walking up to within forty yards of the squirrel, closed out the business of a flourishing young pine-cone about two feet from his tail, while the prospective victim twitched his brush away to the tree-top with remarkable expedition.

"Never mind him ; there's another," said Belville, pointing to another gray-coat running up a tree perhaps eighty yards away. "Rest the rifle on that fallen tree-top."

She did so, and the ball, glancing from the limb beside the squirrel, went singing up into the air, while the squirrel effected his disappearance again without stopping to sing.

"I haven't seen much of you alone lately," said Belville to Laura, as they strolled on toward a pigeon that sat bobbing its head on a dead limb, some distance beyond. "I have been quite lonesome."

"Oh ! I have to be more attentive to Charley now, you know," she answered lightly.

"He don't seem to be failing as fast as he was."

"Why, no, indeed! I think, on the contrary, he is improving. He seems so much happier too."

"Laura—I cannot call you Mrs. Norton," said Belville, after a long silence—"I see now that I have let my prize slip away from me irrevocably."

She made no answer.

"Laura," he said, after a pause, "do you not pity me? Have you no part in my regrets? Did I really, in my too hasty considerateness, give away the heart that I had as well as the hand that I hoped for?"

"Dr. Belville," replied Laura, "you must not talk to me so now. I am another man's wife."

"I know I am saying strange things; but the circumstances are also strange."

"I shall make every allowance for that," she responded, "but you must never refer again to that wild episode of our lives. When I married Charley I loved him only a little less than before. I married him without regret. I love him now more than ever. I am his wife, and you must treat me as such."

Belville stood abashed for a moment at her firm and decided tone, and said, with suppressed feeling, "Forgive me if the pain of losing you has made me forget the respect that is due you."

"Why do you laugh?" he asked solemnly, as with a smile she turned to go again to the camp.

"Why, Doctor," she answered, "with all that is awful and sad in this unhappy affair, there is still something very absurd in the entire situation."

"It is anything but absurd to me. It is digging my grave," said he with quivering lip, as he left her side and strolled silently back to his hammock.

Mid-day came, and the ring-doves began to come into water. And now and then a squirrel came hopping along the ground toward the little stream that ran away from the spring. Belville seemed indisposed for shooting, and lay in his hammock smoking. Eveline Norton had brought a novel with her—*verbum sat.* And Norton and his wife took their guns and strolled off beyond the spring and sat down on the soft carpet of pine needles to watch for pigeons coming in to drink.

"You are feeling a great deal better, ain't you, Charley?" said Laura, with a glad sparkle in her eyes.

"I surely am improving and I feel much better in this high soft air."

"I am so glad!" she exclaimed.

"You may thank yourself, then. You have saved me!"

"I meant that I was glad—any way," she murmured, with faint, hesitating tone.

"And I too. It would have been the same if I had been well."

"Perhaps—not, Charley. I am afraid I should not have been so happy."

"Why not?"

"There's a secret that I cannot keep. I know you will forgive me, because you know how glad I am that it has turned out all right. Charley, I have been a very naughty girl, and came near losing you—oh, how near!"

"Of course I forgive you. I could forgive you anything. But please explain. I am in the dark."

"There was a time—thank Heaven it passed so quickly!—that I liked—him"—with a glance toward Belville—"too much. Yet I loved you too."

Norton smiled. "Laura," said he, "I too have a secret to tell, and I believe you will as readily forgive me as I do you, when—"

He was interrupted by hearing a light step on the ground at one side, and turning, saw that the noise was caused by a big yellowish-brown doe with glossy sides, followed by two little dark-brown fawns, all mottled with white spots, which walked to within twenty yards of where they sat, and stopped at the little spring run to drink. The fawns lagged behind, and one of them, straggling off to one side, came to within ten feet of Norton and his wife. Petrified with amazement, both sat perfectly still, when suddenly the doe raised her head, uttering a hollow-toned "*phew !*" long-drawn and penetrating. In another second she sprang several feet into the air, landing on the other side of the rivulet, bounded like a ball from the touch of the ground, and was ricocheting rapidly towards the camp, with the fawns springing rapidly after her, when she caught sight of Belville scrambling out of his hammock. Quick as a hare she turned at an acute angle to her course and went back directly towards Norton and wife, whom she had not yet seen but only scented, without knowing their exact direction. But now she went no longer with the high-glancing curve, but lay down and hugged the ground like a scudding hare. Straight towards them she went until within twenty feet, when they made a very expeditious removal of physical obstructions to her further progress. This turned her a little, and she fiew past them slightly to one side, and with the small shot from Norton's gun pattering harmlessly on her tawny coat, she vanished down one of the dark vistas of pine and oak.

The fawns, on account of some brush in the way of sight, had not seen the mother turn, and ran on the course they had first taken, straight into camp, where with a dismal "*maa!*" they stopped until they saw Belville, when they turned and scampered off in the direction the mother had taken.

"Don't shoot! don't!" said Norton, as they came on, seizing Laura's gun, which she was raising, deceived by the appearance of the fawns, which always look much larger than they really are.

They went past in safety, just in time to run into the loving embrace of Belville's dog, which was coming back from a fruitless dash he had made after the old one. One of the fawns uttered a piteous "*maa!*" as he grabbed it by one of its long ears and it went rolling over on the ground, kicking like a little fury. The dog let go with a yelp as one of the little sharp hoofs struck him in the head, but grabbed again as soon as the fawn got up. Norton was soon on the scene and seized a hind leg, which he held about as long as a man can hold an electric flash. Although, like the dog, he was useless to hang on, he was equally good at grabbing again, and between them they managed to keep the fawn from getting away until Belville arrived on the double quick. Belville seized both hind legs at once, one in each hand, and at the same time lifted them clear of the ground. A few swift, tremulous kicks were given with the hind legs, but there was not force enough in them, and the capture was complete. A rope was soon brought and fastened around the captive's neck, and after half an hour's caressing it followed its new friends back to camp, where it was christened "Doc," and henceforth became the most contented and familiar member of the party, until the time came to leave and they tried to get it in the wagon. Then ensued a scene such as can be appreciated only by one who has tried such a job assisted by one invalid who is afraid of his lungs, and by two ladies—who are not.

Then came "Doc's" day of triumph, and after a long struggle he was left in his native home, with many farewell caresses and regrets from the ladies and various remarks from his breathless and exhausted namesake, who had left all his court-plaster at El Cajon, and had not even a needle along to mend the rents in the only coat he had left with which to pass through the fashionable city of Julian.

CHAPTER XX

THE MOUNTAIN QUAIL.

LET us follow Belville and Eveline as they start after breakfast one morning to go to the top of the Cuyamaca. It is only a short walk, not over a thousand feet of elevation, and we will see where we are.

Half a mile up a pine-covered slope and we reach a shoulder upon which rests a rocky, pyramid-shaped head, about three or four hundred feet high and easily climbed. A few minutes' time brings us to the top of this, and we stand upon its loftiest rock. A vast sea lies far below on the west, with tumbling waves of snowy white rolling like great masses of carded wool; with long shafts of golden light, touching, as they are shot through the eastern mountain-gorges from Apollo's fiery bow, the crests of these billows; with its hundred islands of different heights looming up here and there, some in a full blaze of light, others just tipped with gilded spires, others standing dark and somber in the shade of greater peaks. Even as we gaze upon this sea its masses begin to break. Great rifts of bluish green with edges of gold and pearl begin to yawn along its rolling surface, and through them appear the dark blue chaparral of the hills, the long green winding strips of river bottoms and cañons, and the silvery-gray heads of rocks and cliffs. And now through the farthest rifts shimmers the distant Pacific, with its high rocky islands looking like small ant-hills. Soon the great white sheet is entirely broken up and is scudding away to sea in a thousand rolling clouds, the whole western slope is bathed again in sunlight, and the far ocean shines like a lake of quicksilver.

Rising thousands of feet below, in the yawning gulf in front, the San Diego River winds its green way to the sea through immense rocky walls. Far to the right the serpentine bottoms of the San Bernardo and San Luis, and on the left the verdurous trails of the Sweetwater and Tia Juana rivers, gleam among plains of brown or yellow, or thread the gorges that lie between the dark bluish hills of chaparral and the bare, dreary heaps of rock and boulder. Towards the south roll in wild confusion the ragged mountains of Mexico, and for hundreds of square miles the eye wanders over a tumbling sea of rock, cliff, chaparral, boulder-studded peaks all cleft with deep valleys, and cañons shining in their winding courses with bright green timber. Here and there the eye rests upon a bright little valley like the emerald lake of Pine Valley, sunk in the mountain's back and eternally green with timber and grass or the golden stubbles of Viejas; but nine-tenths of it all is primeval wilderness that will remain so forever, broken only by the tread of the herdsman's or the hunter's horse.

Westward, the eye rests upon more pleasant scenes, though here, too, it is nearly all boulder, chaparral, towering heights or yawning cañons ; yet many a fair valley or broad open plain, nestled in a girdle of hills or sunk in some mountain-gorge, greets the eye. And nearer by and more to the north the mountain chain breaks away into smooth rolling hills, clad with golden carpet of dry grass and studded with oaks like some old Eastern apple-orchard. At various points one sees many a little vale, pocket, or flat, where the corn nodding along the road and the little house embowered in heavy live-oaks or surrounded by a garden, still green in midsummer without irrigation, bring up sad memories of a land better loved than this. One hundred miles to the north, the bald pate of Grayback looms high through the hazy blue, and around him are clustered his smaller brethern, our former friends San Jacinto and Cucamunga rising at his side. Scores of lesser peaks, that in the East would be considered "Cloud-Cleavers" or "Sky-Splitters," lie between and all around, but they are so numerous, and so overshadowed by their more aspiring brethern that they here pass unnoticed and unnamed.

As the eye naturally wanders around to the east, it ranges over more crag and cliff and scar with a few fine valleys between, descrying the fair meadows of Treat's ranch almost beneath; until in a few miles the country tumbles rapidly away in dismal desolation, without a gleam of green or blue or golden yellow, or other sign of life, into the wide-reaching ghastly gleam of the Colorado Desert.

In all this vast circuit of the eye, sweeping a space larger than Massachusetts, Rhode Island, and Connecticut combined,* the eye rests not upon a single city, town, or even hamlet, except the far-off town of San Diego and the little pile of culled lumber struck by a whirlwind that lies nestled in the fairest part of these mountains and goes by the name of Julian. No churches, no railroads, no anything is seen except a few ranches at wide intervals and little school-houses still more widely scattered, with here and there an Indian *rancheria*, or group of huts. Yet nowhere in all this country are property and life safer or health and comfort more secure. The judiciary is not excelled in the State; in few places are taxes as low; nowhere is there a better set of county officers, nowhere less stealing among officials. And many a day, and far and wide over the United States, may one travel before he will find people more cultured and refined or better educated than the upper half of the white population of this county. Few indeed they are, and scattered, but among them one will look in vain, even among the many "forty-niners," for the Californian of the novelist, half fool and half scamp, or for the typical muderous character of fiction, or the "galoot" of the Eastern scribbler who writes of California life.

What mellow tones are these, like the taps of the leather hammer on the glass plates of the harmonicon, that arouse Laura from her novel, and her husband from his after-breakfast nap—a thing so easy to take in this mountain-air. " *Quoi, quoi, quoi, quoi, quoi!*" it

* This country alone is about as large as these three States.

goes, seeming far yet near, half plaintive and half joyous, half calling and half answering. The sound is evidently made four or five times by one bird, and then taken up and carried along by another.

Taking their guns, Norton and Laura went slowly toward the sound, which grew louder until they reached the little spring run, a hundred yards below the camp, when it suddenly stopped. While waiting for it to sound again, they heard a "*queeah, queeah, quit-quit-quit-quit, queeah, queeah !*" so tender and plaintive in tone that they stopped in wonder. This new sound came again, accompanied by a faint rustle in the dry grass and weeds some twenty yards ahead. Upon their walking closer, the "*queeah, queeah !*" became more distressingly anxious, and out walked in plain sight, almost in single file, two dozen or more graceful little birds a trifle larger, but of about the same shape, plumpness, and easy motion of that dear little friend of the Eastern stubbles, "Bob White."

The leader hopped upon a low stone, the next one mounted a log, another fluttered upon a rock, while the rest walked about with sober visage and dignified pace ; all with frequent cries of "*quit-quit-quit-quit, queeah, queeah !*" or a simple "*queeah, queeah !*" and a mild inquisitive gaze at the strangers, in which curiosity and not alarm was plainly predominant. Their colors were not those of any Eastern game-bird. With coats of brownish gray, vests of brilliant cinnamon mottled with white below a full open bosom of blue, four white bands along the back and sides and around the throat, a broad white collar of antique cut tied with a wide cinnamon cravat, a jaunty cap of grayish brown upon the neat little head, from the center of which nodded two long sable plumes, they walked and wheeled, cocked their heads from side to side to survey their visitors, and repeated steadily their peculiar and plaintive note.

But though they showed little alarm, evanescence was most decidedly a part of their programme, and all this while there had been a manifest purpose to gently steal away. Now they began to vanish in earnest. But not with the buzzing wing or active leg of Bob White or the little valley-quail of California. There was only an easy grace smacking both of politeness and impudence, as the dead leaves rustled to the patter of their little feet and they began to fade in the grass and brush.

"Hold on!" came a voice from behind the amateurs, as they raised their guns to shoot before the birds should get away. "We'll have better fun than that with them. Put up that murderous gun and bring forth the plaything of the immortals, Mrs. Norton. You, Norton, keep your gun, but don't shoot at anything until it flies."

"Why, when did you—"

"Just dropped," said Belville. "And just in time to prevent sacrilege, I see. I'll show you some sport, however, for compensation."

Old Prince stood by his master's side as he spoke, the very incarnation of *business*. His tail no longer hung, but projected. Stiff as an icicle, it fairly quivered at the tip with rigidity. One fore-leg was bent double, and the other three trembled with his efforts to keep still ; while his body was firm as a garden statue in a Minnesota winter. On his aged brow sat grave importance, and mighty wisdom shone from his staring bright eye. His nose was wrinkled with seriousness, while his chaps quivered and watered like those of ye city epicure what time he beholdeth on one of Delmonico's plates a June woodcock, killed while feeding its helpless young.

The bow and arrows were soon brought and the party moved on, Mrs. Norton ahead and Prince waddling along in the rear with the anxious solemnity of a circus elephant walking over his master. His legs rivaled his tail in stiffness, and he looked up occasionally at his master with intense satisfaction, licked his chaps and sniffed the air, which was laden with that fragrance the dog so loves.

The birds were soon overtaken, and as they huddled up with inquiring "*quit-quit, queeah, queeah!*" about fifteen paces before, an arrow decimated the feathers upon the brownish-gray tail of one of the number and sent half a dozen of his immediate neighbors towards the four points of the compass. They went hardly twenty feet away, however, just flying up and alighting again. One of them lit upon a stone, another on a piece of dead brush, while the others stole back to their companions who still mingled with the soft rustle of gently vanishing feet a steady and dolorous "*quit-quit, queeah, queeah! quit-quit-quit-quit, queeah, queeah!*"

Whizz! went an arrow over the head of the bird on

the dead brush. He cocked his head, nodded his long dark plumes, and said "*quit-quit, queeah, queeah!*" *Zip!* went another arrow through the brush just by his side. He said again, "*quit-quit-quit-quit!*" hopped leisurely off the brush, and started off with a "*queeah, queeah!*" to join his companions. The bird on the stone also made some remarks about "quitting," and was preparing to suit the action to the word, when another arrow skipped gayly from the string, and Mortality knocked at the lattice-door of his little ribs in a way that invited an immediate response.

An arrow that scattered the pine-needles among the rest of the flock caused a decided increase in their pace, and as shaft after shaft flying wild from the archer's now trembling hand hissed over the birds or scattered the dirt around them, they broke into a run and some flew a few yards, alighted, and then ran again.

"Now we shall have to scatter them," said Belville. "You had better keep quiet and let me do it. Hold Prince back."

Belville started on a run after the birds, while Norton collared Prince and tried to hold him. He discoursed most touching strains "to the rocks and rills, touching the tender stops of various quills," as his master ran ahead without him. The quails quickened their pace as Belville charged on them, and stuck to their legs with provoking pertinacity for a few moments, until Belville made a "spurt" and got within ten paces of them, when suddenly the air was filled with buzzing wings and wheeling and darting streaks of blue, white, and cinnamon.   Quickly his gun came to his shoulder and covered the dark green shrubbery of a *manzanita* behind which a bird had flown. The gun cracked; a shower of blue and cinnamon feathers puffed out from behind the bush; a dull sound of a falling body was heard; and *Norton* lay prone upon the earth !

As he picked himself up and brushed the pine-needles out of his sleeves, he announced to the universe at large his intentions of sub-letting all future contracts to hold a dog while his master goes ahead to shoot.

Prince didn't seem at all inclined to object to this arrangement, but displayed remarkable equanimity as, nearly wagging his tail off, he went in to pick up the fallen bird.   He then trotted away over the ground ahead with his nose in the air and his tail vigorously whipping his sides.   He had not gone a hundred yards when his pace slackened.   So did his tail.   The tail got slower in motion.   So did the legs.   The legs seemed to slacken the tail and the tail to react upon the legs, until he had settled down to a pace suitable for a fashionable mourner at a snail's funeral.   Then he stopped altogether, stood for a minute with his eager eyes fixed in a stony gaze; then he turned his head and glanced at his master.

"Come on quick, now, with your guns," said Belville.   "These birds do not lie long."

As Norton came up, three birds rose from the dead brush ahead of Prince, and almost at the first buzz of their wings his gun went off and rent the raiment of a flourishing young *manzanita* about three feet to one side of them.   One of the birds went to Belville's side and came whirling down out of a shower of feathers, while another plunged like a wet rag into a pile of rocks at the crack of the second barrel.   The birds were soon picked up, and the dog sent on.

He at once began to stiffen and crawl, sniffing the air and straightening out occasionally into a dead point.   But no birds rose.

"Too slow for these chaps, Prince.   You will have to go faster," said Belville, as he started ahead of the dog on a rapid walk.   "Hie on! boy, or you'll get left!"

But Prince had not been trained upon California quails, and followed along behind as if he had a bag of shot on each foot and his tail was spliced with a poker.   By running and cheering him on, Belville soon got him pretty well stirred up, and he overtook a little bunch of birds that had hidden in a fallen tree-top when they saw him coming.   Belville went to one side of the tree and Norton and his sister to the other, while Mrs. Norton was to look for the game and flush it with an arrow when visible.   Carefully she looked into the brush, but there was no sound or sign of life for two or three minutes; then Laura suddenly drew back, and with a vigorous pull at the bow-string sank an arrow half way to the feathers in the white and brown mold on a rotten stump beneath the brush.   As the arrow *chugged* into it, a "*quit-quit, quee-ah!*" was heard within, and Prince, who had been standing off at some distance ran close up, turned his head to one side, crouched low, and, looking intensely anxious, settled down stiff as marble.

Belville kicked upon the opposite side, and out came four birds, whizzing in various directions. One came down before the combined effect of a heavy battery opened by Norton and his sister, and another's machinery was deranged by a shot from Belville.

These birds were soon picked up, and the hunters started for the rest of the covey, the trail of which the dog soon struck. But Norton and the ladies were unable to follow at the rate required to overtake them with the start they had now gained, and Belville went swiftly on alone.

Note.—The mountain quail of the Pacific slope seems to be little known to sportsmen. I have seen some very absurd statements about it by those who have attempted to describe it.

It is *not* " twice as large as Bob White."

It is *not* "very fine eating."

It is *not* " extremely rare."

It is *not* " extremely wild and difficult to shoot."

It is *not* " found only in the roughest or most inaccessible places."

It does *not* " run faster than the valley quail."

I am fully aware that it would have made a far better subject for a good chapter if these things had been true. But while not averse to good subjects, my main object is accuracy, and I describe these birds just as I have found them.

I have seen them only in their natural state, and not as they might become if much hunted. But I have not only hunted them with a shot-gun, but have time and again met them when deer-hunting, and have sat down and watched them until the last one had stolen softly away. I have seen them often so close and unconcerned that a good archer could kill half a dozen with a bow, and it is no trick for a good rifleman to decapitate three or four before they leave. I do not know what they may be in the North; but in Southern California, when not hunted, they are the very embodiment of guileless simplicity.

Owing to fuller feathers this bird looks much larger than Bob White, but is only a mere trifle larger in body, if at all. In flavor it is almost exactly like the valley quail, which is about equal to a tolerable grade of chicken. Though by no means plenty, it is not *extremely* rare. In the Cuyamaca Mountain I once saw four coveys without leaving the road, yet they are by no means abundant throughout the country generally.

It is not quite so swift a flier as the valley quail, although swift enough. I have found it in good easy ground to hunt, though it generally likes rougher ground than the valley quail. I have found it at altitudes as low as one thousand feet above the sea: though I believe these were the increase of escaped tame ones. Its habitat seems to be above four thousand feet.

It does not run as fast as the valley quail, though it will depend upon running much longer, and is much harder to force into flight.

It is very easily domesticated and makes a charming pet, though I do not know whether it will breed in confinement.

CHAPTER XXI.

DEER-HUNTING.

IS this a hunt, or only a stroll through some old English park? Head to head in silent conclave stand the grand old oaks as they have stood for centuries. The shady ground below them is laid with a golden carpet of fine dry grass. Here and there the ground rolls in wavy swells, then spreads away in little flats, then sweeps again into billowy form. On either side it undulates more than in the middle, and finally breaks away into little bluffs, tables, and benches, with gulches, pockets, and ravines between. On these benches and tables the large oaks begin to dwindle away into scrubby oaks, which in turn fade into oak-brush, and this again into chaparral of various shades of green, running up the sides of the mountains which inclose the little park. In various directions run paths well beaten and smooth, on one of which Belville may be seen strolling lazily along, while Norton is tying his horse a little way behind.

Norton has very much recovered since the time last chronicled in this narrative; but he still keeps his horse near him in hunting, a precaution no invalid should neglect, and one that even a well man soon adopts when he gets acquainted with the magnificent distances of California and its vast proportion of out-of-doors to the acre.

"Do you see that track?" asked Belville, pointing to a track in the trail like a cross between an enormous human foot and a huge misshapen pancake.

Norton looked for a moment, and a cold sweat started all over him as he looked up in undisguised dismay.

"You needn't be alarmed. He's far off by this time, tucked away in the thick brush of some howling cañon that it would be impossible to travel through except on hands and knees. There are a few grizzlies left in Santa Rosa, and this is one of the biggest, but it is almost impossible to get sight of them. But here are the tracks I care most about," he added, pointing to some sharp-toed-foot prints in the dry old cattle-trail in which they were walking.

San Diego is not a "deer-country," as that term is generally understood; and, from all that can be gathered from the old Spanish residents, it never has been. There are too many acres to the deer, and too much land to the acre. Yet for him who knows how and where to hunt them, deer are abundant enough to furnish good sport. And it is doubtful if the world can show easier or more pleasant still-hunting than in the oak cañons of the northern part of San Diego County, at the time of year when the deer are most numerous in them.

This favorable time is generally the Autumn, when the acorns are ripe on the scrub-oak along the edges of the cañon, and hang-thick on the low sweeping branches of the large trees in the middle of it, or fall pattering from their tops.

Autumn in this country is only a palace-car on the long train of summer days. On, on, on, the season rolls until about the middle of December, when, without jolt, jerk, or jar, the traveler is suddenly swung into Spring, for that is what Winter really amounts to here. Nature dons no gorgeous burial-robes. The drowsy ear of night remains unvexed by endless disputes as to whether Katy did or didn't. No bobolink peeps his sad farewell above our heads. No bloody sun struggles down through smoky air. No maple or gum tree flames in crimson; no beech or hickory wears a golden crown; no oak puts on its russet mantle. Here and there at the extreme end of the season the sycamores or cottonwoods along the river-bottoms begin to furl their green banners for a few weeks, and the grape-vine's bright green fades for a while. But the hills hang out no gaudy standards of decay, and their velvet vests of checkered green show no sign of change. The serpentine trail of the cañon is still filled with glistening green ; the old oaks shine as brightly as ever ; the sun rolls daily through unclouded skies; the air grows even drier than in summer; the crimson of the sunset deepens in the valleys, and the peaks glow at evening with a deeper purple. If Nature has not spilt her paint-pots over our landscape, she has also sent no blustering scouts of Winter to buffet our ears; and if she has withheld the sentimental haze of Indian Summer, she has at the same time withheld the scowling sky and chilly breath that in other lands too quickly arouse the Indian-Summer dreamer.

Norton had been wise enough to stay and finish off the recovery that had plainly begun, and Belville, appearing to be as glad as any one about his improvement, had still remained with the party.

With easy sauntering pace, but with keen and restless eyes, they strolled along the smooth paths, peering around the corners of the gulches and scrutinizing the dark green recesses of the pockets. Suddenly Belville stopped, and, pointing far away down a vista among the trees, exclaimed, as he dropped out of sight,

"There is a deer lying down under yonder big live-oak! Take off your hat and rise up carefully, and see if you don't make out a pair of ears."

A cautious inspection showed Norton two dark points like fine inverted "V's" in plain relief against the yellow background of grass. Presently, what at first glance appeared to be a piece of dead log developed into a head with trim tapering nose and a bit of graceful neck beneath it. And what had seemed to be only a dark shadow turned out to be a body ; for these deer at this time of year are dark gray in color. While Norton and Belville were still looking, the head was suddenly turned directly toward them.

"Keep still and don't move!" said Belville. "They cannot make out our heads from so far if we don't move them."

The turning of the distant head brought into view another trim little nose and the delicate point of one ear, just visible on the other side of the first one, and lying near it.

"There is a big fawn beside her," said Belville. "Now there is as fine a chance to shoot a deer as you will be likely ever to get. You take my rifle and try her. Do you see yonder little ridge that juts out toward them, and is covered along its back with scrub-oak brush? If you can make the point of that you can get a splendid shot. You can reach it easily, but it will take you some time to do it with the care that is necessary to make sure of a shot. So the first thing to recollect is that there is positively no haste. Those deer are good for two hours where they are, and even if they were not, you might lose more by haste than you would gain. Back out of here now, and swing around into that next little cañon to the right. Go to the head of it, and there you will undoubtedly find an old cattle-trail that leads over the next ridge and around the head of the next little cañon. But, whether you do that or not, cross the heads of the cañons until you get on to the ridge that leads out to where the deer are. Get on the back side of it, keep out of sight, and go as quietly as you can possibly move until you get behind the last bush on the point. Then lay your rifle under the bush, and try and shoot from under it without showing any part of yourself. If you do this carefully, they will be more sure to stand in case you miss the first shot or two. But whatever you do, remember above all things to take a fine sight. and shoot low down on the body, or you will be apt to overshoot."

Taking Belville's rifle, Norton started, and going slowly, so as neither to tire himself or make a noise, he reached in about half an hour the point of the ridge that ran out towards the deer. Raising his head very cautiously behind the bush, he at length saw, about sixty or seventy yards away, the old one with head raised, her long ears pricked up attentively, and chewing her cud. The young fawn by her side was still in the same position as when first seen. But Norton now discovered another fawn beyond the deer lying with its head turned over upon its side, apparently dozing.

From the time Belville first showed him the ears and suggested his trying their owner with his rifle, Norton had recognized some serious demoralization in his capillary harmony. But when he looked through the bush and saw the shapely forms of glossy dark gray, the long mulish ears, and the trim black and gray noses pointed towards him, every hair on his head felt as though it were raging in deathly struggle with its neighbors.

"Pshaw! I have plenty of time. I will be cool," he thought.

It is very easy for the mind to legislate for the nerves. But it is quite another thing for the mind to enforce its edicts. Norton discovered this when, after waiting about five minutes to cool down, he began to raise his rifle. As he brought the sights up in line with the glossy chest that, with the legs folded beneath it, formed so plain a mark, a deluge of shivers flooded his back and his hand trembled so that he could not shoot even with the rifle rested on the ground.

But Norton was naturally cool and collected; he cared nothing for the nonsensical, imaginary glory of killing a deer, and he had none of the base sensations that thrill the ordinary meat-hunter.

He remembered what Belville had said about having time enough, and resolved not to throw away a good chance by a little excitement which would soon pass off. He therefore lay and watched them some fifteen minutes, trying all the time to persuade himself that he would not give a cent to shoot the whole three. And in this he so far succeeded that his nerves soon reached a delightful state of composure.

Again he looked along the sights, and now at last he *was* cool. What in hunting is more delightful than that calmness, born of confidence and not of indifference, with which the rifle-hunter raises the sights upon large game, knowing that success is dashed with sufficient uncertainty to require the best of care, yet exulting in his own skill to accomplish it? Yet what in rifle-hunting is more brilliantly illusive than that same confidence when it first begins to dawn after the dark night of uncontrollable nervousness?

Norton now saw the sights full and clear upon the shining breast of the mother-deer, and with exultant soul he pressed the light trigger. Swift as the hammer falls under the loosened spring, so swiftly under the spring of three sets of steel-like legs, loosened by the report of the rifle, the three gray bodies bounded fifteen feet into the air at the first jump. They landed at the three points of a triangle, and the graceful forms stood for a moment, the bright eyes and ears all attention, as they looked at the trees and hills around them, and then at each other.

Again Norton drew the sights upon the doe's breast and pulled. *Bang!* went the rifle, and *bump!* went the simultaneous stroke of twelve hoofs upon the hard dry ground, as from the three points of the triangle in which they stood the three jumped at one bound to the center. They stood there together, one fawn looking over its mother's back and the other standing under her neck, but all looking and listening with trembling curiosity.

Again Norton drew, as he supposed, a cool sight and fired; the ball like the others whizzed harmlessly a foot or two above the mark, and again the three deer shot outward with simultaneous bound. One stopped at the first jump; another took three or four jumps; the third a dozen; and then all stopped again.

Thus deer often act that have never seen man or heard the music of his rifle. And thus often acts the man who makes his first effort on them with the rifle. The deer were confused by the echo from the hills, and, seeing nothing, knew not which way to run, even if they thought there was any necessity for running at all. And Norton, getting more and more confused by the consciousness that he was doing his best and yet failing, yielded more and more to that fatal delusion which often makes even experienced riflemen uncertain on a down-hill shot. And as faster and faster he dispensed the singing lead at the retreating deer, higher and higher it flew above them, until the last bullet of the repeater was gone, and the last gray rump was undulating away in the edge of the chaparral on the other side of the valley. And then for the first time he happened to recall Belville's last advice about shooting low and taking a fine sight—a caution he had utterly forgotten.

"Never mind," said Belville consolingly, as he came up with Norton's horse. "It will all be the same a hundred years hence. And you will have another chance before we are through with this country."

They sat down and took a smoke in the breezy shade, and then, with Norton riding well in the rear, so as to make no noise, and Belville well ahead as scout, they started on.

For an hour or more they sauntered along the old trail, looking with eager eyes down the shady vistas of yellow and green, and into every opening in the hills on either side. Already the slope upon the western side of the valley was shading into a bluish haze, the air began to feel cooler, the breeze began to fail a trifle, and a shadow crept slowly up the slope on the east. Evening was coming on; the deer would soon be afoot; a sharper watch must be kept. Something must also be done pretty soon unless they wished to return empty-handed to camp.

The mountain-peak on the right was purpling fast, and they had decided to turn back toward camp when, at Belville's suggestion, they decided on a last look around the corner of a little projecting ridge that lay before them.

"Thanks to the man who invented the last chance ! It's the last slippery log in the slippery path of the still-hunter from which he often slides head first into a perfect mire of good luck," said Belville to himself, as, peering cautiously around the ridge into a gulch, his eye caught sight of a small white spot in a bush, a dark gray bit of shiny fur a few yards farther on and a few feet to one side, and he saw a couple of glistening points rise from the chaparral, and below them several more similar points.

He backed down and returned to Norton as quickly as possible, and said,

"There are three, and perhaps more, in there. One is a big buck and must be absorbed by all means. Tie your horse here and slip up this little cañon and hide on the end of this side ridge, and don't move unless something comes. I'll go around on the other side and let them know we have arrived. They will probably come this way, and you can have a good chance to bid them farewell."

Keeping in the dry bed of a little creek, Belville passed the mouth of the cañon in which the deer were, without danger of being seen by them. He then passed into the next little cañon, and up the ridge that lay between it and the one in which the deer had been seen. Moving cautiously up the ridge, he came at length in sight of the bottom of the cañon, and his eye rested at once upon the lithe body and dandy legs of a sleek young "spike"-buck (a yearling buck) that,

with head erect and ears pricked forward and outward, seemed to think he discovered something. At
the same time, just beyond him, the glistening points
that Belville had noticed before came surging up out
of the chaparral, accompanied by the gray tips of
another pair of ears.

The reader has seen that with all his faults, Belville
was not swinish about game or fish. But as there is
a little strabismus in the straightest of moral optics, so
is there an ineradicable tarnish of greed on the brightest shield that culture and a native sense of propriety
can throw before our brute nature; and we must all
plead guilty to the weakness of preferring a big buck
to a small one. This weakness captured at the first
dash the sound principles that Belville approved most
thoroughly in the abstract: never to take a shot with
the rifle at a dim or uncertain mark when you have
a clear and distinct one, even though the latter be
inferior game. With a contemptuous glance at the
spike-buck, he drew a sight about six inches, as he
thought, below the tips of the second pair of ears,
which he could easily see must belong to an unusually
fine buck, and fired.

A distinct *whack* such as a bullet would make on
a heavy skull came back to him: there was a heavy
crash and smash, together with a *bump, bump, bump;*
the spike-buck, a doe, and two large fawns went
plunging out of the head of the gulch ; while a vigorous kicking and thrashing of brush went on in the
place where the big buck had stood. Belville hastened the speed of the others with a wild bullet or

two, and then dashed down the hill and into the brush where his buck had fallen and had now ceased struggling. In he walked with rifle on his shoulder; yet all was still but the echo of Norton's gun bellowing back and forth among the hills. Belville felt spreading over him a glow of happiness such as he only knows who has been in his place.

But suddenly there was a long-drawn hollow-toned "*phew!*" about twenty yards from him, a crash of brush and the stroke, not of bounding, but of fast-running hoofs, moving with stumbling and erratic pace, but still running and smashing rapidly away through the brush. Belville fired a vain shot or two in the direction of the sound, and then went to look where his buck had fallen. There were the marks of scuffling feet, the signs of a fall and a struggle on the dry ground, but no sign of blood.

Belville stood for a moment, puzzled, and was about to go, knowing how vain is the pursuit of a wounded deer in chaparral without a good dog, and sometimes even with one, when he suddenly saw something among the bushes. He stooped and drew out the single horn of a large deer. It was shivered to pieces at the very base, and told the story too plainly.

The buck, hearing Norton's shots, had turned and gone down the ridge toward the main valley. About this time, Reche of Fall Brook and another hunter, whose name, in modern Latin, is *nullum tui negotii*, were coming down the valley. Reche had a yellow Scotch terrier tied to his waist with a bit of rope—a good way to keep a dog from "breaking shot" provided he is not big enough to break his master. Hearing the shots, they had naturally hastened to get in the way of being run over by anything that might feel inclined that way. They had just reached a point opposite the end of the ridge, and, hearing the crackling of brush, had stopped, when the buck burst from the brush along the top of the ridge and, with its head laid back, came tearing at full speed down the slope directly towards them.

Diego, the dog, straightened the rope and gave a yelp ; the waist-band to which the rope was tied gave way with a rip ; a bullet plowed the hill-side behind and above the deer, another fanned his tail with its cooling breeze just as he turned short around with dog and rope flying towards him. Reche recovered the symmetry of his back-bone just in time to scollop the bark of a live-oak monarch behind the fast-scudding racer at the same time that a ball from his companion's rifle sped through its lungs.

The lungs of the tree, that is. For the deer's white rump dissolved in the chaparral

> " Like the snow-flake in the river,
> A moment white, then gone forever,"

with Diego yelping far in his rear, leaving Reche and the other, each declaring that he had shot off a horn, but both taking particular pains not to look for it.

Then there came a call from Norton. While the other deer were bounding through the chaparral up the hill, he had disencumbered himself of two buckshot cartridges that he had got weary of carrying and putting in and taking out of his gun. And though it was a long shot he made, he was sure he saw a deer stumble.

Belville went to look, and found marks of a fall and a few drops of blood, and called to Reche to bring the dog. Diego was finally retrieved from a bush in which he had tangled his rope, and taken to the place where Norton's deer had fallen. In a moment he had the scent, and bounded away up the hill with sharp yelps. He had gone a hundred yards or more, when the yelps doubled in intensity and frequency, a crack and crash of brush was heard, and soon the chaparral was parting and smashing in a line down the hill, towards another gulch. Down, down, down, goes the racket, not with the regular *bump*, *bump*, *bump* of springing legs, but with a crashing discord of breaking brush, yelping dog, and stumbling hoofs

Down they go into the bottom of the gulch, where the nimble terrier seizes by one of his long ears the deer, which now turns out to be the spike-buck that had first been seen. In a twinkling the dog is shaken off, and as he is thrown against the side of a bank he narrowly escapes impalement by one of the sharp spike-horns. But Diego is like hope in the bosom of a mining-stock verdant. He bounds again and again anchors his teeth in the ear. The sharp hind hoof of the deer tickles his ribs with a thump that sends him whirling to earth once more. With hair erect and bright green eyes glaring savagely, the buck stands at bay, and, as the dog gathers himself, he makes a thrust with his sharp horns that would suffice to finish a much larger dog. But the plucky little terrier dodges and, before the deer can recover for another charge, catches him a third time by one ear. And there he dangles for a moment as the buck tries to shake him off, lets go with a yelp as another hoof fondles his ribs, then grabs again just as a rifle-ball pacifies the savage buck forever.

CHAPTER XXII

DEER IN THE OPEN HILLS.

IN the north-eastern corner of Don Juan Forster's great ranch the Santa Margarita winds its way through high and rugged hills. Their sides are cleft with cañons and gulches, and their tops break away into basins, pockets, ridges, and small peaks, more or less begemmed with the solid granite jewels of the land and half-dressed in tattered robes of chaparral.

Up one of these cañons, on a trail made by cattle that had never felt the *riata* or the branding-iron, and that surpassed the deer in wildness, Belville and Norton on horseback were winding their way. Reaching the top, their eyes wandered over miles of rolling rubbish, green, gray, brown, yellow, black, and bluish, everything lying in wild disorder, stacked, packed, jammed, and crammed as if Nature knew not how to get it all stowed away. Here and there the vast area was cut by long cañons, filled with winding green, which, splitting into branches, encircled the waist of some somber peak ; and deep ravines yawned with bottoms also of timber or chaparral. Everywhere was the everlasting boulder. Yet almost every point and pass, basin and gulch, was connected by the trails of cattle; for the California breed are at home on the wildest and most rugged hills.

"Here, you see, are deer-tracks," said Belville, pointing to several in the trail.

"I declare! There are about a dozen," exclaimed Norton.

"Yes," said Belville, "just a dozen—hoofs. But only three deer: a doe and two fawns. You make the common mistake of counting a deer to every footprint."

The trail wound around the heads of two or three little gulches and the breast of a little peak, and then descended into a basin about two hundred yards wide and a hundred feet deep. The bottom of the basin was cut up into little ravines and pockets, with an abundance of boulder, brush, and chaparral.

"It is too early in the day for deer to be on foot yet," said Belville, after a careful survey of the bottom and sides of the basin. "And it is extremely probable that those deer whose tracks we saw are lying down in there. Or they may even be standing up; for they can almost keep out of sight in brush a yard high, unless they move or the sun happens to shine on their jackets. We had better leave our horses here, for if they are in there they will be sure to hear and see us when we go down into the basin; and if once they start, they'll stop for nothing."

They tied their horses, and Belville went around by a circuitous route to the opposite side of the basin, and took a position on a rock commanding the two trails, on one of which he thought the deer were most likely to come out. Norton then began a cautious descent into the basin through a gulch at the side. He reached the bottom and took an old trail leading up the middle. With the stealthy tread he had seen Belville use, he sneaked along with watchful eye, thinking himself a pretty smart chap, after all, for a city verdant, who knew a trick or two about hunting, when his blood was suddenly curdled by an unexpected apparition.

About twenty yards from him, on a quite open slope, all at once he saw a big gray doe, with a fawn on each side above and below and a little behind her. Six great flaring ears of light gray, six eyes of bluish black, and three black muzzles were all aimed directly at him. He was shot through and through with amazement. "Where in the world did they come from so suddenly? How could I have missed seeing them before? Aren't they beauties?" These questions skipped through his mind without waiting for answers; for all were swamped in the great and delightful thought: "And how close!"

The two fawns took a step ahead of the mother and stopped. Norton raised his gun. It was loaded with buckshot wire cartridges, and a faint pang flitted across his tender heart as he thought of the havoc they would make among those pretty innocents. Better feelings almost triumphed as he thought that the camp could not use such an immense amount of meat after he had killed them; but then he thought of some rabbit-fed settlers near by, and concluded that he might play almoner of Heaven to advantage.

One of the great beauties of hunting is the grand opportunity it gives to the play of the highest faculties.   Norton might have passed through life without thinking of the stupendous paradox that one may often bag more by aiming at nothing than by aiming at something.   But no sooner did he see the two fawns step out ahead of the mother, with a strip of light between the back of the lowest and the belly of the highest one, than he saw, with that transcendent power of judgment which only such occasions can develop, that he could bag both by aiming between them.   For this delightful contingency Messrs. Eley & Bros., of London, neglected to provide when they made their buckshot wire cartridges—a very great piece of carelessness on their part which once cost a hunter three wild turkeys he hoped to get at one shot by firing at a hole between them—and hit it !

So Norton, like that brilliant and greedy youth (as the aforesaid hunter then was), was ignorant of the fact that these cartridges often go like a bullet for many yards before breaking.   And when he took a cool aim at that strip of light between the fawns, and sent a cartridge whizzing straight at it, he very naturally looked astonished as he saw the dirt fly from the dry bank beyond, and beheld the three deer spring unharmed high into the air and ricochet with airy lightness up the slope.

But then, what of it ?   We don't want but one, any- how.   They are still within easy distance ; and who ever missed a deer with buckshot ?   Something like this flashed through his mind as he raised the other barrel on the big doe, and saw the curl of her white and gray rump just in line with it.   He pulled the trigger and sixteen buckshot whizzed directly to where the doe *was*, while she struck the ground some distance beyond, after leaping through the space nearly a yard above where she had stood when he pulled the trigger. The trio waltzed over a ridge near by, the last little black tail fading out of sight just as the discomfited Norton got his gun snapped shut on two more cartridges. Whereupon he delivered himself of some wisdom to the effect that a deer is accompanied by more circumambient space than anything else in creation. Which the same is herewith most cordially indorsed.

Belville's face was illumined with joy as he heard the two shots from Norton's gun, and fairly blazed with delight as he heard the inspiring *bump, bump, bump* on the hard ground coming closer. He looked out from behind his rock and saw a beautiful fawn, large and sleek, come bounding up the trail. Just as he raised his rifle, the old lady herself leaped into view with the other baby skipping high behind her. With magnanimity unparalleled Belville let the fawn pass, and raised his rifle on the old dame. It is sad to find the brilliancy of apparently noble motives turn out to be only the tinsel of a false pretense. Yet candor compels the statement that Belville meant to invert the old one, in order that when her heels should kick at heaven instead of spurning earth, her loving offspring might tarry to see what was the matter, and thus give him a good chance to inform them.

On came the doe, glancing so high from the ground

at each touch of her fairy feet that Belville, after a few vain attempts to tell where she was going to strike next and get his sights trained on that spot, took down the rifle and said, "*Maa!*"

This did not appear to be any news to her; so she kept on, and he called out "*Maa!*" again, in a louder tone. This stopped the foremost fawn, and as Belville raised his rifle on that one so as to make sure of something, the old one stopped to see what the fawn was doing. She looked so much larger that Belville shifted the rifle onto her. Just as he pulled the trigger she rose, and the ball shaved the hair of her chest just back of the fore-legs. Full fifteen feet she went at the first spring, bounded four or five feet into the air at the next touch, and landed in the head of a little brushy ravine; when, before Belville could load again his swift-firing repeater, the lofty head and graceful neck were lowered, the high rolling rump vanished, and in the head of this little ravine, scarcely two feet deep, and in brush scarcely three feet high, the billowy beauty had disappeared.

But the hindmost fawn was still in sight, curving high among the rocks and bushes and fast careering towards the place where the mother skulked away. In another moment he too will reach it, and he too knows right well how to sneak out of sight in brush hardly big enough to hide a rabbit. But Belville is following his course, with the rifle held well ahead of him, and now, as he descends from an arching spring, the sights are held four or five feet ahead of him and fully two feet below. The *bang!—bump!—spat!—*are simultaneous; for the deer reaches ground just as the bullet gets there and his shoulders are square in its path.

Two more hours slide down the hill of time, never again to draw up their sleds, and Belville, half a mile from the scene of his last performance, is trying to slide himself down a sloping face of rock so as to get into a trail that will bring him fifty yards nearer to a dark shiny spot in the brush three hundred yards away. The silver sheen of the still visible ocean is changing fast into burnished gold ; the distant peaks of gray and green are reddening fast into carmine and purple; the tide of crimson haze begins to flow up the western valleys; the soft green of the chaparral on the eastern slopes begins to darken into blue, and on the western slopes to glow with brighter green; the bee is humming on his homeward way; and the roaring wings of hundreds of quail flying to roost resound from the cañon's depths a thousand feet below. Evening is fast falling, and something must be done soon if that shiny spot is to be investigated and camp reached before dark.

So thinks Belville, and he proceeds to commit that supreme folly of being in a hurry after a deer that is not in haste. Why does he not send Norton to camp on this trail, and take time enough to reach that hill that commands the object in question at so short a distance? Or why does he not let the quarry go undisturbed to-night and come again early in the morning? Either course is surer than the attempt he is now making to approach it while in sight of it. He gets into the trail, and by stooping low keeps out of sight until at the end of a few yards the trail turns down a slope, and brings him into plain sight of that shining spot, on one side of which several fine points now glisten in the light of the sinking sun.

Sure as man who is falling behind the world thinks himself ahead of it, so sure is the hunter to think he is outgeneraling a deer just when the deer is out-generaling him.   And Belville chuckles with satisfaction as he finds himself drawing closer to the game and yet it does not move.   He has hunted much, but not before now has he seen a deer stand in the brush with his head down but turned to one side, quietly watching something at a distance.   And yet he has hunted enough to have seen it.

Still he creeps quietly on, and still the spot moves not.   Soon he is within two hundred yards of it, and concludes to try a shot; for he doubts the chances of getting any closer.   He adjusts the sight in a second, raises the rifle, and the spot is gone!   No jump, no crash of brush, no sign of anything.   And yet the brush seems scarcely three feet high, and thin at that. The fellow had only dropped his head, crouched a little, and sneaked away.   This is only one of the many pleasing little idiosyncrasies of this kind of deer.

As the stars were paling in the blue strip above the river-gorge, Belville and Norton finished their breakfast at their camp beneath a royal live-oak, on a little bench of land by the water's side.   And before the sunlight began to skip along the topmost boulders they were mounted and off; for this morning they were to ride the river cañon to find a deer or two before they went into the hills for the day, perhaps to find some deer that had decided to spend the day in the cool shades of the breezy gorge itself. Breakfast over, they mounted their horses, which carried them along through the mica sands of the river-bed, which sparkled like gold in the whirling water, over little strips of rank green grass along its sides, around big boulders, through green groves of sycamore, cotton-wood, and willow, under the limbs of great live-oaks and the heavy tangles of grape-vines, while the sides of the cañon, clothed with evergreens of dozens of varieties and besprinkled with a most liberal assort-ment of rocks, ran through a hundred hues and shades as the light grew stronger. Here and there on the sandy bars or along the wet margin of the river they saw where deer had crossed the bed of the stream or stopped at its edge to drink. And wherever a gulch or cañon broke from the hills into the main cañon, tracks were generally to be seen on the trail that wound up its side or along its bottom. There was a line through a patch of grass that was of a different shade from the rest, and Belville said, as he pointed it out,

"There has been a deer through that this very morning. That difference in color comes from the slight bending of the blades of grass, which makes the light strike them differently. We must be quiet now."

They went in the direction indicated by the line for a few yards, when suddenly they heard a long-drawn "*phew!*" which was repeated at intervals of several seconds like the snort of a Mississippi steamer, and the sound was getting farther away. Yet there was no cracking of brush, no bump of feet, no sound upon the ground. Quickly Belville sprang from his horse and ran. But not towards the sound; and Norton stood for a moment in wonder to see him run backward and directly *away* from it. Through the water and over its bars and shallows he dashed, until he reached the trees on the other side of the river, when he stopped, turned around and cocked his rifle, looking at the hills on the side whence the sound had come. In a moment he saw, stalking deliberately with kingly coolness up the hill, a splendid buck, with broad branching horns and body round and sleek as that of a mule with fatness. Stopping a moment to look, the buck caught a glimpse of Belville, who was raising his rifle, and in a twinkling he was in the air.

How is it possible for a deer to run up such a hill? And even if that is explained, the greater difficulty remains of explaining how one can *bound* up such a hill. Yet up he goes nevertheless, much as a ball would go *down* the side of the pyramid of Cheops. Boulders, bushes, *barrancas*, and ledges stand thick in his pathway, yet he ricochets along, on a slanting course indeed, yet still up, up, up, rapidly up. *Bang!* goes the rifle, and the dirt flies from the place he has just left. *Bang!* it goes again, held higher, and the shot goes too high. *Bang!* goes another, held a whole jump ahead, and this time it strikes too far ahead, for no two jumps are alike. *Bang!* goes still another shot, held closer to him to avoid the cause of the last miss, and the dust flies from the bank just in line with his tail.

And now he has continued his swift career to where the sunlight, six hundred feet above, shot through a cañon on the other side, makes the rugged hill smile with morning freshness.

O Nature, why dost thou ever mingle some alloy of weakness with thy greatest strength? Yet when we ourselves so often in the very moment of triumph allow some infirmity to dash to earth the victor's plume, how can we blame that buck for yielding to that strong curiosity for seeing what is below him that a deer always exhibits when running up hill? In charity let us forgive his weakness for pausing after such a splendid escape. He stops, rears his proud head with all its tines glistening in the morning sun, turns his thick massive neck and points his black muzzle and forehead downward. He shines all over as the sun lights up his dark jacket and slim legs, and stands there, the picture of grace and strength.

He starts as the rifle cracks again; but not with the former ease as of a spring released from coil. He starts forward with a crouching convulsive jerk, and runs, not with the high spring or the low scudding gait he well knows how to take when in haste, but with the lumbering gallop of an old cow. And alas! no longer upward goes he, but this time he turns downward, and with a plunging crash, among the brush. He reels, struggles and stumbles, turns a somersault and comes tumbling down as fast as he went up, and rolls dead to the foot of the hill.

CHAPTER XXIII.

TRACKING DEER ON BARE GROUND.

A FEW miles from the ranch-house of Santa Margarita is a huge basin or amphitheater of several
thousand acres, sunk deep in the great dark hills of
Santa Rosa. A brook of pure cool water traverses it,
winding through heavy arcades of alder, sycamore,
ash, cottonwood, and grape-vines. Low hills, sprinkled with white-oaks, roll away on the one side into
the heavy chaparral of the mountains, which tower
thousands of feet above; low meadows or little plains
thick set with live-oaks spread away towards the hills
on the other side. Tremendous gulches filled with
bright green timber break here and there into the
mountains, winding upward towards their tops until
the timber is lost in the wild chaos of boulder and
bristling chaparral.

In a grove of live-oaks close by the brook our hunters were now encamped, and as they looked at the
cool shades and listened to the bubbling water, as
they heard the quails calling all around and the doves
with whistling wing scudding in arrowy flight, as they
saw the rabbit's white tail flicker along the edge of
the brush at evening, and found the deer's track by
the brook in the morning, they concluded they had
found a pretty comfortable place. And who that drank

of the pure cool water, lounged in the deep shades, looked up at the soaring hills robed in dark chaparral, cleft with stupendous cañons, and fringed along their tops with oaks; or bathed in the warm sulphur spring, and felt the cool air descend at sundown like an angel of sleep, would have thought that this place was not fifteen miles from the bare and dreary coast, and but a few hundred feet above sea-level?

For several days Belville had been trying to get sight of an immense buck of the *burro*, a large "mule-deer" variety that is found on the desert slope of the mountains, and only at rare intervals on the coast slope. Thus far he had been able to find only his tracks, and occasionally an abandoned bed; and he now determined to try another plan.

Floods of inky twaddle have been shed from the goose's quills about the difficulties of tracking game on bare ground. There is not a *vaquero* of twenty in California who would not laugh to learn, as many have from books and magazine articles, that the ability to do this was an almost superhuman power reserved by nature to the gifted Indian alone, grudgingly bestowed even upon him, and refused to the white man. It is not to be denied that in the case of animals as light as a deer it is no easy matter to follow them upon bare and dry ground, which is nearly always hard; and on some kinds of ground, impossible; and even the keenest Indian finds this difficult. But, on the other hand, there are places where a deer may be tracked on bare ground, not as easily, indeed, but almost as surely as upon snow. And this, too, upon ground so dry, so hard, and so covered with grass or brush, that to the tyro it would seem a hopeless task. Yet it requires no natural gift, no lifetime of schooling, none of the qualifications we generally read about as indispensable; but only patience, a sound and *tolerably well* practiced eye, and, above all, a knowledge of the deer's habits and movements.

"The chap has been here early for water," said Belville, one morning about sunrise. He pointed to a large clear-foot-print in the sandy margin of the brook, half a mile above the camp.

Norton looked at the track, and took Belville's word for its age; for to his untrained eye the freshness, plain as that of a newly-plucked rose, was not quite apparent.

But where is the next track? The bank behind shows along its edge a light fresh scrape, where the dew-claws of a hind foot had touched as it came down on to lower ground, and between that and the track in the sand was a pebble the size of a walnut, one side of which was moist, showing that it had been lately displaced. But no other sign of a foot was visible on that side of the brook. The rocky and pebbly bed of the brook showed no trace of anything, and the rocky ledge on the other side, closely bounded by dead weeds, grass, and brush on the bank, gave slight prospect of finding any indications.

" He has gone across, that's certain," said Belville, looking in vain for any trace of backward tracks. "And as deer very seldom spend much time around water in this country, he is probably several hundred yards, perhaps half a mile or more, away by this time. So we won't waste any time hunting the tracks here, but will depend upon picking up the trail farther on."

Outside the timber a cattle-trail ran parallel with the brook on the other side. Belville walked up and down this trail for fifty yards each way, looking carefully in it for tracks. It was not traveled enough to make its bottom dusty, so that nothing was very plainly seen; but here and there was a faint scrape on some bare spot, a faint ridge of fine dust coming to a point with a slight opening in the center, and occasionally the clear imprint of two sharp toes upon some spot more dusty than the rest. All these were of the width of the track he had seen in the sand. There was, however, no clear outline, only a smooth appearance to it all, as though ants had been traveling or the breeze blowing over it, and in the shade the color was the same as the rest of the ground. So Belville decided that these were yesterday's tracks, and not what he was looking for.

Across the trail, the ground stood thick with white sage, dead grass, dead weeds; scarcely one twentieth of the bare ground could be seen. Running through the weeds in places there were faint lines of different shades of color, but the sage and grass showed none, the sage being too scattered and the grass too low and fallen. And even the traces left in the weeds were of no use; for dead weeds, when pushed aside and so deflected as to indicate a different shade, do not recover as they do when green; so that the animals that made those lines might have passed there several days previously.

Must then the romancer's Indian triumph after all? Must the pale-face give it up?—especially a pale-face who is plainly city born and bred, and not a professional hunter, reeking with whisky, tobacco, bad English, buckskins, long hair, flop hat, and the rest of the novelist's regulation outfit?

The Indian would not waste a moment in trying to pick out tracks on such ground. Neither does Belville. Though only an amateur hunter, he knows the habits of deer too well for that. Two hundred yards ahead he sees where the ground rolls up into swells with "sags," or little passes, between them. He knows that deer do not feed on this kind of ground; that they rarely lie down in it by day; that it is still much too early for a deer to lie down anywhere; that through each of those sags is probably an old cattle-trail; and that traveling deer, like men, will take to a path almost every time when it is convenient. He knows, too, that half a mile farther on the ground breaks at the foot of the mountains into higher hills, clad with chaparral and with timbered vales or brushy gulches between—the very kind of ground in which deer most love to spend the day. He knows also that it is time for the buck to be nearing this ground, and that he is undoubtedly on his way there now. He will, of course, lounge and browse a little on the way, but there is not much time to throw away if he is caught standing or in ground open enough to offer a good mark for a running shot.

So Belville went straight and swiftly for the deepest of the little sags among the hillocks. There in the bottom, as he expected, was an old trail, little used but still a plain trail, in which grass had grown and had been long since trampled flat and cut up by cattle-hoofs. Quickly his eye ran along a few yards of this and caught sight of a faint scrape on a hard bare spot. There was no outline of a track, no print of toes, no dust thrown up, no grass or weeds bent, no leaf moistened on the under side by being pressed down, no fresh side of a stone or chip or moss turned up; only the faintest change in the shade of color on a spot of hard dirt as large as a quarter of a dollar. Could there be a wilder flight of fancy than calling this a track?

Yet the eye that was used to reading the ground decided in a second that that mark was positively made that morning; that nothing but a hoof could have so ground the fine particles of dust as to make them show such a different shade of color, and consequently that the mark was not made by panther, wild-cat, coyote, or other soft footed animal. Just as quickly it was decided that this track was not large or heavy enough for the track of cattle.

But where is the next track? Little Belville seemed to care, for he traveled rapidly on in the trail almost without looking for any further sign. And behold, it led through dead grass, weeds, and white sage, ground for which a deer could have no use at this time of day. And it only went one hundred and fifty yards before it turned over a little rising tongue of low

chemisal which ran out from a large patch on the left,
And in this *chemisal* the ground was almost bare.
When Belville reached this, he found the bottom of
the trail both bare and dusty, and in the very first
foot of it was a print as distinct as if made by the
point of a flat-iron. Two or three more were beyond
it, beside which no more were seen. But a moment's
glance at the ground on either side showed on the
left a bright spot with a little fine ridge of dust cast
up ahead of it; a yard beyond it was another, and just
beyond that a slight spot of grayer shade on a bit of
friable granite. Yes; the deer had turned that way.

And now, you see, it is comparatively easy to follow
the track. And that is just what the tyro would do.
But Belville does quite the contrary. He knows that
this bit of brush is too low, too open, too near the
Santa Rosa trail for a deer to pass the day in, and
that he will leave it at the other end, or at the side
that lies towards the higher and more broken hills.
But he also knows that at this early hour of the morning a deer may have stopped at any point on his way
from water back to the hills. Hence he quickly
reasons thus:

1. If he has passed on, I can pick up the trail where
he left this *chemisal* patch quite as easily as I can follow it through; perhaps more easily.

2. If he is still in here (and he may possibly be behind
those rocks or among those higher bushes), it will
take all my eyesight to find his fur without wasting
any time or attention on his tracks.

He now motions to Norton to sit down, and then

reflects how best to inspect the ground.   Four things he considers in this order:

1. The wind.

2. The best ground to travel without noise.

3. The best ground from which to see the game; that is, the highest.

4. The sun.

The wind question is quickly disposed of, for the land-breeze has just stopped and the sea-breeze has not yet begun; so that the deer can scent a person no better in one direction than another.

The question of noise in walking vanishes as easily, for the brush is about equally dense and brittle in every direction, and on the outside the dry crackly sage-stalks are so disposed about as to leave little opportunity for selection.

There is also little choice of elevation of ground, certainly not enough to counterbalance the advantage of having the sun fall right.

So he takes the course that will give him the sun on his own back while it shines on the deer's coat and horns—an advantage sometimes worth all the rest put together.

Futile are all these manœuvers, however, for neither glossy fur nor glistening tines nor crash of brush nor bump of hoof greets eye or ear, as Belville passes over the ground.   But then, more than three fourths of the painstaking of good still-hunting is care thrown away.   It takes Belville but a few moments to find where the deer left this brush, which seems to be on a course that leads over another *chemisal*-crowned ridge two hundred yards away This ridge is so thin and low that Belville at once decides that the game is not there, and he therefore goes straight to it without looking a moment for intermediate tracks in the dead grass and weeds. For not only does the ridge lie in the direction of the last track, but it is directly in the course of the broken hills and brushy vales mentioned before, and so long that a deer would not go around it; and it is, moreover, on a kind of ground that deer like to travel through, though they seldom lie down in it.

Reaching the ridge, Belville finds the track readily by making a short tour along the edge; and it proves to be a simple matter to follow it across, as every other track shows quite plainly on the bare ground. Reaching the other side, the track is found to lead towards a large piece of low ground covered with dead grass and sage and liberally sprinkled with white-oaks.

And now, be careful, Doctor. This is the time of year for acorns—those white-oak acorns the deer loves more than any other kind; he has undoubtedly stopped to get some, and is probably eating them yet. Remember, too, that those tree-tops shut out much of the view, and that if you try to enter that place from higher ground he will be almost certain to see your feet and legs before your eyes get low enough to see him; for a deer's eyes are marvelously quick to detect a motion of any kind.

All this Belville knows right well. For see how he backs out and starts away off to the right, so as to get into the dry sandy bed of a little creek that leads out of this ground. Traveling cautiously up the water-course for two or three hundred yards, his eye at last rests on a spot of white, flanked with a line of dark gray with a center of black, supported by a couple of knock-kneed gray sticks, perhaps three hundred yards beyond. A shiver of satisfaction runs over the hunter as he drops his head almost out of sight and watches the object before him. Presently some shining points rise from behind it, and a huge head, surmounted by great branching horns, appears. Motionless at first, it shortly turns a moment to each side, and then disappears again.

"Too far!" says Belville to himself. "I stand a better chance of getting closer than of hitting him from here. Besides, he must be killed dead with a sure shot and not sent hobbling into yonder chaparral to die."

So saying, he starts on a very hazardous, yet, if properly performed, quite easy, operation — to approach a deer when in plain sight of him. This is almost impossible unless the deer is feeding from the ground. For if he be on the watch, it is quite impossible to come near him; and if browsing, his head is so high that he is quite likely to see you.

Leaving his hat behind, Belville starts on hands and knees toward the deer. In a moment the buck's head comes up, and at the first motion upward Belville stops still as a statue. The animal takes a look all around and lowers his head again to the ground; whereupon Belville begins again to crawl forward as fast as possible. At the next moment up comes again the heavily-antlered head. The buck looks carefully all round the horizon, scratches one ear, turns around broadside, and stands a moment with the sun full on his shining coat. He appears much larger, higher shouldered, and thicker necked than any of the deer yet described, and his horns are longer and more branching. It is without doubt the old boy that made the track. Down goes his head once more for acorns, and now Belville drops flat upon the ground. He no longer dares trust himself on hands and knees; for the deer's eyes are now too nearly turned in his direction. So he adopts the more laborious but much safer process of worming his way on his elbows and toes.

He advances in this way about fifteen yards, when the deer takes another observation, while Belville stops the instant he raises his head. Feeding resumed, Belville advances another twenty yards before being again interrupted by the upraised head. This time the deer takes a good look, moves a few paces, wiggles his tail with evident satisfaction, then decides on another bite. And as soon as he drops his head to the ground Belville continues his cautious and painful progress.

And now the dark muzzle and huge gray ears are turned full on Belville as they come up; every shining tine on the horns seems to be pointing directly at him; he almost sees the dark blue eyes looking through him; he can almost see that tight firmness of the mouth that a deer wears when suspicious of danger. The deer does not run or move. He only looks straight on, and keenly. What is Belville to do? What would you do if in his place?—if you had been crawling for ten minutes, feeling as if every hair on your head were caught in a whirlwind, with delightful expectation waltzing through your heart, while hope and fear were executing a contra-dance along your back-bone?

You would no doubt shoot from where Belville now is. It is only two hundred and fifty yards. And what is that distance for the great modern rifle? Do they not now score bull's-eyes at a thousand yards? And are not hunters constantly shooting game at five hundred and six hundred yards? Are not two hundred and fifty and three hundred yards the regulation distances for killing game? Yes, with the quill. But Belville has tried too often the difficult operation of estimating distance to be deceived by the ridiculous stuff of such writers. And he reasons like one who knows.

"I ought to get at least one hundred yards closer for anything like certainty, and even that is not enough for a center-shot. But then, the old fellow seems suspicious. If he starts, I can't hit him running from here. If I wait longer, he may decide that there is danger in this quarter and vanish. Besides, it is getting to be time for him to be moving; he may be through feeding; and if he starts off for the hills even on a walk, I cannot overtake him. I guess I shall have to try him, though it's a very long shot."

So thinking, he begins very slowly to raise his gun. But why does he not stop to consider the other side of the question? Perhaps he does not see any other side. People often view more important questions in the same way. But if he would ransack the lumber-garret of experience a moment, he would recognize some very important considerations. He would remember that deer often look steadily in one direction for some time without suspecting anything; that to raise the rifle now and adjust the sights while the deer is looking his way is dangerous, especially with the sun shining as it now is; that in his present position he cannot look over the intermediate ground, without doing which the estimation of distance, always unreliable enough, is doubtly untrustworthy; that unless alarmed the deer will either begin feeding again, or, if done feeding, will probably stand around a few minutes before going off; and that even if he is suspicious, the chances of his running a few paces only and stopping again for another look are just about as good as the chances of making a deadly shot at an unknown distance.

But how hard it is to reason calmly at such a time! How hard, with the game in sight and the rifle in hand, to have that patience and coolness of judgment upon which in the long-run success most depends! It is more than Belville can stand, and he slowly raises the rifle.

And as it comes to a level, the shapely glossy statue is changed into a cow-shaped brute on a long springy and awkward trot—a gait that deer sometimes take. And this trot the deer holds regardless of bullets spinning around him, until he fades over a low ridge.

Belville made a few observations on deer in general and this one in particular, which will not do to print, and then made his way back to Norton, to whom he recounted his adventure, laying, however, more stress upon his success in tracking the deer than upon the results obtained after he had found him.

"It's too late to go anywhere else this morning," he said; "so let's take a smoke;" and he sat down by Norton, and consoled himself with a fragrant pipe.

NOTE.—Selection has, of course, been made of an easy case of bare-ground tracking, to exemplify its most important principles. There is much ground on which it would be far more difficult. But it must be remembered that on the greater part of such ground still-hunting, either by tracking or otherwise, is almost impossible. So that bare-ground tracking over country worth hunting at all is generally no such wonderful thing as it is represented.

CHAPTER XXIV.

THE MUTUAL JOKERS.

YOU don't seem a bit tired with your walk; you must be getting much stronger," said Belville to Norton, as they sat down on a rock.

"I have certainly gained very much, and have good reason to hope for a complete cure."

"Yes, if you don't make the usual mistake of going back East and resuming your old mode of life. Fully sixty per cent of invalids who do recover undo themselves again in this way."

"How many do you suppose do recover?"

"Very few. Very small is the percentage of those who recover in any climate, or could recover in any climate in the world. Fully fifty per cent start from home too late to be cured by anything. Of the other fifty, one half look upon climate as a direct and positive medicine, and think there is nothing to do but to sit down and take it. They take no amusement, no exercise, do nothing to increase the appetite or build up the system. They find that they don't get well at once; and in a few weeks vote the climate a fraud, and skip away to some place more lively and unhealthy. A very few do as you have done: look upon climate not as a direct *means*, but as a *condition* of cure, and go to work to build themselves up by out-of-door amusements that give just the right amount of exercise, increase the appetite, and keep off the blues. And yet a large number of these, after life is saved and assured, throw it away by returning to the climate and habits of life in which the disease originated."

"I shall look out for that mistake and avoid it," said Norton. "I believe I owe my recovery entirely to the life I have led since I came here. If I had not fallen into your hands, I might have gone the way of the great majority. I shall always be grateful to you for advising me to spend the time as I have, and for helping me to do it."

"I knew it would save you if anything would; but I felt quite alarmed about you at one time."

Norton here began to laugh.

"There's a joke about that that is almost too good to keep," he said at length.

"Any joke is too good to keep. Unlock the casket," said Belville.

"I played the dying man pretty well that time!"

"Yes. I thought you did. But I wondered how you could make yourself thinner in flesh without real injury. Of course the cough part of it was easy enough to manage," replied Belville, coolly.

"You don't understand me," said Norton. "I saw how it was going between you and Laura, and I played that trick to head you off."

"Going between us? Please elucidate."

"Come, now; you need not play the innocent. Laura has told me all about it."

. "Oh—yes," said Belville, scratching his head as though trying to rake up his recollection. "You mean that little transient affair. I declare, I'd almost lost sight of it in the light of a brighter matter. Oh, I knew that all the time. Well," he added flipping the ashes from his cigar with his little finger as delicately and artistically as if in a city club-room, I can tell a joke worth two of yours, and one that has the additional advantage of being news. You see, that was only a little matter of rapid growth and equally rapid decline; it was a mere phosphorescence, a transient gleam of moonlight that I mistook for sunshine. I found out right away that I had not chosen as I wished, and so I made no objection to her marrying you as the easiest way to arrange the affair. It was your sister that I really wanted, and true love being always blind, you know, I did not see it at first."

Norton sat staggered at the cool impudence of the fellow, and said not a word, although he wondered whether he ought not to resent such talk; while Belville continued calmly smoking.

"Now, my dear fellow," contiuued Belville, flipping off with elegant ease the slight crust of ashes that had formed again on his cigar, "if you feel under any obligation to me for my share in bringing about the turn things have taken, I'll give you a receipt in full, if you wish. Your sister has canceled the whole obligation."

"See here, my friend, I don't relish such allusions to my sister, even from you," said Norton, with a decidedly frosty crackle in his tone.

"I can readily understand and sympathize wit!

your repugnance to allusions.   In fact, I have myself·
a most pronounced antipathy to the article. What
you mistook for an allusion was a fact. But your
mistake was very natural.   No apology is necessary."

"Do you mean that my sister—"

"*Pre-e-e*-cisely," interrupted Belville. "She gave me
her heart some time since, and will give me her hand
this coming winter."

"Why! she is already engaged to a young physician in Boston!"

It was now Belville's turn to be astonished, but he
suppressed all outward signs of surprise.

"Ah, well, you know it is common for patients
having a severe complaint to change physicians," he
replied pleasantly.

"But I can't believe it. She can't be false to him,"
rejoined Norton, still struggling under his astonishment.

"Of course not false. She couldn't be false to any
one. Only slightly fickle. Others have been so
before her," said Belville, soothingly.

"No indeed; I don't believe she could," said Norton, shaking his head solemnly and talking mainly to
himself.

"Then she could not have been engaged to the
other man. I shall cheerfully accept that view of it,
for I dislike fickleness."

"Well, you shall never marry her," said Norton,
at length, with firmness.

"Oh, perhaps not; perhaps not. She said I should,
however. But then I didn't know about the other

doctor in the case. There is no depending on fickle persons. I really regret to learn that she is so fickle."

Norton's response to this was angry, but Belville's rejoinder was conciliatory, and they finally agreed to have no more words about it; Norton vowing inwardly, however, that his sister should never transform their hunting companion into a brother-in-law, and Belville being complacently satisfied with his own purposes.

"May I be immediately and eternally jilted if I don't believe I behold venison on yonder ridge!" said Belville, suddenly fumbling for his glass. "Bang my hair, if I don't!" he continued, as he turned it upon a small dark speck in the brush nearly half a mile away.

"What is it?" asked Norton.

"It is either a spike-horned buck or a doe, I can't tell which. If a doe, she has likely a fawn or two with her. It acts as though it were going to lie down on that point," he said, as he saw the distant object move around the shady side of a large *heteromeles* that was now shining with bright clusters of crimson berries amid its lustrous green leaves. "The surest way is to wait here and watch it until it does lie down," he continued; "for if we attempt to approach that ridge while it is on foot, it will be sure to see us; unless we could make a wide circuit, which you see we cannot do on account of the chaparral. But if it once reaches that line of thick brush where the ridge joins the main hills, farewell deer! But the chances are very strong that if let alone it will lie down just about where it is, because it is now very near the time of day for deer to take a rest, and that is just the kind of place they like to lie down in."

He watched the spot a few minutes longer, and then it gradually shifted out of sight around the bush. Several minutes more of steady gazing failed to catch another glimpse of it.

"I think it has lain down," said Belville, at length. "But it won't do to rely upon that. There are more deer lost by haste than in any other way; and this is most decidedly a case where it is dangerous. If it has lain down at all, we can take half the day to approach it. If not, we will gain nothing by going while it is standing up, for it will be no easy matter to keep clear of its eye-range even when lying down. It would be quite likely to lie still if it did see us, especially if we were at a considerable distance. But it is never safe to presume on that. And if it should see us while it is standing, it is far more likely to run than if the discovery is made while lying down. I think we had best retire to the shade of that big oak and camp for an hour or two, so as to give the fellow a chance to settle down and get composed."

An hour and a half passed away, and then Belville said,

"Well, it's late enough and warm enough now for the deer to be down. Suppose we close in on him now and try him."

They rode to the other side of a branch of the creek that, lined with timber, ran to within three hundred yards of the point, and when they had come opposite the point they tied their horses and crossed the stream on foot.

"Now if you can travel up the bottom of this gully until you get a hundred and fifty yards or so beyond that point, you are all right," said Belville. "You will find it rough and warm, but take it slowly, and take an occasional rest in the shady parts of it. When you get there, climb out of the gully and sneak as quietly as you can up to the back-bone of the ridge. I shall probably be there by that time; but if I am not, wait for me. I'll swing around and work up the next gully, and so get on the ridge from the other side, and if all goes well we will meet there without the deer's seeing, hearing, or smelling us."

Then they separated, each going his way. In about twenty-five minutes Norton had reached the back of the ridge, where he found Belville awaiting him.

"Now," said Belville, "the wind is all right, in our faces; and we can take our time to it. You keep down along the side of the ridge just high enough to see anything that runs along the back, yet low enough for a shot at anything that goes along the side. The deer will be almost certain to hear one of us before the other, and will whip around the point to the other side and offer there the best shot. But it may also run along the top of the ridge; and it may run off the point and across the creek: either of which would give us a very bad shot. So make as little noise as possible."

Belville now allowed Norton to walk faster than himself, knowing that his companion's boot would make more noise than he did with moccasins; the purpose of this little scheme being to let the deer hear Norton first and run around to Belville's side of the ridge. As Belville was far the best shot, this was quite a pardonable piece of selfishness, for it increased the chances of securing the game; but whether pardonable or not, it was a weakness such as often lets down the underpinning of the most magnanimous sportsman's good intentions.

It was one of Belville's faults to be an extremist; a regular radical in nearly everything he undertook. And he was not less an extremist in some of his ideas of hunting than he was in his ideas of the pleasure and propriety of flirting—a subject upon which he had once ranked high as an authority among the crushing young men of festive "Frisco." Hence it was not "remarkably remarkable" that, before he heard or saw anything like a deer and before he got within fifty yards of where the animal had been last seen, the visage of Norton, clouded with disappointment, should heave in sight around the point, and quite low down, too. The gloomy aspect of Belville's face at once eclipsed Norton's melancholy countenance; but the expression lasted but a second, and was changed into a flash of triumph as he started and ran to the top of the ridge.

Reaching it, he looked a moment all over the surrounding territory and then went down the other side a little way. Just below the level of the top a faint scrape on the ground attracted his eye. It was only the freshening of the color of half an inch or so of the dry hard earth; but there was certainly a change in the shade caused by the grinding of the lightest particles of dirt under something heavy. Three, six, nine, fifteen feet ahead of it his eye quickly runs, yet detects nothing till the twentieth foot, when a slight rim of dry dust, the thickness of a thread and half an inch long, catches his eye, being noticeable mainly by reason of the difference in the color. By its side is another scrape on the hard ground, only four inches from the rim of dust! And in this last scrape is something looking powerfully like the print of a small nail-head.

"May I encounter a female book-agent if he hasn't stepped square in Norton's track since he passed here!" exclaimed Belville. He turned around and went straight to the bush where he had first seen the deer. Norton was already there. Belville gave a look at the ground under the bush and a glance along the ground for some twenty feet in the direction he had just come from. But nothing was visible except here and there a faint scratch or a broken twig or crushed bit of dry springy moss.

Then he said to Norton, "That deer has let you pass him and then quietly sloped with that low sneaking trot that will take a deer out of sight in a potato-patch and carry him over a drum-head without making a particle of noise. It's one of the tricks of the trade. I was intending to get higher up on the ridge in another minute or two, but did not think you were so far ahead."

"To tell the truth, I suppose I spoilt the thing by

trying to play a little trick on you. I tried to get ahead so that you would drive him on to me," said Norton.

"A capital joke! Only you got it tail foremost. You should have stayed back," said Belville. "There's nothing now to do but quit," he added, as he shouldered his rifle and started for the horses.

"That wild-cat thinks he's pretty sharp now, don't he?" said Belville, as they got about half-way to camp. He pointed to a round head with two tufted ears that was peering at them from a granite boulder about a hundred yards distant at one side.

"O—o—oh! yes," said Norton. "Ain't he a rouser? Just wait till I—"

He slipped off his horse and handed the reins to Belville.

"Here, take the rifle," said Belville. "It's too far for buckshot, and you can't get any closer, probably."

Norton took the rifle, and the first shot sang across the rolling ground beyond. But Puss seemed to enjoy the tune and lay still.

The second shot, striking the edge of the rock, made a spiteful "*mee-aa-oo*" as it spun away aloft, but Puss, as if it were the voice of one of her angel-kittens calling from above, remained yet perfectly quiet.

"Don't be in such a hurry," said Belville as Norton shot again without effect. "Take it coolly; they don't move generally unless hit."

Ball after ball hissed, sang in the air, and splashed in pieces against the face of the rock, until the magazine of the rifle had been emptied of the fifteen shots it had contained.

"Here is the last one. Now make it tell," said Belville, handing him another cartridge.

"Then you shoot him, for I couldn't hit a barn now; and it won't do to go home without anything," Norton dolefully replied.

"Oh, I don't care about shooting him again," said Belville, carelessly.

"Again?"

"Yes. I shot him yesterday."

CHAPTER XXV.

THE DOCTOR'S LAST HUNT.

WHERE is there a grizzly-bear country without its "Old Club. Foot"—that old varlet that years ago lost part of one foot in a trap ; that always prefers to bag his own game, and so cannot be baited; that does not affect cold victuals, and so cannot be poisoned or waylaid; that traveling lead-mine from which no hunter has ever yet recovered his investments, and even from prospecting which so few have returned?   Even poor San Diego, unknown, forsaken, and despised as it is by the state of which it is a part, has—or did have until Belville got after him—its "Old Club Foot."   Like all other "Old Club Foots" he does not go an ounce under two thousand pounds, and if the last two men who weighed him ever send in their figures he will probably weigh a few hundred more.

"Old Club Foot" ranged from Santa Rosa to Temescal, and from there to the San Jacinto Mountain—all famous places for grizzlies in the olden time, and a few still linger there.   When this fellow was on the southern end of his beat, one of his favorite places was the great cañon that, nearly opposite the camp of our friends, wound its way a mile or more into the dark bristling mountains.

It was three days after the hunt for the big mule-deer—days that had been spent in lounging along the shady stream, shooting at doves as they whistled through the timber along its sides or rose with twittering wing from bathing in its rocky basins of clear water; enlivening the dullness of rabbit life at morning and evening; or stimulating quails in the low brush. Belville had started down the creek at dawn to look for a deer, and before he had been gone half an hour he returned. Finding the camp all quiet and probably still wrapped in sleep, he tore a leaf from his pocket-book, wrote a few lines on it and fixed it on the coffee-pot, where it could not fail to be seen. Then he shouldered his rifle and started for the mouth of the big cañon.

When the remaining campers went to get breakfast, they found the note and read as follows:

"Have just found fresh tracks of 'Old Club Foot' leading to the big cañon on the west. Did not wake you for fear you would dissuade me from going after him. But I have never before had a chance at a grizzly, and am not going to be scared out of one by his size, or by the chaparral, rocks, or anything else. I know it is dangerous, but so is everything else in this life. Should anything happen—There can't, though; my rifle can get away with anything; so there is no use in providing for nothing. Don't worry. I shall probably be back by noon.

B."

"Mercy!" exclaimed Eveline. "Charley, can't you find him and stop him?"

"Oh do!" said Laura, pleadingly. "It is horrible

to have him go there alone into that dreadful brush and among those rocks and hills."

Ah! Belville, why not think of that before? What bravery in following such a monster into such a bristly tangle of stiff chaparral, where you stand no chance with the raging giant if the first shot is not instantly fatal, where he may rise upon you unseen from behind some bush or rock at less than ten feet distance, where flight is impossible and no friend can reach you if hurt, or perhaps even find you? For neither the *vaquero's* horse nor the wild bull of the hills can traverse those rugged glens and the dark shaggy steeps that form their sides, so nearly impenetrable are they to all but the grizzly and the madman who follows him. Yet what makes man more stupendously insane than false ideas of bravery?

"A dozen well men could not stop or even find him in there now," said Norton. "It's a crazy piece of work, but I see no help for it. But it is said that the odds are always greatly against finding a bear, even when hunting him; so it may be all right."

Sorrowfully they got their breakfast and sat down to eat. Scarcely had the coffee been handed around, when sharp and clear upon the cool morning air came ringing down the cañon a distant rifle-shot.

Eveline spilt some of her coffee in her lap; her brother suspended half-way a very energetic and so far very successful bite into a biscuit; and Laura dropped into the ashes a quail she was broiling. Before the echo of the shot had died along the hills, another shot came rattling down, followed in another second or two by a continuous *bang, bang, bang, bang, bang, bang, bang, bang, bang !*—as fast as nine shots could be rolled out of a Winchester repeater.

They said not a word until the last echo was buried in the dark sepulchral hills.

"I shouldn't wonder if he had got him now," said Norton.

"Wh—which one?" said Miss Norton, in a tone of very anxious doubt.

Hour after hour sped from the bow of time, feathered with surmises, fears, hopes, and doubts, until the last one transfixed the raven night and brought it down with the sudden fall characteristic of this southern latitude. And yet no Belville came. They built a big fire and waked the long night with signal-guns, but no answer but the echo came back from the looming black hills.

At dawn Norton started off for help, and by noon all the men that could be mustered at Santa Margarita and San Luis Rey were scouring, or trying to scour, the cañon into which Belville had gone. But what avail kind hearts and willing feet in chaparral where the hard, dry ground shows no trace of a moccasined foot ; where the brush turns back the toughest mountain-horse, yields only to the crushing weight and tough hide of the bear, and must in most places be threaded on hands and knees? Two days were spent in the search, and on the afternoon of the second day one by one the searching parties returned unsuccessful, and the quest was sorrowfully given up. The last *vaquero* left at dark, and Norton and the two ladies sat by the camp-fire alone, bewildered and dazed by the tragic ending of their sport.

Suddenly Eveline Norton burst out crying. Mrs. Norton's large dark eyes began to look very dewy. Norton himself wore a very abysmal countenance.

"I'm so sorry you told me what you did!" said Evy to her brother's wife.

"So am I. But it would have made no difference," said Norton, soothingly.

"It might have. Maybe he wouldn't have been so reckless if we hadn't—"

"What?"

"Quarreled about it. It was Charley's fault. He ought not to have told me about that, or told him about my foolish affair with Dr. Hart. I liked Dr. Belville twice as much," sobbed Evy.

"He was worth a dozen Dr. Harts," said Mrs. Norton, with judicial firmness of tone.

"He was certainly a very clever fellow," replied Norton, "and has been very kind to me, and to all of us. He has done his best to give us the best shooting and to make everything comfortable. We should have had little pleasure here without him, for we would not have known where to go, how to go, or what to do. Just think how different our impressions of everything would have been without him."

"We could not have stayed here at all. How could any one stand such a lonely country without traveling about and amusing themselves as we have?" said Mrs. Norton.

"I hope you didn't treat him badly on account of

that trifling matter I spoke to you about," said Norton to Eveline.

"Why didn't you call it a trifle the other day when you told me about it?" she replied, half indignantly, half sorrowfully.

"You were as good a judge of its nature as I was."

"You know I always look up to you as my only brother, and depend upon your advice."

"But I certainly gave no reason why you and he should quarrel over it."

"I didn't mean to. I spoke mildly enough about it, and he retorted with my engagement to that stupid Dr. Hart. I got a little provoked at discovering that he knew of it, and he began joking and teasing me until we got into a downright quarrel, and I finally told him—"

"What! you didn't break the engagement?" exclaimed Mrs. Norton, in dismay.

"I didn't mean to. I meant to make up yesterday," were the words borne out on a fresh flood of tears.

"It has made him desperate. He was a man of very deep feelings—very deep," said Mrs. Norton.

"Yes, indeed he was. I—shall never—marry—any —one—now," sobbed Eveline.

On the following morning they sadly packed their things and drove away. Sadly they rolled over the bare sheep-trodden *mesas*, the sorrowful-looking brown hills, and through the dreary cañons of the coast-road between San Luis and San Diego. How different everything seemed from the fresh bloom they saw in spring! a melancholy sight enough to those whose eyes are undimmed by any saddening associations, but doubly so to our friends, to whom even the fullest blaze of California's spring beauty could now be only dull and dreary.

They endured two days of San Diego's quiet life, and then fled to Miner's. But most of El Cajon was now bare and brown; the roads were dusty from the travel of heavy teams; the days were hot; the winter boarders had not yet arrived, and would not arrive until after the rain came; there were no ducks yet; the quails were as lively as they were numerous, and vanished up the hills at the first sight of a gun. Though Miner and his family, after their custom, did everything possible to make it pleasant, El Cajon seemed hopelessly gloomy and full of depressing reminders, and until after the rain came there was no hope of an improvement even in external nature.

So our friends soon fled to Los Angeles in search of more diverting life. The beautiful surroundings, the orange-groves, the vineyards, the gardens and orchards of the City of the Angels relieved the dullness for a while. But none of them could forget the lost friend, and Norton could not repress his sorrow when he thought of how kind Belville had been to him, and pictured to himself the sad and graveless death and lonely resting-place. Nor could any of them compare even the beautiful orange-groves they saw with the live-oak grove in the wild cañon, the bustle of the street with the uproar of the blue-plumed myriads of the valley, or the beautiful drives of San Gabriel with the rough and rugged boulder-washes of the San Bernardino Mountains, without a sigh of regret for those wild scenes.

So they soon fled to Santa Barbara, and landed once more full in the loving embrace of dullness with the memory of Belville closely haunting them; and from there they beat an immediate retreat to the Ojai Valley.

They had been in that place but a week, and were meditating still another flight, when among the mail forwarded from San Diego came a paper for Eveline. Broad pen-marks called her attention to the marriage-notices, and she read:

"At Oakland, Cal., on ———, by ———, Edward Belville, M.D., to ———, of Oakland."

On the margin, by its side, in Belville's handwriting, were the words, "Not false, but slightly fickle."

Blank astonishment and perplexed bewilderment were at first visible on every face as this was read aloud. Joy beamed from the ladies' eyes as they gradually realized that their friend was still alive. But after these transitory phases of feeling had been manifested, their countenances settled into an expression of determined resentment, as they contemplated the full extent of the imposition that had been practiced on them.

"Why, he's been engaged to this girl all the time!" exclaimed Mrs. Norton, with flashing eyes. "Nearly all his letters were postmarked 'Oakland,' but he always said they were from his sister."

"I just knew he was a contemp—" said Eveline.

"I could have told you—" said Laura, in the same breath.

"Be chary of your wisdom!" interrupted Norton "It's a trifle late. The best cosmetic for the face of affairs is humility. He has painted all three of you pretty well at one stroke—not false, but fickle."

"Charley," said his sister, after a pause as long as her countenance, "did any of the men look to see if there were any *bear*-tracks that morning?"

"I declare! I never thought to ask them to look. It was only about ten miles across to the stage-road, too! Perhaps—"

"Why, of course," interrupted his wife. "There's no *perhaps* about it."

THE END.